# THREAT RISING

KJ KALIS

# ALSO BY K.J. KALIS:

*The Moscow Brief*

*Threat Rising*

*Tainted Asset*

# 1

The heavy black clouds of a passing thunderstorm left the squat brick building that housed the Washington County Coroner's Office plunged in blackness. Just after midnight, an equally dark black van pulled up in the back of the building directly behind the double bay doors reserved for use by law enforcement, funeral homes, and the county coroner herself, Dr. Ava Scott.

Two men sat in the front of the black van, wearing matching dark navy uniforms complete with jackets, patches, and baseball caps that identified them as EMTs. They'd only met a few hours before. They didn't know each other's real names, only that they had been assigned to work together that particular evening. They had been briefed in separate rooms by separate people before meeting for the first time when they'd been handed the keys to the van, given the codenames of "Blue" and "Green." There was no conversation between them other than what had to be said.

"Ready?" Blue asked.

"Ready."

From inside the nearly empty van, Blue opened up a black

nylon backpack that was set at his feet. From inside, he unzipped a case that contained a handheld meter that looked like something an electrician might use, but wasn't. As he flipped the switch, his tongue gave his lower lip a little flick. His eyes narrowed, watching as the screen turned from red to green. "Jamming is on. We're good to go."

Green picked up his cell phone and checked the screen for service. "I've got no service. Confirmed. We are good to go."

The two men exited the van simultaneously, closing their respective doors and walked to the back of the van where they opened the back, working silently. From inside, they pulled out a gurney, the bed covered in thick black vinyl. The van had been borrowed from one of the local funeral homes, one of the many makeshift hearses used to transport the dearly departed from the coroner's office to one of the many local funeral homes where they could be prepared for viewing and burial by distraught families and friends. Blue reached inside and flipped the latch, unlocking the gurney that was secured to the rails in the bed of the van. The two men simultaneously tugged at the frame, the legs from the gurney unfolding as it came out of the back. One, the taller of the two, pushed the gurney toward the back doors as the shorter man closed the back doors of the van, the engine still running.

Pushing the gurney to the back door of the coroner's office, Green gave the door a double rap with a single knuckle, avoiding the doorbell that had been installed for the use of anyone who wanted to get into the building and didn't have a key card. A second later, the latch on the heavy metal double doors popped open and a man stuck his head out. He was dressed in blue scrubs, the sleeves of a long white T-shirt sticking out from underneath his blue shirt, the white fabric glowing bright against the blackness of the night.

The man in the scrubs gave a short nod as if he recognized the men although he'd never seen them before. He pulled the doors open without saying anything. They walked as a group following the man in the scrubs, the only noise the clatter of the wheels of the gurney as it turned a few corners.

Ninety seconds later, the three men and the gurney were in the autopsy room in front of the cold storage bays. The man in the scrubs said nothing, just pointing to the door marked 113. The taller of the two men from the van opened the door and slid the interior tray out. He reached for the zipper on the black bag inside, giving it tug.

"You don't want to do that," the man in the scrubs said.

"Why? We were told to check the identity."

"Even if you had a picture of him, it wouldn't do you any good."

Blue stopped, his fingers still pinching the tab on the zipper. "It's that bad?"

The man in the scrubs nodded, "Yes, it is. It's the right body. Take it."

Without saying anything more, Blue pulled the rack from the cold storage out, extending it the entire way out into the space. There was no noise around any of the men save for the clock on the wall, an old-fashioned kind with a second hand, dully ticking in the background.

Forty-five seconds later, the three men had managed to heave what was left of the body wrapped in a black bag onto the gurney. As the two uniformed men began to roll the body away, they waited as the man in the scrubs closed the cold storage door and secured it. He stepped in front of the two men and led them back through the twists and turns of the coroner's office to the back doors where they had entered only a few minutes before.

As soon as they pushed the gurney out into the night, Blue gave the man wearing the scrubs a curt nod. Without responding, the man in the scrubs closed the broad doors to the coroner's office and disappeared back inside.

Opening the van doors, the two men pushed the gurney with the black bag inside, secured the rails with thick metal clamps, slammed the doors shut, and returned to their positions inside of the van, every movement efficient and rehearsed as if they had somewhere important to be. Back inside the van, as Blue started the engine, Green fiddled with the jamming equipment, turning off a set of black switches. "Jamming equipment off."

Blue checked the signal on his cell phone. "Confirmed. Back to normal. No one will ever know we were there."

As they pulled away, Green shrugged off his hat and his jacket while Blue drove, glancing at the scar on his right wrist. It matched Blue's wrist, a short white mark making his dark skin look like he'd been cut with a straight razor, the holes where it had been stitched up still evident on the surface. Green looked down at the scar and then back at Blue, "We'll be back to base in twenty-two minutes."

"Confirmed."

## 2

By the time Travis pulled into Sarah's Barbecue, he was starved. He'd gotten up early, managed to get the horses fed and watered, and cleaned their stalls before heading out to Big Al's Tack and Feed to get worming supplies.

It was spring, the air dry and cool for just south of Austin, Texas. The bluebonnets were blooming, the northern mockingbirds and brown-headed cowbirds called to each other from a stand of Texas Ash trees on the other side of a dilapidated fence as he parked the truck, the smell of smoke and meat filling the air.

Travis glanced at the bags of supplies on his passenger seat. His vet insisted on worming every eight weeks. After loading up on tubes of paste Ivermectin, Travis spent a little time walking around the tack store picking up a couple of extra halters, two new shedding blades, a three-pack of saddle pads that were on sale, and a box of apple-flavored horse treats that he knew Scarlett, the mare he'd bought for Kira before she passed away, liked.

Travis slammed the door to his truck and walked over to the little shack that was the home of Sarah's Barbecue. Humidity hung in the air and made the scent of the smoking meat even stronger after the storms from the night before. The thunder and lightning had been intense, rolling in and out like waves on the ocean. A couple of times he'd woken up drenched in sweat. Whether it was from a nightmare he couldn't remember or the storm, he still wasn't sure.

"Hey, Travis," Sarah called to him from behind the counter. She was dressed in her normal restaurant uniform, a red T-shirt, sometimes with a red flannel shirt over the top, sometimes not, her long blonde hair tied into a braid that rested on her right shoulder, a few wisps of her soft hair escaping from around the side of her face.

"Hey, Sarah. How are you today?" Travis hadn't exactly become friends with Sarah, but at least they were on a first-name basis. It wasn't as though he had a lot of friends. Travis wasn't that way. But he was a particular fan of Sarah's Barbecue and that made it worth the conversation. "What's good today?"

"Everything as usual. What are you having?" she said, glancing down at the register.

Travis studied the menu written on a chalkboard above the counter for a minute. Sarah's Barbecue was typical of Texas smoke shacks. It wasn't much more than a small building with a prep kitchen in the back and the wood pits behind that. There wasn't proper restaurant seating, only a counter inside with a matching one outside and a few picnic tables scattered under arching trees on one side of the parking lot. Unless people were willing to sit outside or stand at the counter, Sarah's Barbecue was entirely takeout. From the brief conversations Travis had had with Sarah, he knew her grandmother had started the business out of the back of her house to make a little extra money for the family. Eventually, it got to be a big enough operation that the family had bought that piece of land where Travis was standing, converting the single building — an old ramshackle garage — into the pits and the kitchen prep area.

"'No need to make it complicated,' as my grandma used to say," Sarah had told Travis months before.

Travis had immediately adopted that motto as his own, except for the fact that things always seemed to get complicated for him.

Looking away from the menu, he caught Sarah's eye. "How about if you give me one of your famous brisket sandwiches and if you have some extra, I'll take two pounds home for later on."

"You can eat all that brisket by yourself, Travis?" Sarah said, her fingers flying over the cash register keypad.

"Don't you know it. Gotta keep my girlish figure," Travis said, patting his stomach.

Sarah raised her eyebrows, "Looks like that ranch work keeps you in pretty good shape. I should probably send you home with three pounds so you don't wither away to nothing."

Travis chuckled. He enjoyed their friendly banter. Someone watching might think they were flirting, but Sarah was married and had two little girls with the same beautiful blonde hair as she did. He'd never encroach on another man's woman, not after what happened with Kira. Turning away for a moment, he ignored the flicker of sadness in his chest.

"Your order will be right up. I'll get your drink for you." Sarah said, adding a slip of paper to the line of orders the kitchen was already working on.

Travis stepped off to the side to make room for the line of people that had formed behind him. He leaned against the wall, listening to the hum of the employees in the back talking to each other and Sarah's easy conversation with everyone who approached her register. There was a radio playing somewhere in the kitchen, a new country tune floating above the din of the voices. Travis glanced at the ground, nudging a little piece of white paper that looked like it was from a straw wrapper with the toe of his boot, scooting it against the rough concrete floor.

"Travis?" a voice called. He looked up. A woman from the back, wearing an apron smudged with dark stains from meat grease and the orange from barbecue sauce, had a Styrofoam box in her hand and a bag in the other. She lifted her chin, "Here's your order. Have a good day."

"You too."

Travis looped the plastic bag over his wrist and grabbed the drink with one hand, picking up the Styrofoam box with the other. He walked outside into the sunshine, the ground was still a little damp from the storms the night before. The day was pleasantly warm, even if it was humid. He walked to the end of the outdoor counter and set his food down. A few gray metal stools were tucked underneath the ledge. They were new. The last time he'd been to Sarah's place, there'd only been room to stand at the counter. He pulled out a stool and grabbed a couple of napkins from the dispenser before opening the box that had his lunch in it. Inside, a sheet of red-checked wax paper framed the bottom of the box, the juicy brisket sandwich covered in grilled onions on thick bread flanked by a scoop of coleslaw and a matching scoop of potato salad.

Travis settled in, fishing a fork and knife from inside the bag, feeling a nagging weariness in his body. He felt like he'd been going nonstop for the last few weeks. The contractor he'd hired to build the new barn had just about finished. When he'd left that morning, they were installing the stall doors. Travis had watched for a few minutes, shaking his head, not sure they'd ordered the correct hardware to latch each of the doors closed. He'd have to check that when he got back to the ranch. The noise of the construction had put several of the horses on edge, which meant there was extra exercise for them and time in the paddocks where they could find some peace and quiet. The construction had set him on edge too. It had been Kira's dream to start a breeding program. The new barn had been part of that plan. And although Travis wasn't sure he'd ever get a breeding program off the ground, he did need the stall space, especially with new training clients coming in to take advantage of his reining skills.

Travis picked up the sandwich and took a bite, the tang from the homemade barbecue sauce was a sharp contrast to the richness of the fat in the beef brisket. Sarah's Barbecue was a hidden gem, he thought to himself, wiping his face. She did Texas barbecue the way it was supposed to be done — just salt and pepper on a good cut of meat smoked slowly over a wood-burning pit. He wasn't interested in any of that fancy spice that so many pit masters tried to use. Plain and simple was the way he liked it.

As Travis chewed and swallowed the first bites of his sandwich, he thought about the afternoon ahead. Once he went back to the ranch, he'd have to check in on the contractors and then return a phone call from a new client that was ready to bring four horses out for him to train. With any luck, the new barn would be ready in time to house them together. He and Ellie, his assistant, had walked through the new barn the day before, discussing which horses to relocate to the new stalls and which ones to leave in the existing barn. Ellie had mentioned they needed to finish setting up the tack room in the new barn as well as get the stalls outfitted with corner feeders and water buckets. Travis took another bite of his sandwich, chewing slowly, shaking his head. There was a lot to do. He might need to hire another assistant to come in and give them a hand. Although he loved his time in the barn with the horses, it was getting to be too much. Even if he could get someone to come in and clean stalls in the morning so he didn't have to do it, would be helpful. Travis made a mental note to think that through when things settled down, if they did.

He shook his head. The work at the ranch, combined with his skip tracing business, was getting to the point when there weren't enough hours in the day. As he stabbed his plastic fork into the pale-yellow potato salad, he thought about Kira. He wished that she'd been by his side to build the business the way they planned. But it turned out she had her own agenda, one that didn't include him.

Travis's mind flashed back to the moment a few months before in the Oval Office of the White House when he'd pulled the trigger and shot her as she held the President hostage. He'd watched her body collapse as the bullet penetrated her skull. He blinked, pushing the thought away as he picked up a forkful of coleslaw and bit down on it. It had been months since Kira's death, her second one, after she'd faked her death in Ecuador. As far as he knew, there'd been no funeral, but he wouldn't have gone anyway. There was no inquisition either. The record was clear. Kira and one of his former coworkers, Gus Norman, were double agents for Russia. They'd managed to kill two of the Joint Chiefs with a banned nerve agent smeared on their briefing books before Travis and John Spector, the head of the Secret Service could stop the assault. John Spector had lost his life in the process and Travis had increased his body count.

Travis took a sip of his soda, sucking the cold liquid through the white straw and leaning back a little bit on the stool. He wiped his mouth again, looking at the food left in the box. It wasn't as if killing them was so problematic. Kira and Gus were in the wrong. That was clear. But he'd trusted them. It was the breach of loyalty and trust that still ate at him to that day.

Travis sighed, shrugging his shoulders and adjusting the heels of his boots on the rungs of the base of the stool before continuing to eat his sandwich. He took the thoughts about Gus and Kira and put them back where they belonged — in a wooden box in his mind with the top nailed shut. He had other things to think about. The horses. The new barn. The three calls on his voicemail for skip tracing services that he hadn't had time to return. His life was full and exactly the way he wanted it to be.

"Travis?"

Travis looked over his shoulder. Washington County Sheriff Brandon Burnett stood behind him, his thumbs hooked into his gun belt.

"Hey Sheriff Burnett," Travis said, wiping his face for what felt like the thousandth time. "How are you doing today?"

Sheriff Burnett walked up to the counter and rested a meaty forearm not far from the white plastic bag that held the two pounds of brisket Travis was ready to take home for later. Travis glanced at the sheriff. He didn't have his hat on. A few strands of his thinning hair lifted off the top of his head and twisted in the breeze, threatening to fly away. "Doing pretty good. Yourself?"

"Better than I deserve." Travis looked down at his meal, staring straight forward, hoping that looking back at his unfinished food would encourage the sheriff to move on and find someone else to chat with. He picked up his sandwich and took another bite, chewing slowly, not making eye contact.

A moment passed before the sheriff cleared his throat, "I'm sorry to bother you while you're eating, Travis…"

Travis turned, closing his eyes for a second and then opening them, "But…"

Sheriff Burnett gave a little nod as if he was acknowledging the fact that he had something to say, "I need your help."

# 3

"You think you need my help with what?" Travis said, staring at the sheriff, who pulled one of the napkins out of the dispenser and wiped his forehead.

"It's not something I can talk about here." Sheriff Burnett glanced over his shoulder as if he was expecting someone to be listening to their conversation. Travis pivoted slowly on the stool, checking to see what the sheriff was looking at. Standing a few feet away was a mousy woman wearing a red wrap dress pushing her glasses up higher on her nose. Sheriff Burnett looked back at Travis, "This is Dr. Ava Scott. She's the county coroner."

Travis furrowed his eyebrows and gave her a curt nod, trying to remember if they had met before, "Ma'am," he said looking at her.

"Mr. Bishop, it's nice to meet you."

Travis narrowed his eyes, "How did you find me?"

"I called the ranch office. Ellie picked up. She said you drove into town and guessed you might stop for lunch. She mentioned how much you like this place."

"So you tracked me down?" Prickles went up the back of

Travis's spine. He shouldn't be that easy to find, but apparently, he was.

Sheriff Burnett tried to smooth a few more wisps of flyaway hair back down on his head as he looked at Travis, "Should've worn my darn hat today, but you know, the thing is so hot." He dabbed at his forehead again. "Listen, Travis, we need you to come back to the office with us for a talk."

"About the thing you need help with?" Travis led.

Sheriff Burnett nodded, "Yeah. You have a reputation for finding things in the area."

"So you're trying to tell me you lost something you shouldn't have?"

The muscles in Sheriff Burnett's meaty jaw flexed. He looked at Travis as if he was a two-year-old that had just sworn in public for the first time. His eyes got wide, "It's better if we talk at the office. Can we do that?"

"All right. I've got some stuff going on, but I can swing by for a little bit." The last thing he wanted to do was to get caught up in one of the sheriff's messes and lose the whole day.

"Thanks."

After shutting the lid to the box that held half of his uneaten lunch, Travis followed Sheriff Burnett and Dr. Scott in his truck as they drove the police cruiser out of Sarah's Barbecue and down the road. Questions filled Travis's mind as he followed the cruiser in front of him, the tires kicking up plumes of dust and grit despite the rain they'd had the night before. The dry Texas countryside never stayed damp for very long. Travis stared straight ahead as he drove, thoughts pounding in his mind. Sure, it bothered him that Sheriff Burnett had been able to track him to Sarah's Barbecue, but what bothered him more was the fact that he'd brought the coroner with him and wouldn't say exactly what he needed help with. Travis's stomach tightened into a little knot around the lunch he had just eaten, acid burning the back of his throat.

The heartburn he was feeling wasn't from the barbecue, he was sure of that. It was from Sheriff Burnett. The expression on Sheriff Burnett's face told him there was more to the story. It might not be a story Travis would like.

Pulling up in front of the Sheriff's Department, Sheriff Burnett and Ava parked in one of the reserved parking spots noted on a small white placard posted on a green metal pole that read, "Official Vehicles Only." Travis's pickup truck wasn't official, so he parked on the other side of the lot and caught up to them at the front door of the squat brick building.

The Washington County Sheriff's office housed more than simply the hub of law enforcement for the county where Travis lived. It also held a small jail, a smattering of legal records, the dog warden, and the coroner's office, which was located in a suite of offices and labs off the back of the building. A single-story dusty red brick building with a gray roof and black shutters around each of the windows on the edge of town, the Sheriff's office had been built ten years before, or rebuilt as it were, after a tornado ripped through the county and damaged the original building beyond repair. After a lot of grumbling by the county trustees, they finally approved building a brand-new structure with necessary upgrades that included five jail cells, up from the three they'd had previously, two of which were full at the time of the tornado. The two men being held in the jail at that time had never been found. Although people in town didn't talk much about it anymore, from the relationship he had with Sheriff Burnett, Travis knew the sheriff still felt bad about it. "Hope they were whipped right up into that cyclone," Travis had heard the sheriff had grumbled at the time. Whether that was true or not, Travis didn't know.

By the time Travis walked across the parking lot, Sheriff Burnett and Dr. Scott had already disappeared inside. Spring had come fast to Washington County, Texas, the heat and humidity surging a bit higher each and every day until the climax in the middle of the summer. Stepping inside the door, Travis could feel the air conditioning already running in the building, a cascade of cool air washing over him, penetrating the T-shirt and jeans he wore along with his worn cowboy boots.

Sheriff Burnett smoothed the hair on his head again, this time having better luck since he was out of the wind. "Why don't you come on over to my office? We'll talk there."

Travis nodded. As they walked down the hallway, Travis glanced behind him, seeing Dr. Scott following. She had her hands laced behind her back and walked slowly in their wake without saying anything, staring at the floor. Travis could see circles underneath her eyes as if she had been up late or something was draining the life out of her. Which one it was, Travis wasn't sure.

The sheriff's office was located in a corner of the building just beyond the lobby area. An officer buzzed the door to let the three of them in and they walked directly to Sheriff Burnett's office. They passed up a bank of desks and two officers, one that was manning the lobby area and one that seemed frustrated by something he saw on his computer, a single white tooth biting into his lower lip. The building smelled like a combination of burnt coffee and lemon cleaner, as though someone had started a pot and left it on the heat for too long while they were mopping the floors. Other than the occasional chatter from the police radios, the office was quiet save for the noise of their footfalls on the tile as they followed the sheriff to his office.

The door to Sheriff Burnett's office was closed but unlocked. The Sheriff pushed it open and waved Travis and Dr. Scott inside, quickly closing the door behind them and flopping himself down into the chair behind his desk. He tugged at his gun belt at the same time, adjusting it on his soft hips. Travis sat down in a chair on the opposite side of his desk. Dr. Scott pulled up in the chair next to Travis, crossing her legs, folding her small hands in her lap after pushing her glasses back up on her nose again.

Sheriff Burnett glanced out the window and then back at Travis. Travis waited. He learned that sometimes the most powerful position in negotiation was the silent one. People didn't like silence. It felt like a vacuum. If he didn't say anything, it was more likely that Sheriff Burnett would get to the point, and do it quickly, not getting caught up in casual banter that delayed the entire process. Travis narrowed his eyes, staring at the sheriff. From the look on his face, banter wasn't on his mind, which was unusual. Sheriff Burnett was usually a friendly man, more interested in public relations than arrests. Travis chewed the inside of his lip, waiting.

As Sheriff Burnett looked back at Travis, he shifted in his seat and sucked in a breath, "I'm sorry to take you away from your lunch and your work this afternoon, Travis, but like I said, we need your help."

Travis didn't say anything. He glanced at Dr. Scott. The sheriff had said we. A red flush had crawled from her neck up into her cheeks that nearly matched the color of her dress. Whatever Sheriff Burnett was about to say clearly had something to do with her. Her reaction told him she was uneasy at best, mortified at worst.

Sheriff Burnett cleared his throat and swallowed, his Adam's apple bulging up and down in his meaty neck, "This morning, when Dr. Scott arrived here at the office, she was finishing some paperwork on a body we recovered a couple of days ago."

Dr. Scott chirped, her voice high and thin. "Male. A John Doe."

"Anyway, when Dr. Scott went to check the body, she discovered something quite disturbing."

Travis looked at Dr. Scott again. Her cheeks were now aflame, the same color as her red dress. Her fingers were knotted tightly in her lap, the knuckles white. Travis knitted his eyebrows and looked at Sheriff Burnett, "Spit it out. What's going on here Sheriff?"

He cleared his throat again and then turned, staring at Travis. "The body that Dr. Scott went to find this morning is gone."

# 4

"Gone? How do you lose a body?" Travis said, frowning at the sheriff and Dr. Scott.

Sheriff Burnett pulled a thick white handkerchief out of his pocket and dabbed at his forehead again. Even with the arctic level of air conditioning pumping through his office, he was still sweating, beads of perspiration clinging to his high forehead. "I have no idea. That's why we need your help."

Dr. Scott shifted uncomfortably in her seat as though every muscle in her body had just suffered through a major cramp. She pressed her lips together in a grimace, the corners of her mouth jutting downward. Travis stared at her for a moment. She seemed deeply embarrassed. Whether it was because Travis was there or because the sheriff had exposed her secret, Travis didn't know. A heavy silence settled over the room as Sheriff Burnett kept sweating and Dr. Scott seemed to shrivel even smaller in her chair.

"I don't understand. How did you lose a body? It's not like they could get up and walk away." Travis's response probably sounded callous, he realized, but he didn't care.

Sheriff Burnett's lip puckered as he blew a long breath out of his mouth. "That's what we don't know."

"And that's why I'm here? You think I can find this missing dead body that somehow walked itself out of your autopsy room?"

"I didn't say it was in the autopsy room," Dr. Scott hissed.

"Where else would it be?" Travis countered.

Sheriff Burnett tilted his head to the side, dabbing at his face with his handkerchief again, "Now Ava, don't get defensive. No one is accusing you of doing something with the body. We simply have to figure out what happened to it. There has to be an explanation."

"Are you saying it wasn't in your autopsy room?" Travis frowned.

"No," Dr. Scott said through pursed lips. "That's not what I'm saying."

Sheriff Burnett didn't give her a chance to finish. "Listen, Travis, you have a reputation around here as being somebody who can find things. And I know about your background. I know that you've been through more than most. That's why we thought maybe you'd be the one to help since this is, as you can imagine, kind of a sensitive subject. People need to trust the coroner's office. They need to know their loved ones are safe, even if they are departed. We wouldn't want this kind of information to get around the community; if you know what I mean."

Travis stared at the ceiling for a second. Sheriff Burnett was right about a couple of things. Travis knew he had a reputation for being someone who could find things that were lost. That was the definition of what a skip tracer did. Whether it was a truckload of cattle that the Orlando family lost when a competitor shipped them into another county, a valuable piece of family jewelry, like the gold Rolex presidential watch he'd found the month before, much to the delight of the Warner family, or finding a person, like how he'd found Elena Lobra-nova when Gus had come calling a few months before, that was what he did. He was a finder and a fixer.

Sheriff Burnett's voice droned on in the background as Travis ran through the possibilities of what could have happened to the body. His words cut into Travis's train of thought as he said, "And you know, we've always worked together well..."

At least that much was true. Maybe not completely true, but true enough. Travis and Sheriff Burnett had worked together on a few cases, the sheriff giving Travis access to some of the law enforcement records that civilians weren't typically privy to in order to help him solve his cases. "It's all in the name of justice," Sheriff Burnett had said to him on more than one occasion when Travis had come calling. Low crime rates and people living in peace were good for the sheriff's career. And Sheriff Burnett had cut Travis a break when Travis got into a fistfight at the Sleepy Rooster Bar right after Kira died.

A woman had sidled up to him after Travis had a few too many beers and started talking to him. Travis didn't make a move on the woman, but her husband felt otherwise and threw the first swing. Unfortunately for the husband, Travis's training proved to be too much. The man left the bar with a broken nose, three fewer teeth, and a nearly dislocated shoulder. Sitting in Sheriff Burnett's office a few hours later, the sheriff had questions for Travis when he ran his background and couldn't access the records. Travis couldn't tell him a lot but managed to let Sheriff Burnett know about his time with the Delta Force and CIA. A few hours later, with a signed affidavit that Travis was only defending himself sworn to by the bartender, and after hearing about Kira's death in Ecuador, the Sheriff managed to somehow put the issue to rest.

Travis focused again on Sheriff Burnett's words. "As you can imagine, this could potentially be a serious problem if we can't recover the body. The family might take offense to that, if you know what I mean."

"Family?" Travis blurted out. "I thought you said it's a John Doe."

"It is." Dr. Scott stammered, "Or, it was. I should know something soon." She shook her head like her neck was having a tremor and stared down at her hands again.

Travis sighed and raised his eyebrows. The day had started off with his only concern getting worming supplies for the horses and now he was sitting in the sheriff's office dealing with a missing John Doe. Travis swung his head from side to side, trying to get a grip on what Sheriff Burnett was asking him to do. He'd never been asked to locate a dead body before.

"Now, before you make up your mind, Travis, I know how busy you are. I've heard in town all about that new barn you're building out there and I know you've got other skip tracing clients, but there's a little more to the story that we haven't told you yet. Can you reserve judgment for another minute or two?"

Travis scowled. "More to the story? There is more than you somehow lost a dead body?" The words came out in a way that was harsh and accusing, but it was the truth. That was exactly what had happened. The question was how.

"Ava, how about if you show Travis what else we found before he tells us he's too busy to give us a hand?"

Ava didn't say anything. In a smooth move, she pushed herself up out of the chair in front of Sheriff Burnett's desk at the same time she uncrossed her legs. Based on what Travis could see, Ava might be a trained medical doctor, but she didn't seem to have a strong enough constitution to deal with the living. Perhaps that was how she ended up being a coroner in the first place. Dead bodies didn't get emotional, at least not in the way that families in hospitals did. She motioned to Travis to follow her as Sheriff Burnett struggled to get out of his cushioned chair behind his desk.

Travis followed Sheriff Burnett and Dr. Scott down a few white linoleum floored hallways, glancing at pictures of historical places in Washington County. Each image was framed and encased in glass and hung artfully on the walls — the clock tower in the county square, the interior of the courthouse, the front of the local library, and a cluster of kids all dressed in their soccer uniforms beaming and smiling, their arms wrapped around each other, medals around their necks from a local soccer tournament. Travis glanced at each of them as he walked by. It was as if the pictures had been hung on the wall to prove there were still noble things that happened within the county. It was a subtle and ineffective foil against the jail cells and dead bodies. Travis knew bad things happened all the time. There was literally no way to avoid the fact that someone could be minding their own business and bad luck could crash into them like getting T-boned by a semi without any warning, all the normal parts of life getting twisted and turned, thrown in the air, bodies broken with lives turned upside down. That was a fact of life. Or at least it was a fact of Travis's life.

By the time they got to the autopsy room, Travis was in a mood. The only thing he wanted to do was walk back out to his truck, drive back to the ranch, and be left alone. He gripped his fists into tight balls and shoved them into his front pockets as he walked along behind Dr. Scott and Sheriff Burnett. It sounded like they had a problem, but why it was his to fix, he wasn't sure. He sighed, everything in him wanting to turn on his heel and bolt, but something kept him there.

After pressing a code into a keypad on a locked door at the back of the building, Dr. Scott went ahead of the two men into the examination room. Travis glanced around. He'd been into the sheriff's office on several occasions, but he'd never gone any farther than the portly man's office. Visiting the coroner's wing was an entirely new experience.

"The body was housed in rack 113," Ava said, pointing to the bank of cold storage units that had been installed against the wall. There were fifteen of them, far more than Travis thought Washington County might need, unless, of course, a potential mass casualty disaster from something like a tornado counted.

"You always call them racks?" Travis frowned.

Ava nodded, "Yeah. That's the common term. Why?"

"Sounds like something from the Navy." Travis thought back to one of the many times he had to travel aboard an aircraft carrier on his way to a mission. With thousands of members on board and no way to house everyone comfortably, the Navy built "racks," small beds stacked one on top of each other in tightly shared quarters. Sailors frequently had a hard time sleeping when they got onto the aircraft carrier until their bodies adjusted to the noise and thrum of nearly constant conversation and lights on all the time, many of the sailors collapsed after being on the ship for a few days with little or no sleep, their physiology finally realizing they'd have to give up their need for peace and quiet at some point.

"It is. The design was adapted from the military. Maybe you've seen something like this in the past?"

Travis shook his head. Clearly, Sheriff Burnett had told her something of his history. He cleared his throat, suddenly feeling uncomfortable. The idea that people were talking about him sent his stomach into a tiny knot. "No. I've seen racks, but this is my first trip to an autopsy room."

Travis took a moment to scan his surroundings. Off to his right, there was a set of gleaming stainless-steel worktables, a variety of scientific equipment lined up neatly from one end to the other, including two different computers. He recognized what looked to be several different types of microscopes, but as for the rest of the medical equipment besides the computers, he wasn't sure what they were. In the middle of the room, there were two equally shiny examination tables with metal head-rests built into one end with a drain hole in the center of each of the tables that extended into the tile below. A hose with a spray nozzle at one end of each setup was coiled neatly, the hose draping close to the floor, but not touching it. Operating room lights were centered above each one of the tables, their handles covered in thin plastic covers that resembled bags, the kind he'd seen last that Dr. Davey's office, his dentist, on his last visit. Trays were next to each one of the examination tables covered in blue fabric, a black box of latex gloves was stationed at the edge of each of them as if they were just waiting for the influx of instruments to be used on the next body. The walls were painted a gleaming white that matched the white floors. The whole room reeked of sterile things. A shiver ran down Travis's spine. There was definitely no life in that room. Only death.

"The body was housed over there. Best I could tell, based on the damage to the tissue, it was a male of unknown ethnic origin, probably somewhere between his late 20s to mid-30s. If I had to stake my life on it, I'd lean more toward the mid-30s."

"Why don't you have more information about him? Color of his skin? Any ID? Anything like that?"

Travis glanced at Sheriff Burnett in time to see the sheriff stare at the ground and jam the toe of his boot into the tile as though he was kicking at something, but there was nothing there. Travis pressed his lips together and looked at Ava, waiting for her to answer.

"I can't give you more than that because there isn't more to give."

## 5

"Why can't you tell me more? What do you mean? You examined the body, didn't you?" The questions came out of Travis's mouth like rapid fire from a rifle, one after another.

Dr. Scott's shoulders slumped and she glanced at the floor before looking back at Travis. Her words came out barely louder than a whisper, "I can't say I've ever seen it before in my career, but the body was very badly burned, almost down to the bones. It had to be a very intense heat to do that much damage. That's all I can say for sure."

Travis ran calculations in his mind. At that moment, Sheriff Burnett was asking him to try to find a badly burned and mangled body that had somehow been whisked away from rack 113 in the Washington County coroner's office. "When did this happen?"

Dr. Scott sighed, "Sometime last night. I can't tell you exactly when. I left here a little after six o'clock. I was here late finishing some paperwork."

"And you don't have surveillance? I've seen cameras all over this building. Have you looked at the feed?"

Sheriff Burnett looked at Travis, "I think we can actually be more specific about what time the body disappeared than Ava is saying. The surveillance feed went down for some reason right after midnight. While I can't tell you that the body disappeared during that time frame for sure because no one checked right after, it was gone when Dr. Scott got to work this morning."

Travis took a couple of steps forward toward one of the autopsy tables. He wrapped his fingers around the cold stainless-steel edge and looked down at the surface, dreading what he might see, the image of Kira's dead and broken body appearing before him, her skull split in two from the round he'd put into her brain in the Oval Office. It was her second death, the first one faked in Ecuador, but the grief he felt from both of them was real. He blinked and pushed the thought away, his chest tightening. He closed his eyes for a second and then looked back at Sheriff Burnett, "You have a missing body and somehow the surveillance cameras went off at midnight. It wasn't some sort of software update or your vendor making improvements or something?"

"That was the first thing we looked into this morning. I called them myself," Sheriff Burnett said, hooking his thumbs into his gun belt. "I thought for sure it was a glitch or maybe we had a power outage or something. You know, that kind of stuff happens. The technician I talked to said that wasn't the case. The system was operating perfectly. Something messed up the signal."

"Like a jammer?" Travis watched the two of them for their reaction. Ava dropped her eyes to the floor and Sheriff Burnett stared at the ceiling as though the answer would magically appear up there. "Maybe," Sheriff Burnett said, sighing. "The tech didn't know. I can show you the feed if you want?"

Travis nodded. He had access to jamming equipment in his war room. He found it helpful from time to time. He'd used it last when he was with Elena a few months before. Jamming devices could be used to interfere with all sorts of electronic equipment. They could do everything from making it impossible for cell phone signals to send and receive, to dampening the ability of listening devices installed in a home or office to collect data. He pressed his lips together. Espionage was a tit-for-tat business. As one side of the equation improved their listening devices, finding newer and more high-tech ways to invade people's privacy, the other side of the equation — whether it was a government, business, or even a criminal enterprise — figured out a way to block that same technology. It was like watching two people climbing ladders next to each other. One might get ahead of the other by a rung or two only to turn around and realize their opponent had actually passed them. The worst part of it was that no one knew who was winning. The game was never over.

"Yes, I'd like to see that." Travis turned on his heel to go back to the door. Despite all of his training, the autopsy room was giving him the creeps. He was ready to leave. Dr. Scott's voice stopped him. "Wait, Travis. There's one other thing I need to show you."

Travis pivoted in time to see Dr. Scott walk toward the wall adjacent to the morgue's cold storage racks. He hadn't noticed it before but there was a closet door. As she opened it he saw a four-drawer file and above it, a safe. As she turned the knob for the combination on the dial, she glanced over her shoulder, "When I started working here, I asked them to install this safe. We had one at my previous job. It's the best place to keep people's valuables until their families come to get them."

"You have this guy's wallet or something?" Travis knitted his eyebrows together, curious about what she was getting out of the safe.

"Not quite." Ava pressed down on the handle for the safe and pulled the heavy door open, reaching inside. From the interior, she pulled out a small bag, sealed with red tape. Travis had seen those types of bags a million times before. Evidence bags. She walked across the room, her low-heeled pumps making a dull clipping noise on the floor as she held the bag in front of Travis's face. Inside, he could see a small glass vial, oblong in shape, about the size of half a pen cap.

"What's that?" Travis said as she dropped the bag into his hands.

She raised her eyebrows, her eyes wide. "I was hoping you could tell me."

# 6

Travis looked at both Dr. Scott and Sheriff Burnett before looking back down at the bag Ava had dropped into his hands. He scowled. Whatever was in the bag was something he had never seen before. "Where did you get this?"

Ava leaned her hand on the autopsy table and crossed her ankles, shifting her weight to the side. She looked more like she was posing for a casual photo than she was discussing something she'd retrieved from a dead body while she was standing in an autopsy room. "From what was left of his right forearm, just above the wrist." She pushed herself off the table and uncrossed her legs, recrossing her arms in front of her chest in one smooth movement. "When the body got here it was so badly damaged I decided to do a full set of x-rays."

"You were looking for bullets or shrapnel," Travis mumbled.

"Correct. Instead, I saw what looked like a blip on the x-ray. Couldn't really tell what it was. I ended up excising the area and found that implant or whatever you'd like to call it. I thought it was strange so I bagged up and stuck it in our safe."

Travis studied the capsule. The best he could tell it was

made of some sort of clear glass or polymer. Inside, he could see something that looked like a white substance along with what appeared to be a green circuit chip and a few wires. He frowned. It was clearly electronic in nature. It reminded him of listening devices he'd run into on CIA operations. "What do you think this is? Some sort of a tracking device?"

Sheriff Burnett shrugged, "That's the thing, Travis. We don't know. This whole thing is a mystery. We don't know who the body was. And now we have this."

Ava tilted her head to the side, "That might not be entirely true, Sheriff," she said, the words coming out of her mouth slowly. "I might have something of an idea who our victim is." Ava walked over to one of the computers on the stainless-steel worktable against the wall, entering a password and scanning what looked to be her email. "There!!" she pointed. "It just came back. It looks like our John Doe has a name. Jake West."

"How did you find that out?" Sheriff Burnett said, mopping his forehead again.

"In addition to the capsule in his wrist, the x-rays showed that Mr. West had surgery on his foot. I checked with the manufacturer. All of the rods and screws that are used for medical devices generally have some sort of serial number to them. Well, maybe not the screws, but the larger pieces do. It's a way for the biomedical companies to keep track of the performance of their devices and also to track if there's a problem. It's like the way that a vehicle identification number, or a VIN, is attached to every car that's manufactured. If there's a problem, the manufacturers can quickly figure out which vehicles have the issue and who owns them. It's the same with medical devices. The serial numbers give us a good idea about identity too. I'm happy that it worked in this case. Let me see if I can pull up some more information about Mr. West."

Travis walked toward Ava and stood behind her shoulder as she tapped away on the keyboard, impressed by her skills.

Maybe there was something more to her than he originally thought. "We've got a lot of Jake West's here, don't we?" Ava mumbled, staring at the screen. She frowned. "According to the records, he did live in Texas, or at least at the time of his surgery he did. Near Dallas. Let me see if I can cross-reference an address so we can get a picture of him." After a couple more keystrokes, Ava sucked in a breath, "Here!" she pointed.

The screen showed a man with blond wavy hair, green eyes, and pale skin. His face was long and thin with a pointed chin and ears that were tight to the side of his skull. "That looks like the same skull shape I saw on the body."

Travis scanned the record over her shoulder. It said that Jake West was a resident of Dallas, was five feet eleven inches and one hundred ninety pounds with blond hair and green eyes. "That's not a lot to go on, but at least it's a start."

# 7

The conversation in the autopsy room had gone on for far too long. Edward saw Dr. Scott and Sheriff Burnett disappear inside with a man he didn't recognize, tall and muscular with a fringe of clipped brown hair evident under the back of his baseball cap. What they were talking about, he wasn't exactly sure. The fact that he didn't know made him nervous.

Edward stood outside the door of the autopsy room, listening. Although the building was newer, the walls were thin. With his exceptional hearing, he was able to take in a good chunk of the conversation. He heard one of the racks open and close as if Dr. Scott was showing Sheriff Burnett and whoever the other man was where the missing body had been. At that point, the conversation became more muffled. The only explanation for why Edward couldn't hear them was that they were at the back of the autopsy room, far away from his listening ear. His stomach clenched into a knot. Everything the night before had gone exactly according to plan. But he hadn't counted on Dr. Scott discovering that Jake West's body was missing quite so fast. Later on that day, certainly, when it was time to finish the paperwork. But first thing in the morning when other bodies were waiting? He hadn't accounted for that. He shook his head and sighed, pressing his ear up to the door again. He should've known better. Dr. Scott was extremely detail-oriented. She was the kind that would come in the morning and double-check every bit of the work she'd done the day before. She was a hard worker, that was for sure. But her obsessive personality made her difficult to work with. Luckily, Edward wasn't working in the office because of her personality. He was placed there.

Turning on his heel as he heard voices approaching the door, Edward disappeared down a hallway that twisted away from the autopsy room and out through the back doors where the van had taken away Jake West's body the night before. He'd checked the surveillance feed himself that morning. There was nothing to be seen except for Edward moving around the building as he normally would on the night shift.

Outside, the afternoon had turned balmy. He walked to the other side of the parking lot, striding toward a stand of trees behind the building. It was a spot where the people that worked at the Sheriff's Department who still smoked took their breaks. There was no one there now, only a smattering of used-up cigarette butts stinking up the ground near a stand of pine trees. A few birds chirped overhead. He pulled the phone out of the pocket of his scrubs and dialed.

"Yes?"

"It's Edward." Edward identified himself by his cover name. Everyone on the team had them.

"Yes, Edward."

"They know the body is missing."

"Is that all?"

"No."

"Continue."

Edward turned his back toward the building in case anyone

watching through the windows could read lips, "They're discussing the matter with someone else."

"Who is it?"

"His name is Travis."

"Additional information?"

"I have the license plate number to his truck..."

# 8

"So you'll help us?"

"I'll try. Honestly, there's not a lot for me to go on here," Travis said. He glanced down at the capsule in his hand. "I need to take this with me."

Dr. Scott glanced at Sheriff Burnett who gave a single nod. The Sheriff moved toward the door of the autopsy room. "Sure. If that thing can help you figure out what happened to the body, then yes. And I know you have access to help we might not be able to get otherwise."

Travis felt his body stiffen. He knew Sheriff Burnett was referring to his time with Delta Force and the CIA. Sheriff Burnett was right, it was possible that he could get some additional help if he needed it, but there was no part of him that wanted to tangle with the Agency again. Not after what happened with Gus and Kira. Not if he could help it. "I'm hoping I don't need to," he said, licking his lips. "But I'd like to get a closer look at whatever this thing is. It might give me a better idea of who Jake West was and what he was up to. Clearly, there's more to his story, especially if somebody has gone to the trouble to steal the body."

Dr. Scott had a scowl on her face. Travis could tell by how stiffly she held her body that she wasn't happy that he wanted to take the implant with him. That was too bad. If they wanted his help, they'd have to cooperate. "Is there a problem, Dr. Scott?"

She glanced at the floor, her cheeks turning ruby red, and paused; as if she was measuring her words. She looked at Travis, "No. If the sheriff says it's okay for you to take the implant with you, then it's fine with me, I guess."

Her words hung in the air for a moment. Travis didn't respond. She cleared her throat, lacing her fingers in front of her, her eyes glued to the evidence bag with the implant inside. "Mr. Bishop, there is one other piece of critical evidence you should know."

Travis shifted his weight, resting it on one hip watching her, his lips partly open, "What's that?"

"Jake West was dead long before they burned his body."

K eaton Callahan pulled his thick glasses away from his face using his free hand to wipe his eyes. They were bleary from staring at the computer screen for too long. He picked up a bottle of moisturizing solution from the desk and put a single drop in each eye before replacing the glasses on his face. The frames themselves had set him back a couple of thousand dollars. When he started his career, spending more than fifty bucks for glasses would have given him pause. No more. He picked up the bottle of eyedrops and tossed them in the drawer in his desk. "Using these things all the time makes me feel like an old man," he grumbled to himself, pushing his padded black leather executive chair away from the expansive desk in his office. He stood up, walked to the window, running his fingers through his wavy dark hair.

The view from his office window in Miami was nearly as spectacular as his office itself. Surrounded by three sides of glass windows, his office on the top floor of Explority Biotech had more square footage than most of the homes in the area. Off in the distance, Keaton could see the Atlantic Ocean, gentle waves blowing into shore in orderly lines of white surf.

He pulled open a long patio door and stepped outside, instantly feeling the breeze blowing around him. Miami was known for its breathtaking ocean views and hopping nightlife. Being able to take advantage of at least one of them while he was at work was just another perk as CEO of Explority Biotech.

Scanning the distance, he could see some boats in the harbor going in and out, hear the buzz of traffic below him, and a few pedestrians wearing brightly colored clothes moving in clusters up and down the sidewalks. On nice days like the one they were having, stepping outside and getting some fresh air, untethering himself from the wall of monitors set up on his desk, gave him just enough energy to finish the day's work.

And it never ended.

Explority Biotech was responsible for researching and developing biomedical devices that helped people, or at least that's what the mission statement on their website said. Keaton had started off in the biotech business with a good heart, wanting to make people's lives better.

That lasted until he figured out how much money there was to be made. That money had funded a house and a condo in Miami, a house in Aspen and a fifty-foot Sea Ray express cruiser with twin diesel engines docked at the local marina, in addition to a Ferrari painted in gloss black parked in the garage downstairs, and entry into pretty much any of the best restaurants that city had to offer at any time he wanted.

Keaton propped his forearms on the railing outside, staring off in the distance. Realistically, he had enough money in the bank that he could walk away from the business and go live on his boat for the next several years if he wanted to. The business would manage itself, he was sure. Part of him thought peace and quiet sounded like a good idea. Another part of him wasn't so sure he'd ever be able to give up the adrenaline rush that came with a brand-new idea or the satisfaction he felt as they guided one of their products through clinical trials and out onto the open market.

His favorite day running Explority up to that point had been when his company had gone public. He'd hired a private jet to take him and his team to New York to ring the bell at the New York Stock Exchange, closing the market for the day, his face peppered all over the national business news, calls of congratulations coming in as far away as India and China. His skin tingled thinking about the moment he pressed the button. One man had single-handedly stopped trading on one of the largest markets in the world. That was a lot of power. Power was something he liked.

Straightening up, Keaton pushed his glasses back up on his nose and drummed his fingers on the rail. He took a couple of deep breaths, ones that his therapist and yoga instructor would have been proud of. Along with the pressures of his job came nearly constant tension. Headaches, an upset stomach, and trouble sleeping were nearly constant companions on his journey. Keaton glanced toward the marina, squinting toward the spot where his boat sat. Maybe someday he'd be able to relax enough to properly enjoy it.

But that day was not today.

Striding back inside and closing the door behind him, Keaton stopped for a moment and surveyed his office.

Directly in front of him was his desk, a fourteen-foot-long span he'd had custom built out of burled wood that held three oversized monitors, an open section where he could sit and write, and a third section with chairs where he could meet with other people. His black leather executive chair had wheels on it that allowed him to push himself from one end of the desk to the other depending on what he needed at that moment. The floors were reclaimed wood from a warehouse downtown that had been custom installed, sanded, stained, and sealed on site. It took more than two months to recover enough wood in order to fill his office space, which topped out at close to two thousand square feet. To his left, there was a tall white painted wall on the two-story ceiling, decorated with an abstract painting in reds and yellows and greens painted by an upcoming Miami artist known only as Naranja. When Keaton had met her at a gallery opening a few years before, he asked her about her name. It meant orange in Spanish. "It's my favorite color," Naranja responded coyly, spinning on her heel and walking away from him. Her response intrigued him enough that he purchased the painting and hung it in his office.

Below Naranja's massive canvas was a custom-made white leather sofa imported from Italy, two matching chairs flanking it with a glass coffee table in the middle. A crystal carafe filled with amaretto sat on the table. Keaton liked his sweet drinks and amaretto was his favorite, allowing himself one at the end of any particularly stressful day, which had been all of them for the last few months.

Beyond the office area and the couch was a small kitchen, not big enough to cook a gourmet meal, but spacious enough to hold snacks and food so he didn't have to leave his office. A full bathroom and a dressing room were the only other rooms in his office. They included all of his favorite toiletries kept in stock by his assistant, Rory, as well as several changes of clothes, depending on what the occasion might require, including a custom-made tuxedo, workout clothes, and business casual outfits, in case an opportunity should pop up at the last second and Keaton didn't have a chance to return to his condo or one of his homes to prepare for an evening. The only thing the office lacked was a proper bed, but the couch was comfortable enough.

Other people might have thought his office was extreme, but for Keaton, it was all about convenience. He wanted everything in his life within arm's reach so he could keep working. And with his current setup, pretty much everything was.

Keaton walked toward his desk, covering one of the many plush rugs on the floor wearing a pair of hard-to-find high-top Jordan's as he heard his phone ring. He flopped down in the leather chair, hearing the cushioning underneath him exhale as it received his body weight. He picked up the phone. "Yes?"

"Sir, we've completed our investigation."

Keaton's skin prickled. He'd been pleased to get the news that the body they'd been looking for had been recovered. The team he had in place had taken it to a private medical lab, transporting it from some podunk location in Texas to one that his company owned on the outskirts of Miami. They'd been instructed to do what they needed to do. He held his breath, waiting for the news. "And?"

"I'm sorry, sir. It's not there."

Keaton exploded out of his chair, pounding his fist on the wooden desk, a crystal cupful of pens and pencils rattling as he did. "What do you mean it's not there? How is that even possible?"

"I don't know, sir," the voice on the other end of the line stammered. "We x-rayed the body and then even put it through a CAT scan. The implant is not there."

"Did you buffoons have Dr. Lyons look at it?" Dr. Lyons was the lead researcher on the majority of Keaton's projects.

"Of course, sir. She was here last night when we arrived. She just left. The implant isn't there."

"It has to be. Keep looking."

"Sir, it's not. Is it possible it was destroyed when they burned the body? Based on the damage, Dr. Lyons said it could have exploded with the heat. Or maybe the coroner found it? We could tell she did have a go at the body before we recovered it."

"Is there anything else? Anything helpful?" Keaton was losing his patience.

"The guy was beaten before he died."

"Beaten?"

"Yeah. Dr. Lyons could see bruising deep under the skin."

Keaton shook his head. "I don't care about how the guy died. I need the implant."

"I'm sorry, sir. We don't have it, and…"

"I don't care! This is your job!" Keaton bellowed. "I need you to find that implant and get it to me. Now!"

Keaton hung up without saying goodbye, throwing his body back down into the leather chair like he was a three-year-old that just had a tantrum. He needed answers and his team wasn't getting them.

Keaton picked up his phone, thumbing through his recent phone calls. He connected to a single number. "Malcolm? I'm about to lose my cool."

The voice on the other end of the line chuckled, "I heard you already did. The guys at the lab just called me. Said you went ballistic on them."

News traveled fast. Keaton grimaced, "I need that implant."

Malcolm was the lead on Keaton's current off-the-books project. It was only something that a few people knew about. Other than Keaton, Malcolm was the only one that knew all the details. He and Malcolm didn't see each other in person very much. The type of work that Malcolm did for Keaton made it unsafe to do so. The times they did meet, it was usually in the back of Joey's Italian Restaurant, in a private room in downtown Miami that Keaton entered from the back. Malcolm did the same. The owner, a short man with a single strand of hair cutting across the top of his head, served them ossobuco, chianti, and basket after basket of homemade, hot Italian bread while they talked. Malcolm was a good eater. He was Nigerian by birth but appreciated a good Italian meal as much as the next man did.

"I might be able to help with that."

"You might?" Keaton's eyes widened. Malcolm always

seemed to come through with information at the moment he needed it.

"Actually, I can. I got a call a few minutes ago from our contact at the coroner's office. Apparently, the coroner extracted the implant and hid it somewhere in the building. He didn't know until a few minutes ago."

Keaton pushed himself out of his chair and started to pace back and forth. He needed the implant in order to finish the project. If he didn't have it, he'd have to come up with a work-around, but even with all his technical expertise, he wasn't sure that was possible. "She had it the whole time? Where is it now?"

"Well, apparently when the coroner discovered the body was missing this morning, they quickly reached out to somebody in the area for help. His name is Travis Bishop. I'm running a background check on him now. Looks like he was involved in the military. He's a local horse trainer with a skip tracing business on the side."

"I don't care if he's Bobo the Clown! I want that implant back. Get it for me now." Keaton said, ending the call and slamming his phone down on his desk.

As Keaton sat in his chair, he heard a familiar buzzing from over his shoulder. A wave of nausea covered him. As he glanced over his shoulder, he whispered under his breath, "Not now. Please, not now…"

## 10

Keaton closed his eyes for a brief moment, hoping the hum he heard from outside would go away. It didn't. Resigned, he stood up from his desk and walked to the patio door, sliding it open. Hovering just outside the door was a sleek black remote-controlled drone. As Keaton walked back into his office and sat down, the drone followed. Keaton looked at the ground, not saying anything.

The drone visits had started nearly a year before. Keaton had first noticed it while he was working, thinking it was a case of industrial espionage. He quickly assigned his assistant, Rory, the task of making sure that his monitors had privacy screens attached to them and that thick blinds were installed on every window in his office. If someone wanted to see what he was planning, they'd have to work for it.

Industrial espionage in the biotech sector was the real deal. New drugs and devices could cost billions to bring to market by the time the research, development, testing, and the legal loopholes the FDA made everyone jump through were completed. That didn't even begin to deal with the investment of human capital — the long hours of brainstorming, problem-solving, and legal wrangling it took to get patents and protections put in place. And even if everything was done correctly, there were always spies from competitors lurking about, people from other companies posing as a wide variety of contractors, from plumbers to caterers, who were paid to steal information. When Keaton had started Explority Biotech, he'd discovered the window washer one day hanging outside not only washing his windows but also taking pictures of the information Keaton had displayed on his computer from the suspended position he had on the high-rise. Keaton calmly walked to the kitchen area of his office, grabbed a long knife hiding it behind his back, and walked out onto the patio as the man quickly stuffed his phone in his pocket and resumed his washing routine. Keaton approached one of the lines the man was using to keep himself on the side of the building and held the knife to the nylon rope, demanding his phone, "Or, this will be the last window you ever wash." The man quickly handed over his cell phone and descended the side of the building, never to be seen again.

But the drone that had been visiting him wasn't industrial espionage. It was the single person that had a death grip on Keaton's life and his business.

"It's nice to see you again, Keaton," a male voice said, projected from the inside of the drone with a thick Middle Eastern accent.

"Hello, Raashid. What can I do for you today?"

"I've come for an update on our project. Has the implant been recovered?"

"Just about. The body has been recovered."

"And the implant?"

Keaton slumped down onto his desk chair. He knew Raashid Al Khan was watching his every move from a hidden location. Where, Keaton had no idea. Keaton had researched the drone after the first time it had spoken to him. Drone technology had evolved greatly over the last decade, going from something fun that could be flown by the neighbors, to high-tech equipment capable of carrying out pinpoint assassinations in parts of the world where the United States had no business being. This particular model, the one piloted by Raashid or one of his henchmen, included full video capacity, navigation, and speakers for voice communication. And that was just what Keaton could figure out on his own. Raashid was probably the only person he'd interacted with that was his match in terms of intellect, not that he'd actually met him in person. Whatever Keaton could imagine about the drone, he was certain there was more to it.

"It wasn't with the body. We have a lead, though." As much as Keaton wanted to lie to Raashid, or the voice coming out of the drone, he knew that wasn't a good idea. Raashid had his ways of confirming information. How exactly, Keaton had never been able to figure out.

"Do I need to remind you that we need both implants in order to complete the assignment?"

A single bead of sweat dripped down the side of Keaton's face. He flicked it away, hoping that his sudden movement on camera looked more like him pushing hair away from his pale face than sweat gathering on his brow. "I know. I know. You've told me that a hundred times."

"Then handle the problem, Mr. Callahan. I don't want to have to remind you again of the consequences of your failure."

The drone buzzed out of the open door and disappeared out of view. Keaton didn't bother chasing after it. He stood up from his desk, walked to the patio door, his hands shaking as he closed it.

## 11

A fter Dr. Scott and Sheriff Burnett handed over the implant to Travis, he spent the next hour in Sheriff Burnett's office with them, going over the details of the case. Sheriff Burnett passed Travis a copy of the police report from when the body had been found. "We don't see too many injuries like this around here. You know that, right?" Sheriff Burnett mumbled as if he was trying to reassure Travis that finding a burned body wasn't normal for the peace and tranquility pretty much guaranteed by the trustees of Washington County.

"I know that. But that doesn't change the fact that it was found on your turf. Where exactly was it?"

"A company is rehabbing an old elementary school building out on route five. They showed up to work and found the body tossed in one of the dumpsters. It was the smell that got their attention. I guess the guy that saw it threw up his breakfast before calling the police."

Travis raised his eyebrows, "Can't say I blame him." Travis stared at the photos in the file. Jake West's body was nearly unrecognizable as human remains. The skin, what was left of it, was black and charred, the tendons and ligaments holding the muscles to his arms visible from where the flesh had burned away. The only thing that identified the remains as human right off the bat was the menacing grimace of the man's teeth white against the black flesh. Travis quickly flipped the page, looking at the description. There wasn't a lot to go on. He frowned and then glanced at the Sheriff and then Dr. Scott, "You have any more information other than this? We know the guy's name is Jake West. He's from Dallas, he had a strange implant in his arm, he was dead before he was burned, and that's it?"

Dr. Scott nodded, her voice so quiet it was nearly imperceptible, "That's it. I wish I had more for you..." she muttered.

Travis shook his head and closed the file. If he had to guess, any background check he ran wouldn't reveal very much. Anyone who was killed the way Jake West was and had a strange implant in his arm was clearly involved in something off the books. Whether that was criminal or governmental remained to be seen. Working for the CIA, Travis had seen his fair share of bodies brutalized at black sites, but the trauma Jake West's body went through was probably the worst he'd seen. Whoever had gotten his hands on the man left no stone unturned, no secret left unfound. Travis stood up, holding the manila file in his hand and shoving the implant in his pocket, "One other question, Dr. Scott."

She blinked, "Sure."

"You said he was dead before he was burned. How was he killed?"

Dr. Scott shifted in her seat, "A single shot between the eyes. Dead instantly. Whether that was the only thing that caused his death, I have no idea. It wouldn't surprise me if other damage had been done to his body but it was masked by the fire. The only reason I know he was shot is from the hole in the front of his skull. I sent out a toxicology report. That might tell us something. But I can't go back and do any additional research, obviously," she said, throwing her hands in the air.

It was the first crack in Dr. Scott's very professional veneer that Travis had seen. She was clearly frustrated by the situation.

Sheriff Burnett nodded, using his handkerchief to dab at his upper lip, "Now Ava, I told you not to worry about this. Travis will help us out, won't you, Travis?"

"I'm going to try."

---

## 12

With the case file in his hand and the implant shoved in his pocket, Travis said his goodbyes to Sheriff Burnett in Dr. Scott with the promise that he'd update them as soon as he knew anything. He didn't give them any timeline. That wasn't his style. Travis wandered out to the truck, opened it up, immediately smelling the rest of his lunch and the couple of pounds of brisket he bought from Sarah's Barbecue at lunchtime sitting inside.

Starting the truck, he pulled out of the sheriff's office parking area and headed out on route twenty back to his ranch. Thoughts were surging in his mind. He rolled down the window, letting the warm afternoon breeze into the truck, laying his arm on the sill of the driver's side door as he drove. He turned on the radio, hearing a familiar refrain from a country song that came out a few years before. Apparently, it was still popular enough to play.

The lyrics and the melody weren't enough to interrupt Travis's train of thought. He pressed his lips together as he drove, focusing on the road just enough to navigate his way back to the ranch. After a few minutes of pondering, he realized the things Dr. Scott and Sheriff Burnett had given him needed his immediate attention, regardless of the fact that no quick action on his part could undo Jake West's death. He picked up his phone, dialing Ellie, "Hey."

"Hey, yourself. I'm on my way to you."

Ellie had worked for Travis for the last few years. She was reliable, punctual, great with the horses, and even better with the clients. Most of the time, Travis had Ellie do the initial phone calls with potential customers, sifting through who was a good candidate and who wanted him to take their backyard pony and turn it into the next champion. What most people didn't realize about horses is they were no different than human athletes in many ways. Their bodies were built to do specific jobs. While it was possible to take a racehorse and turn them into a reiner, they'd never be able to compete against horses that were bred to do the work, specifically quarter horses. And even among the horses in the same breed category, their physiology made some of them better candidates for training than others. He always looked for horses that had a lower head carriage, strong hocks, a flexible back, and a determined spirit. A lot of the other things he could train into them, but if they weren't built for the sport, there was no way they would succeed.

"Good. I stopped at Big Al's and bought the worming supplies. I'm headed back to the ranch myself."

"You get some of that good barbecue from Sarah while you were on your way back? The sheriff called. He was looking for you."

"He found me." Travis gritted his teeth together. It wasn't Ellie's job to tell anyone where Travis was.

"Everything okay?"

"Okay enough." It felt like a not-so-subtle probe. Travis didn't feel the need to try to explain to Ellie what was going on. What happened in his skip tracing business and what happened at the ranch were two separate activities as far as he was concerned. Ellie was part of the latter and not the former. He needed her to keep her eyes completely focused on what was going on in the business with the horses. Nothing more, nothing less.

He cleared his throat, shifting in the seat of his truck, making the final turn off route twenty to get back to the ranch, "I should be back in the next ten to fifteen minutes. I'm gonna stop at the barn and drop off the stuff I bought at a Big Al's. Can you jump in and get the horses schooled for me? I think there are only three to ride on the schedule today. The rest of them can spend some time in the paddock. When you bring them in, you can go ahead and worm them. I've got some other things to attend to."

"Sure. I'll get it handled. Anything else you need me to do?"

Travis narrowed his eyes. Whether Ellie was still trying to get information about his interaction with the sheriff or not, Travis wasn't sure. "No. That's enough. I'll deal with the rest of it when I get back."

## 13

B y the time Travis got back to the ranch, Ellie was already there, leading a couple of horses out to the paddock, turning them around in tandem and taking their halters off so they could run. Travis pressed the brake on his truck, stopping and watching as the two beautiful animals, their muscles rippling under their sleek coats in the sun, wheeled away from the gate and galloped toward the back fence, kicking up their heels and throwing their muzzles in the air. Travis smiled at their ability to be carefree, then took his foot off the brake and drove to the barn, stopping to look at the new construction as he did, his boots echoing on the new concrete in the empty stable.

The contractors were already gone for the day. Travis walked through the new building, the dusty smell of fresh concrete hanging in the air. He tested a couple of the stall doors, watching as the heavy wooden metal rolled quietly on the wheeled track from above. He nodded, thinking to himself that Kira would be pleased with the results. At least, the Kira he'd been engaged to, not the one that had double-crossed not only the United States but also him. He pushed the thought away. It wasn't the day to follow the ghost of her memory down into a ditch.

Walking back out to his truck, Travis snagged the supplies he'd purchased from Big Al's, hooking the handles from the white plastic bags over his arms and carrying them to the tack room of the main barn. As soon as he opened the door, he could smell the scent of freshly oiled leather. He set the bags on the ground, pulling out the saddle pads and laying them over top of Ellie's schooling saddle, the one she used for daily training. He tossed the shedding blades in one of the grooming buckets and left the worming supplies in a bag hanging on the horn of a saddle nearby. Stopping for a minute and looking around, Travis nodded. Within a few days, they'd move at least some of the equipment and horses over to the other barn. The new space included a better office as well, one that was more secluded from the goldfish bowl view of the arena. He still hadn't decided if he was going to keep his original office where he could look out onto the arena as Ellie schooled the horses or if he wanted to move to the other office. He raised his eyebrows. Maybe he'd use both of them. It was his operation after all.

Closing the door to the tack room behind him, Travis got in his truck and turned it around just as he saw another dust plume coming down the driveway. Ellie. His timing was perfect, he thought, glancing at the manila file folder on his passenger seat with the information Sheriff Burnett and Dr. Scott had given him. The implant was still in the bag shoved into his jeans pocket. He touched it, feeling the lump through the thick denim fabric. His curiosity was piqued, a knot of tension forming in his chest as questions formed in his mind. He started the truck and put it into gear, pulling away from the barn. He made it into the driveway of the log cabin as Ellie passed in her truck. He gave her a wave but didn't stop to talk. It wasn't a good time for questions. He had other work to do.

Inside the house, after dumping off his boots by the back

door, Travis went directly to the war room, using a single finger to unlock the bookshelf filled with a few mementos and history books that hid the entrance and then absentmindedly keying in the code and swiping his thumb across the fingerprint reader. Inside, everything was exactly as he had left it, as it should be.

The war room was a reclaimed space in the log cabin he'd found when he bought the property. Originally, the room was meant as storage behind the kitchen, a place for canned goods, small appliances, and bulky serving pieces that couldn't find a home elsewhere, the shelves dusty, the air stale in the closed-off room. Travis had always been surprised by its size, wondering if the original owners had meant it more for emergency storage than anything else.

For a while, he and Kira had considered blowing out the wall and expanding the kitchen, giving them space to entertain family and friends over barbecue and beers on the porch. But after she died, Travis scrapped that plan. Alone, he didn't have any friends he wanted to entertain and no family nearby. Instead, he closed off the entrance from the kitchen and created a new one behind the bookshelf, spending several months installing a myriad of high-tech equipment and supplies that only he would need. The war room was his, and his alone. As he walked inside, he remembered Elena Lobranova's reaction when she'd seen it and heard him call it his war room. "Are you trying to start a war or stop one, Travis?" she'd asked at the time.

A smile tugged at his cheek thinking about Elena. He hadn't heard from her in a while. She'd resumed her position in the good graces at the CIA after she turned over the Moscow brief that exposed Gus and Kira for what they were — Russian double agents with a covert plan to disrupt the entirety of the US government. It had failed, but just barely.

Travis's war room had built-in cabinets that surrounded the entrance in the shape of a U, finished in a medium brown oak stain with a center island Travis used as a worktable. On the left side of the war room, there were two computers with a bookshelf above them, the volumes including books on history, technical manuals on firearm maintenance, and creative surveillance techniques. Travis wasn't much of a television watcher, so he tended to study those books to help him with his skip tracing business, although it wasn't necessary other than as a refresher. He knew more about surveillance and evasion than most people did about what they'd had for breakfast that morning.

Directly on the other side of the room from the doorway was a bank of locked cabinets, keycode secured handles protecting a variety of rifles, shotguns, pistols, and the ammunition inside. In addition to the firearms, Travis had a selection of smoke grenades and flash bangs — small canisters that emitted a bright light followed by a deafening sound and then smoke — that he had purchased through Sheriff Burnett. He hadn't bothered to explain why he wanted them and Sheriff Burnett hadn't asked.

On the opposite side of the room, the flow of the polished oak cabinetry continued. Above the base cabinets, three large monitors glowed from the walls as they pumped in a constant view of the ranch from the surveillance cameras that were scattered around the property.

Travis pushed the door closed behind him and then waited for a moment as he heard the automatic lock kick into place. A moment later, he heard a soft thud from the other side of the wall, the bookcase sliding back into position. If anyone entered his house while he was in the war room, they'd have no idea where he was. Flipping on one of the arcing lights at the worktable, Travis threw the file Sheriff Burnett had given him down and pulled the implant out of his pocket, staring at it for a moment before setting it down next to the file. He tugged one of the stools out from underneath the edge of the worktable and sat down, facing the door. Glancing to his left, he checked the surveillance feeds on the monitors. He could see Ellie in the barn, one of the horses in the cross ties, the snaps holding the horse into position from each side of the halter as she swung her saddle up on top of the horse's back. Travis narrowed his eyes. Ellie moved with an economy of motion in everything she did. She didn't over cue the horses while she rode, nor did she overcorrect them. Her gentle touch with the animals in his care was one thing that was making his program more and more successful.

A flicker of a frown crossed Travis's face. Recently, Ellie had become bolder with her questioning. When he'd first met her, she barely asked anything, only nodding when he asked her to do something. But now, after they'd worked together for several years, she started to follow his comments with those of her own, usually a pointed inquiry into what he was doing. Perhaps it was just curiosity. Perhaps it wasn't.

But that was a question for another day.

Travis stared at the file in front of him and then glanced at the implant, still in the bag. He flipped open the manila folder, pulling the work lamp closer to him, the glow from the bulb casting a sharp shadow over the edges of the pages. Travis picked at the staples with his fingernail, pulling them away from the cover and tossing them into the trash. Now loose from the file, he took all of the images and put them in one pile and took the autopsy and police report and put them in another pile. He wasn't interested in Dr. Scott's notes or what the police had found at the scene, at least not for the moment. Maybe he would be after he stared at the pictures, but right now, he wanted to form his own opinion.

From the arm of the work lamp, Travis pulled a circular magnifier into place, centering it over the images so he could look at them more closely. He started by looking at the image as a whole and then looking at each portion of the photograph, quadrant by quadrant. It was a habit he'd picked up while in Delta Force as they mapped out missions. Every operator had a different way of processing information. He preferred to look at the whole and then break it apart into its components.

Travis squared a single image of the body under the magnifier, leaning over the lens. Dr. Scott had taken meticulous photographs of the scorched body of Jake West. As Travis looked at the first image, he wondered what the expression on the man's face was that had found the body. Was it shock? Disgust? Fear?

Travis cocked his head to the side as he took in the first photograph. It was a crime scene photo, the charred body nestled in a pile of construction debris, chunks of drywall flaking off near the carcass, a scrap piece of a two by four laying across what was left of the man's legs. Dr. Scott had been right. To anyone who hadn't been looking closely, the body could have been nearly anything, animal, human, or otherwise.

Travis frowned. He'd seen burn victims several times in his career, primarily when he was deployed with Delta Force. The memory flashed in his mind of being on a mission in a remote area of Afghanistan, tired, achy, and hungry after being in the field for several days with his team. They'd come upon a burned-out pickup truck, likely Taliban, that was left as wreckage on the side of the road. Their operational instructions encourage them to evaluate every one of those targets as possible. Sometimes it was and sometimes it wasn't, depending on the situation they were in. That particular time, he and his team, five of them in total, circled the vehicle, checking carefully for IED's that had been placed nearby. Finding none, they moved silently, only using a series of hand signals as they made their approach, M4 rifles raised in front of their faces as they moved slowly toward the truck. A couple of Travis's teammates checked the bed, looking for cell phones, scraps of paper, or any other intelligence that might've been left behind. Travis and another one of his Delta Force buddies checked the interior while the fifth man stood watch.

The windows inside the pickup truck had been blown out, glass crunching under Travis's boots as he got close to the driver's side door. The stench of missile fuel and burning flesh hung in the air, the acrid smell stinging his nostrils. Travis remembered swallowing hard as he looked inside. There were two bodies. The driver was completely burned, his flesh black, only a few shards of clothing left visible. The man in the passenger seat had perished as well, the side of his face blown off, a few burns covering the left side of his body closest to where the driver had been. Travis remembered shaking his head and stepping back away from the body. His mind wondered for a moment what exactly had happened to the bodies. He pushed the thought aside. That hadn't been important at that time.

But it was now, not with the bodies in his memory, but with Jake West. He needed answers if he hoped to help Sheriff Burnett and Dr. Scott find what was left of him.

## 14

Travis reached for the implant that was still in its bag and stared at it. If Dr. Scott had come to him with the burned body, he wouldn't have been interested in the case at all. But the implant — that made things decidedly much more interesting, enough to pique his curiosity. He rolled the implant between his fingers for a moment and then put it down, staring back at the images from Dr. Scott's file. The one thing she was right about was that whatever had burned the body had done it hot and fast, and by the lack of damage to the construction waste, it hadn't been done in the dumpster. Jake West had been killed elsewhere, otherwise, the scrap pieces of drywall and wood from the construction site would have gone up with the body like a funeral pyre sending a heroic deceased Viking away to meet their ancestors. Travis shuddered, wondering what Jake's last moments were like, but then he remembered that Dr. Scott said Jake had been dead long before his body had been burned. At least there was some mercy in that.

Travis went through the stack of pictures in the file and found one from the autopsy of Jake West's face, or what had been left of it. He put it under the magnifying glass and saw the hole Dr. Scott had referred to. He was no expert in forensics, but he was one in firearms. Looking at the diameter of the puncture to Jake's forehead, he imagined the hole was from pistol fire — probably a nine-millimeter or a forty caliber, nothing bigger than that. The bone looked ragged and shattered on the edges.

Travis knew from his training in Delta Force there were two types of shots — a switch and a timer. If a bullet went into someone's head, it was like they were switched off. Death was instant. If the same round went into someone's torso, it was a timer. It was just a question of how much time the person had before they dropped over.

And whoever had killed Jake West went for the kill switch before they torched him.

Travis moved the magnifying glass closer to the image, studying the hole in the front of Jake West's cranium. He absorbed it for a moment and then leaned back, blinking, looking at the ceiling. There was a larger message here, one that Travis was struggling to understand. Why would the killer shoot Jake in the head and then take the time to burn the body pretty much down to the bone? To kill a man was one thing, but to destroy their body was something else, a completely different motivation. In some cases, Travis knew devastating a body was rage. In others, he knew the motivation was about disappearance – removal of any trace the person ever existed.

Except for one thing...

Ruining a body like Jake's had gotten exactly the opposite reaction. All eyes were now focused on what was left, how it had gotten to that state, and why.

## 15

Travis spent another two hours going over the photographs from Dr. Scott's files, stopping only once to exit the war room to retrieve a bottle of water from the kitchen and grab his cell phone. Ellie had sent two texts with questions, which Travis quickly answered as he walked back inside. Going back to his position on the stool, he stacked the images and the documentation from Jake West's case and set them off to the side.

Pulling on a pair of latex gloves, Travis retrieved a knife from one of the drawers below the worktable and slit the top of the evidence bag open, the razor-sharp knife biting through the plastic in one sweep. From another drawer, Travis pulled out a black cushioned mat and rolled it out on the counter. It was one he used for gunsmithing that prevented miniscule springs and screws from rolling away. He shook the implant out on top of it, the bean-sized clear capsule landing in the center of the black examination mat. Travis pulled the light and the magnifying glass over the top of it, doing his first inspection.

Squinting at the capsule under the magnifying glass, Travis took in the things he could say for sure about it. It was clear, probably made of some sort of either tempered glass or polymer. Travis tipped his head to the side and blinked, realizing a polymer was more likely. Even though glass was nonreactive with human tissue, even tempered glass could break if hit hard enough, like in a car accident or while playing sports. If he were making an implant, he would look toward some of the new, clear polymers that mimicked the strength and clarity of glass, but without the shattering factor.

Adjusting the light, he saw a small green circuit board encased in one end of the capsule, the kind he'd only seen before in listening devices when he worked for the CIA. Out of it protruded a couple of small wires. At the other end of the capsule, there was a chamber with a white substance. Whether it was solid, liquid, or a powder, Travis couldn't tell. No motion made it move, at least not under bright lights and magnification. Travis frowned. It could have been vacuum-sealed, but securing that small of a space would require technology Travis hadn't encountered before. Whatever the substance was, seemed to be cordoned off in one end of the capsule as though the capsule had a functional side and a side of cargo.

Travis stood up from his stool, rolling his shoulders a couple of times. All of the bright lights were giving him a headache. He crossed his arms in front of his chest and started pacing, thinking. He stopped for a moment, glanced through the magnifier again, and then ran his hand through his dark hair. Clearly, the implant had a specific use that was reflected in its design. That was a basic premise of engineering. But what the purpose was, Travis wasn't exactly sure.

Another problem loomed in his mind, like a cluster of dark clouds slinking across the horizon. Whether the person or persons who had killed Jake West knew about the implant or not was a completely different question. The fact that someone had stolen the body led Travis to believe something completely different — that whoever had killed Jake wasn't the same person who'd put the implant in him. The people who created the implant probably wanted their work back, and that was who probably took Jake's body.

Travis shrugged, mulling over his hypothesis. Possible, yes. Probable, unknown.

Travis spent the next hour rolling the implant back and forth on the mat, turning it upside down and looking at it from every angle. On one end, he discovered something that looked like a port. It was located near the circuit board. Was it possible this small of a mechanism was designed to be connected to a computer? Travis used a set of tiny needle-nose pliers he had from his gunsmithing kit to remove the plug at the one end of the implant. Staring at it, he realized it was in the same shape as a common cell phone charger. Opening another drawer in his workbench, he pulled out a one-inch dowel that was wrapped with a variety of different cables and cords. He checked the port sizes on them and found one that he thought would fit.

Wrapping the implant in the black mat, he carried it over to the computer, sat down at the desk, and connected the cable between his machine and the implant.

What was on it, he didn't know. But he was about to find out.

## 16

Prickles covered Travis's skin as he pushed the cable into the end of the implant using the least amount of pressure he could, trying not to break it. His hand shook a little at the delicate nature of trying to attach the cable to the port. After a minute of struggle, Travis set the implant down and glanced at it. Satisfied he had the cable lodged correctly into the implant, he plugged the other end of the cable into his laptop and turned it on. A slight wave of nausea ran through him. He was taking a risk. Whatever data was on the implant could easily corrupt his computer and infect some of the other systems he had in place. Luckily, most of those were housed on his desktop and the two computers were kept separate from each other.

Travis stared at the screen, turning on air gap software – a program he'd purchased at the recommendation of a few tech-savvy friends he kept in touch with to isolate his computer from the other devices he owned. Travis waited, watching the screen. He pulled off the gloves he'd been wearing and tossed them in the trash. A few seconds later, an icon appeared as his computer found the implant. The caption underneath it was simply a set of letters and numbers AB753XZT30. Travis frowned. A serial number? A device identification number? He used his cell phone to take a picture of it before double-clicking on the icon.

A few seconds passed. Travis held his breath. At least if whatever was on the implant crashed his system the computer was cordoned off from the network. He'd pick up the laptop, destroy the hard drive, throw it in the trash and go buy a new one. He didn't want to have to do that, but at least it was an option.

While he was waiting, Travis checked the time on his cell phone. He was surprised to find it was nearly ten p.m. Hours had gone by since he'd gotten home. He briefly noticed the sun had gone down on the surveillance video and Ellie's truck was missing from the barn, but he didn't think anything of it. He had more pressing matters to figure out.

After a moment of processing, a black screen popped up on his computer, taking up the majority of the space. Data began to run automatically, a series of letters and numbers white-washed over what looked to be information lurking behind, wide spaces between each line.

Encryption. Travis pressed his lips together and frowned. And a high level of it. He stared as the computer cycled through the information for the next two minutes. It finally stopped. Travis scrolled to the top of the page, trying to make out anything he could, but the coding was complete and indecipherable. There was no way to read it, no way to comprehend what was on the chip inside of the implant.

But at least there was something on it and Travis had been able to access it. He was two-thirds of the way there. He just needed a way to decode it.

Frustrated, the ache in his shoulders telling Travis he'd been sitting in front of the computer for too long, Travis grabbed the implant, dropping it back in the evidence bag and piling the paperwork and photographs from the autopsy back into the file. He stared at the screen again for a moment. No amount of study would be able to decipher what was on it. It was fully encrypted and there were strange breaks in the text as if he only had half of the information. He'd seen some serious encryption before, but this was a whole new level.

Gathering up the implant and dropping it back into the evidence bag, Travis slid the photos and paperwork from Dr. Scott's office back inside the file. From a drawer, Travis pulled out a large manila envelope, sticking both parts inside. There was no need to label it. He knew exactly what it was.

Standing up, he walked to the end of the worktable, pulling open the cabinet door that extended from the edge of the top all the way to the floor. Inside, there was a stack of books sitting on a shelf. Travis set the large envelope down on the floor as he knelt in front of the books, using two hands to lift the shelf. It rose about four inches and then swung to his right exposing a floor safe. Passing his thumb over the reader and dialing in the combination, the door clicked open. Travis turned the handle and lifted it. He grabbed the envelope that contained the file and the implant and set it inside, securing the safe door, giving the knob a twist, and then replacing the shelf of books inside the cabinet. No one knew about the safe. No one. Travis had installed it himself as a way to protect his client's most sensitive secrets.

Staring at the books inside the cabinet, Travis realized secrets weren't secrets if the information got out. And Jake West's information needed to stay hidden for the moment, at least until Travis could start to get some answers.

## 17

Two ATVs rolled down the driveway of Bishop Ranch just before two o'clock in the morning. They approached the ranch from the adjacent property, coming in on a service road that was barely visible except through their night vision goggles. Their handler had been specific. Their target was sophisticated and had surveillance all over his property. This was no common smash and grab. Their opponent was substantial. Their backdoor approach was the only direction that was even slightly unsecured.

Parking the ATVs behind a stand of trees adjacent to the barn, the two men got off their vehicles, each of them wearing black from head to toe and carrying matching canvas backpacks filled with supplies as well as pistols on their hips. They hiked the last hundred yards to the barn, walking against the edge of the open-air arena, the smell of horses, sawdust, and manure filling their nostrils, the aroma of the sweet hay and grain hanging over the barn in the humid Texas night air.

From the information they'd been able to get about Bishop Ranch, they knew it was a working operation, not just an empty stable. The men slid inside the barn door, the horses rustling in their sleep as the men entered. Halfway down the aisle, they found what they were looking for — an empty stall filled with bales of hay and a pile of pine sawdust shavings used as fresh bedding for the horses. One of the men knelt down, opened up his backpack, pulled out a red canister, unscrewed the lid and poured gasoline all over the tinder in the empty stall. The other man did the same, soaking the wood of the stall doors along the aisle, the pungent odor hanging in the air. Giving each other a nod, one of them threw a match.

Using the gasoline as an accelerant, the dry pine shavings became inflamed nearly immediately with their high levels of flammable resin and sap. The two men, still saying nothing, stood for a second watching the flames eat through the tinder as the barn started to burn before striding out the way they'd come, the two of them breaking into a run as they headed back to where their ATVs were parked.

Swinging their legs over the seats, the men started the ATVs, taking the looping route given to them by their handler back onto the adjacent property away from the host of surveillance cameras at Travis's ranch.

Safely away from the smoldering barn, they pulled off the road, one of them pulling out night vision binoculars from their pack, training their eyes on the house. Now, all they could do was wait.

# 18

The screeching from the alarm coming from his phone woke Travis up out of a dead sleep. He'd been in the middle of a dream — a dream where he'd been trapped in a cave in the rugged mountains of Afghanistan, the sound of bullets bouncing off the rock around him. Except that it wasn't a dream. It had really happened.

Sitting up with a start, the alarms puncturing his sleep, Travis swung his legs out of the bed and grabbed his cell phone, squinting at the screen. The perimeter and smoke alarms were going off down at the barn. He checked the cameras and jumped out of his bed, "No!"

Panic surged through him. Running to the bathroom, Travis slid on a pair of jeans and a T-shirt, bolting for the back door, his cell phone in hand, his heart pounding in his chest. He grabbed the keys to the truck and ran out to the garage, barely getting the door open before pulling the truck out.

Travis's mouth went dry as he stomped on the pedal. He could see the flames licking up around the barn. The horses. That's all he could think about. His mind pounded with questions, fear nipping at his heels as he pulled up in front of the barn, the truck coming to a skidding stop. He threw it into gear and shut it off, jumping out.

Charging into the building, covering his face with his arm, a cloud of acrid smoke engulfed him immediately. There seem to be flames everywhere. He opened the nearest stall door and ran in, looping a lead around the frightened horse's neck and calling to him, "Come on, let's go!" he yelled.

The horse followed him out of his stall and Travis ran with him to the nearest paddock where he let him loose. The black gelding, named Gambler, disappeared into the darkness. Travis didn't wait to see where he went. Charging back into the fire, Travis made his way to the next stall and got another one of the horses out. Glancing back at the barn, the flames moving along the edge of the roof, he knew he was running out of time. The fire was burning hot and fast with the pine shavings and the hay as fuel. He went to Smokey's stall and opened it up, throwing a halter over his head and dragging him out. At one point Smokey balked, afraid. Travis used the end of the lead to smack him on the haunches to get him moving. There was no time to waste.

Finally dislodging Smokey from the burning barn, he ran with the gray gelding to the same paddock where he'd released Gambler. Normally, the two horses didn't get along, but at that moment it didn't matter. Travis was just trying to save their lives.

By the time Travis got back to the barn, the heat was so intense, that he wasn't sure he could get back inside. He grabbed a burlap grain bag sitting on the ground near the side of the barn and turned on the faucet, dousing it with water. He covered himself with it as he ran into the fire, opening another one of the stalls. Putting a halter on the next horse, he threw the wet grain bag over the horse's face so he couldn't see where they were going. He yelled, "Come on!" and yanked the lead. After a few hesitant steps, the horse followed him, trotting its way out of the barn and into the fresh air. As Travis released the horse into the paddock with the others, he bent over, his hands on his knees, panting. His lungs burned, his mouth filled with soot, and his eyes stinging, he pulled his phone out of his pocket and dialed 9-1-1.

"Washington County Emergency Services. Give me the name and location of your emergency," the woman on the other end of the line droned.

Travis shouted into the phone, "This is Travis Bishop over at Bishop Ranch. My barn is on fire. I need help. Now!" Travis threw the phone on the ground, not waiting for any more questions from the dispatcher, leaving the line open. If nothing else, they could use his cell phone signal to triangulate where he was, but being a small town, certainly someone in the department would know the location of the ranch.

Travis took off running toward the barn. He grabbed a fire extinguisher that was on the wall near the first couple of stalls and pulled the pin, holding the hose out in front of him. He could barely see the flames through the thick smoke. Extending the hose in front of him, he pulled the trigger, getting enough of the fire doused to be able to extract two more frightened horses from their stalls.

As he pulled the second one out, he could hear kicking and neighing from the back of the barn. It sounded like the horses were screaming. The fire was too hot. His heart clutched in his chest. There was no way to get to the last ones, at least not through the interior of the barn, but if he didn't do something, the last two horses would burn to death.

Running out of the building, Travis stood and stared, out of breath and coughing. In a surge of energy, he ran back to where he'd dropped his cell phone, scooped it up, and jumped in the truck. He might not be able to get to the horses from the inside of the building, but maybe he could get to them from the outside. By his count, there were two left — Joker and Scarlett.

A lump formed in his throat. Scarlett was the mare he'd bought for Kira. He had to try to save her.

Throwing the truck into gear, he spun the vehicle around, aiming for the back of the barn. He pumped the brake for a split second while he lined the truck up with where the back stalls were. Without any hesitation, he pressed on the accelerator, gunning the engine, aiming the truck straight for the outside wall of the barn.

With a crack that sounded like a shotgun had just gone off, Travis felt the impact, his body lurching forward as the wood on the exterior of the barn shattered, the siding falling off. Travis backed the truck out and left it running, not bothering to look at the damage. He could see Joker, wild-eyed, his head angled up in the air, his ears pinned in confusion. Travis ran inside the stall and smacked the horse on the rump trying to dislodge him from the one place the animal thought was safe. "Get outta here!" he yelled, waving his arms and coughing as the horse disappeared into the darkness. Travis sighed. It was better to have a horse loose on the property than have it dead.

Without thinking, Travis jumped back in the truck and careened around the other side of the barn, the tires spinning on the loose dirt. The only horse left was Scarlett. As he pulled the truck to her side of the barn, he could hear violent banging on the back of the stall, as if the mare was desperately trying to get herself out. "Hold on!" he yelled. "I'm coming!"

Travis stomped on the accelerator again, the front bumper digging into the side of the barn and smashing it, a sheet of white siding coming down on the windshield, sending a spiderweb of cracks through the glass. As Travis backed the truck up, he saw Scarlett's rump kicking and flailing near the opening. He jumped out running toward the frightened animal. "Easy, girl!" he yelled, over the crackle of the fire. Scarlett was a spooky horse in the best situation, quick to veer away from danger, high strung and athletic just like Kira had been.

Travis eased his way into the stall, laying a hand on Scarlett's haunches. The barn was hot, flames everywhere, the smoke filling his lungs with every breath. He needed to get her out of the stall. Moving towards her head, Travis waved his arms and pushed on her chest, "Go!" he yelled. But the mare wouldn't move. Travis frantically looked around him. He didn't have a halter or lead or anything, but he couldn't leave Scarlett in the stall to die. Stripping off his shirt, he threw it over Scarlett's face and pulled the belt out of his jeans, wrapping it around her neck. With a tug, he turned the mare around and dragged her outside, yelling and cajoling and clucking the whole time. As soon as she made it outside past the truck and the burning barn, Travis pulled the shirt and the belt off her. The mare went to her knees and then rocked to her side, her mouth open, her nostrils flaring. Whether it was from stress, burns, or smoke inhalation, Travis wasn't sure. Jumping inside the truck, Travis grabbed his phone. The 9-1-1 operator was still asking for him, "Sir? Are you there? We have the fire department on the way. Are you there?"

"Yes! Get them out here now!" With that, he ended the call.

Sliding back out of the truck, he shoved his phone in his back pocket and found a hose on the side of the new barn. Scarlett was still on her side, panting. Travis dragged the hose over, turned the hose on, and sprayed her body down, trying to get the soot away from her eyes and nostrils, cooling her body.

As the water washed over her, Travis stared at the building. There was nothing he could do for the barn. It was fully engulfed in flames and would be a total loss. Even though he and Scarlett were near the new barn, he could still feel the heat on his skin like a giant bonfire celebration after a home football game. The only piece of luck was that he was able to get the horses out. The saddles, bridles, and the papers and records in his office — those could all be replaced. The horses could not. He glanced down at Scarlett, her sides still heaving, as he continued to run cold water over her. Off in the distance, he could hear sirens. He glanced at the driveway and then back at the horse. He needed to get Scarlett up and get her into the corral before the fire department lights spooked her. In the process, he needed to somehow find Joker and get him in the corral as well.

Travis grabbed his belt again and looped it around Scarlett's neck. He clucked at her, giving her a little swat on the side. She eyed him for a second and then struggled, but finally got up, walking slowly, her head hanging down. The two of them walked side-by-side across the driveway to the pasture, Travis keeping a single hand on Scarlett's side.

At the paddock gate, Travis looked around. The other horses were nowhere in sight. If he had to guess they were clustered in the back corner, trying to get as far away from the fire and commotion as possible. He walked Scarlett inside and loosened his belt from her neck. She took two steps and then leaned against the fence, her head hanging down. Travis closed the gate, his eyebrows furrowing, worry running through him. She was clearly injured from the fire, but he didn't know what was wrong with her. As much as he wanted to stay with her, he had to find Joker. The last horse was still missing. Glancing down the driveway, he saw a line of lights and trucks approaching. He knew they'd have to go slow because of the potholes on the driveway. He'd probably get a tongue lashing from the fire marshal about it, but they were there for another reason. He never anticipated it would slow down the emergency services that much. But that wasn't something he could think about at that moment.

"Joker!" he called, taking off at a run, shrugging his T-shirt back on over his shoulders, looking for the loose horse running free and scared on his property. His skin felt hot, as though he'd been out in the sun for too long. "Joker!" Travis stopped and squinted in the darkness, trying to figure out where the last horse went. He didn't see the gelding on the driveway or anywhere near the burning barn. "I just hope to God he didn't go back in," Travis mumbled under his breath, taking off at a run. Horses had been known to run right back into their stalls no matter what the situation was – flood, fire, tornado, or hurricane – only to die in the very place they thought would save their life.

Travis ran back around the far side of the barn to Joker's stall, holding his breath, his heart pounding in his chest. He couldn't get close with the flames eating away at the wood, but from what he could see, there was no animal inside. Running toward the new barn, he darted inside, only to see a dark shadow in the back corner. The layout of the two barns was nearly identical. At this point, the only difference was that one was burning and one wasn't. Travis moved down the aisle slowly, cocking his head to the side, trying not to startle the animal. "Joker? Easy boy."

Travis reached for the light switch and then pulled his hand back before flipping it on. He was afraid any sudden move would scare the already traumatized animal. Taking a few more steps in the darkness, the shadow became the form of a horse, his sides heaving. Joker had pinned himself in the back corner of the new barn, in the exact spot where his old stall was. Travis closed his eyes for a second and breathed a sigh of relief. He walked slowly toward Joker, sliding open the stall door. "It's okay, buddy. You can go to your stall. You just go right on in there and rest, okay?" The horse, his head hanging, seemed to brighten for a moment at the stall door being opened and then walked inside, going directly to the back corner.

At least all the horses were accounted for.

Travis walked out of the barn as the firetrucks rolled up in front, black-uniformed firemen spilling out from inside like ants leaving a hill, shouts and yells echoing off the vehicles and what was left of the barn. A white helmeted man approached

Travis. He put his arm on Travis's shoulder looking at him, "I'm Captain Mason Burke with the fire department. You okay? Is there anyone else inside?"

Travis bent over, putting his hands on his knees. He shook his head, "No."

"Any other animals inside?"

"No. I got them all out. There in the paddock. Except one. He's in the other barn."

"Okay. You stay right here. I'm going to have the paramedics take a look at you. What's your name?"

"Bishop. Travis Bishop."

"All right. We're gonna get this fire taken care of. Like I said, you just stay right here."

Travis stood up in time to see Captain Burke wave a team of paramedics over to him and then point and yell at his crew. Within a few seconds, the fire department had unrolled long hoses and was dousing the fire in the barn with the water they had on the truck, the hissing of the cold water hitting the intense flames. As the paramedics approached Travis, he saw the rumble of a lone fire truck coming down the driveway. He caught the eye of one of the paramedics as she slid her hand under his elbow, tugging him toward the ambulance, "Sir? Can you come over here and sit on the edge of the ambulance for me so we can take a look at you?"

Travis looked at her. He shrugged her grip away, "I'm okay. I think I just need some water."

"Sir," the paramedic insisted, "I can tell by the smoke patterns around your nose and mouth that you've inhaled a whole bunch of fumes. Let's go over to the ambulance and at least get you some water and some oxygen."

Travis hadn't moved, simply staring at the emergency truck moving slowly down the driveway, the red light cycling on the top. Was this help or another threat? He narrowed his eyes, looking at the paramedic, a trim blonde woman with her hair knotted at the nape of her neck, "Is that another department?"

She glanced down the driveway, and then back at him, "No. That's the tanker truck. The firefighters have several thousand gallons of pressurized water on the rig, but out here, where there aren't any hydrants, they call for the tanker right away." She looked back at Travis, "Now, come on. Let's go have a look at you."

Travis frowned. There was something he had to take care of first. "I gotta go check on the horses and make a call. I'll be right over." Seeing the look of concern on the paramedic's face, he held up his hands, adding, "I promise. Give me a minute." Travis knew the paramedic was only trying to do her job. With the way his lungs were burning and the nausea that had come over him, he was sure she was right. He probably had inhaled more than his fair share of smoke, but that wasn't what was important at the moment. It also wasn't the worst thing that had ever happened to him.

Travis strode off towards the paddock, coughing, as he pulled his phone out of his pocket. He dialed Dr. Wiley.

After a few rings, the veterinarian picked up, "Travis? It's late. Everything okay?"

"No. The barn just burned. I got all the horses out but I need you here, right now."

With a grunt, Dr. Wiley replied, "On my way. Give me twenty minutes."

"Make it ten, Doc. I've got horses that aren't in good shape."

As Travis got to the paddock where he'd dropped off the horses, he found Scarlett in the same position she'd been in before, except that she'd laid down next to the fence. His stomach tightened. It wasn't a good sign. She should have been clustered with the other animals, her herd instinct telling her there was safety in numbers, not all by herself and definitely not laying down on the ground.

The other horses had come up from the back of the paddock and were huddled together in a small group about fifty feet away from Scarlett as if they were keeping an eye on her. Travis opened the gate and went inside, walking slowly to the mare. Her breathing had slowed and seemed a bit less labored, but her nostrils were still flared. He laid his hand on her neck and stroked it, whispering, "Help is on the way, girl. Hang in there. I need you to stay with me a little longer." As he stared at her, his heart felt like it cracked in half in his chest. Scarlett was all that he had left of Kira. A wash of guilt and rage and frustration covered him as he knelt in the dirt. He glanced back toward the barn. The flames had died down substantially with the fire department dousing them, the crackle of the wood burning quieter than it had been before, the noise of the streams of water gushing all over the ground in the background like a waterfall. He couldn't imagine what the horses were thinking, and there was no way to explain it to them. There was no way to tell them they were safe and that he would protect them. Travis glanced back at Scarlett, stroking her neck again. "Dr. Wiley is on his way. He's going to help you. Hang in there."

Travis gritted his teeth and then dropped his hands to the ground, barely able to hold his weight, the shock of what just happened rushed over him. He shook his head, unwilling to give up one more thing that was important to him. "Hold on, girl," he muttered again. The horses needed him. The ranch needed him. As much as he didn't want to admit it, he needed them too.

## 19

The next few minutes went by in a blur. By the time Travis turned around again, the two paramedics were on top of him as he sat by Scarlett, guiding his body into a standing position. "Let us help you, Travis," the blonde paramedic said, her arm firm under his.

"I only need a minute to rest. I'm fine here with the horses," he said, trying to struggle away.

"We can argue about that in a few minutes after I get you some hydration and some oxygen, okay?"

Travis grunted but agreed, walking on his own to the ambulance. There was nothing he could do except wait for Dr. Wiley to arrive and watch as the firefighters put out what was left of the blaze.

The steel bumper of the ambulance felt cool through the back of his jeans as he sat down. The paramedic had pointed at the gurney inside but Travis shook his head firmly. The bumper was as far as they were going to get him. Within seconds, there was a blanket around his shoulders and a clear plastic oxygen mask strapped across his face. On his left arm, he felt the squeeze of a blood pressure cuff. On his right arm, he felt the prick of a needle as they started an IV with fluids. "I don't need that!" he grumbled, staring at the blonde paramedic after using his hand to pull the oxygen mask off his face. "I'm fine, really."

"Would you let me do my job, please?" she said, putting her hands on her hips. "Your barn nearly burns down, you managed to rescue all of your horses, and yet you fight me. I think your job is done, but mine isn't. What do you want me to do? Just stand around and be bored while the boys get to have all the fun with the fire?"

Her sarcasm worked. Travis gave a single nod, sucked in a deep breath of the oxygen, and sat for a second, trying to catch his breath. His lungs felt like they were on fire. He felt the cool of a stethoscope on his skin as the paramedics listened to his lungs. "His pulse and blood pressure are fine," the second paramedic, a young man with clipped dark hair, said.

"His lungs are a little clunky, but not too bad. I think the oxygen will fix him right up," the blonde paramedic said from somewhere over Travis's head working behind him in the ambulance.

Travis shifted in his position on the back of the bumper, pulling out his phone again. He blinked, trying to clear what felt like blurry vision. He frowned, staring down, blinking. The blonde paramedic, wearing blue latex gloves, frowned at him. "Your eyes bothering you?"

Travis nodded.

She ripped open a four-by-four gauze pad and soaked it with some sort of solution, tipping Travis's head back. "I'm gonna wipe your eyes. That should make them feel better."

As she pulled the gauze away, Travis could see black soot on it streaked on the white surface. The cool from the gauze pad did make his eyes feel better, though. When he looked down at his phone again, he could see much better and quickly typed a text to Ellie. "Barn burned. Got horses out. Need you here."

As soon as he put the phone down, he looked up to see a large square man wearing a beige set of coveralls standing in front of him, his arms crossed across his chest, a thick pair of glasses perched on his nose. "You okay there, Travis? You aren't giving the paramedics any trouble, are you?" Dr. Wiley said.

Travis had known Dr. Wiley for years. He'd tried a few other veterinarians when he'd started the ranch, but he and Dr. Wiley were the ones that really hit it off. Dr. Wiley was practical and no-nonsense. He didn't mince words. He handled whatever the problem was with the horses with the least amount of drama possible and sent Travis a bill. "Yeah, I'm okay," Travis said, stripping the oxygen mask off his face and stifling a cough. He looked down at his arm and realized he was tethered to the IV the blonde paramedic had put in his arm. In one quick move, he pulled the IV out and bent his elbow up to his shoulder, stopping the flow of blood.

The paramedic, only catching the back end of his actions yelped, "Whoa! What are you doing? You need that IV!"

Travis looked back over his shoulder as he walked away, "I told you. You got to do your job, but I'm fine. Thanks for your help."

Dr. Wiley and Travis walked shoulder to shoulder to the paddock, Travis pointing. "Sorry to get you out of bed. Pretty much everybody's in here. Joker's in the new barn."

"What happened?"

Travis shook his head, his lips pressed together. Tension was building in his chest. "I don't know. The alarms went off. By the time I got out here, there were flames everywhere. I got Gambler and Smokey out first. It's Scarlett and Joker I'm worried about."

Travis pointed at the shadow of the mare, laying on her side in the corral. As soon as he did, Dr. Wiley took off at a run, his wide frame lumbering over the rough ground, sliding inside of the paddock, only slowing as he approached the horse on the ground. Travis matched him stride for stride, closing the paddock gate behind him.

Travis watched as Dr. Wiley laid his hand on Scarlett's neck as he pulled a stethoscope out of his pocket. His jaw was set, his face a stoic mask. "Can we get a halter and a lead on her? I don't want her to bolt while I'm trying to examine her."

Travis turned, looking at the barn. "Except for the ones on the other horses, they're all in the barn."

"I figured that might be the case. I grabbed a couple. They're in the cab of my truck."

Travis ran out of the paddock to Dr. Wiley's truck, coughing a little as he did. Reaching inside, he found four halters and four leads laying on the passenger seat. God bless Dr. Wiley. He scooped them up and ran back toward the paddock. By the time he did, Dr. Wiley had his stethoscope out and was listening to Scarlett's lungs, the cool metal of the stethoscope pressed on the underside of her belly.

Dr. Wiley stood up and gave Travis a nod as he fitted the halter over her head and clipped the lead onto the side. He stared at the mare for a second and then glanced at Travis, "I can't be sure what's happening yet. Probably inhaled a bunch of smoke plus the shock of the fire. I'm gonna get an IV started on her, start her on steroids for her lungs, and give her a tranquilizer to keep her calm. We gotta get her out of this corral though. You got a stall somewhere in the new barn we can use? I need someplace I can take a better look at her."

Travis nodded, "Yeah. The stalls in the new barn are done. No bedding in them, though."

"That's fine. Let's go."

After some clucking and cajoling, Dr. Wiley and Travis managed to get Scarlett to her feet, the mare moving slowly between the two men, her head hanging as she walked with them to the new barn. As Travis flipped on the light, he heard the bang of a hoof against the back of the new barn. Joker. Dr. Wiley gave Travis a glance. "Somebody's not happy."

"I think he just realized he ran back to the wrong barn."

As soon as Travis got Scarlett settled in the stall, he went and checked on Joker. Other than a set of wild eyes, he seemed to be unharmed, but Dr. Wiley would be a better judge of his condition. Travis strode outside, collecting the rest of the horses and bringing them into the new barn, putting them in the same positions they were in the old barn so they could sniff each other through the stall walls. He hoped that would be of some comfort to them after the fire.

Ellie arrived about three minutes after he got Gambler settled into his new stall. Her hair was pulled up in a rough blonde ponytail, no makeup on her face, dark circles under her eyes. "Oh my God, Travis. What happened?"

"I don't know." He glared at the ground, trying to control his anger at whoever had set the fire, and then looked at her. "Listen, I gotta go check on a couple of things. All the horses are back in the stalls. Can you get them some bedding and water and help Dr. Wiley? Do whatever he says. I need to go check the house."

Ellie nodded, her eyes wide, "Of course. Whatever you need."

Walking out of the stable, Captain Burke approached him. "Mr. Bishop?"

"Travis."

The fire captain gave him a brief nod, "Travis." He glanced toward the barn. "We got the fire out. But based on the burn patterns, we're going to be here for a while. I'm going to call in a fire investigative unit. Looks like it was arson."

Travis gritted his teeth. "I know."

Burke frowned, "You know? How do you know it was arson?"

Travis narrowed his eyes, staring at the barn. "It happened

too fast. Seemed to be centered in the middle of the barn. That's where we keep the pine shavings and the hay. Can't be a coincidence. The smoke was acrid, too. Like someone used gasoline."

"I agree. Any idea who'd want to do this to you?"

The options rattled through Travis's mind like marbles in a tin can. The options were endless — the Russians, the CIA or some other unknown enemy Travis had made in the past during his time with Delta Force. He gritted his teeth, "I have no idea, but I'm going to find out."

## 20

The plan worked exactly as designed. The two men hidden in the stand of trees watched as Travis Bishop barreled from the log cabin to the burning barn, only the lights of his truck visible in the darkness. They saw the truck screech to a halt in front of the structure, a lone figure jumping out. A second later, they saw the first horse make it out of the barn, the silhouette of the animal black against the glow from the flames.

"I don't need to see any more. Let's go. That fire isn't going anywhere. He's going to be busy down here for a while."

The second man nodded, swinging his leg over the seat of his ATV.

The two men didn't even attempt to hide the noise from their engines. The crackle of the blaze, plus Travis's focus on rescuing his animals, was more than enough distraction to give them the time they needed. Riding with their lights off, the two men circled through the woods behind the farm heading to the log cabin. They left the two ATVs hidden behind some scrub bushes and moved silently, their backpacks still on their shoulders.

Approaching the back door to Travis's house, one of them pulled an automated lock disrupter out of his backpack and fitted it over the top of the digital lock attached to Travis's door. He waited for a second then heard the lock pop, the digital decoder having done its job. The man gave a single nod as he pulled the door open.

According to their briefing, based on information they'd gathered from the county building department and a contractor they'd bribed, there was no point in checking the entire house. They were looking for a single room, one that was hidden from the rest of the structure. Making their way into the family room, the team moved slowly, pistols out in case Travis had left someone inside. After a minute of searching, they realized they were alone. They holstered their weapons.

The same man that popped the lock took the lead, striding quickly into the family room and staring at the set of bookshelves along the wall. They'd been told there was a latch on the third shelf of one of the bookshelves, but the person they got their information from wasn't sure which one, only that finding it was the key to gaining entry to the hidden room. Their hands covered in black latex gloves, the men started searching, using flashlights, starting at the far end of the room, and working their way back to the kitchen. After a moment of searching, one of the men hissed, "Found it," as the bookshelf popped off of the wall.

In front of them was a gray painted steel door with a lock that included a combination and a thumbprint reader. One of the men looked at the other, "Anyone tell you anything about a fingerprint scanner?"

The other man shook his head no. "The information we had said it was a straight keypad lock."

The men worked in silence for a moment. Using the same decoder box they used for the back door, they were able to get the lock to pop open, but they didn't have a fingerprint scan.

"What are we supposed to do now? We don't have a lot of time," one of them whispered, glancing over their shoulder.

"Get the tools," the other one hissed.

The man unzipped his pack and pulled out a black case filled with small tools – a variety of black-handled screwdrivers, pliers, and picks in several sizes. Using a screwdriver, the man tried to pop the face of the thumbprint reader off. "Sometimes if you can take the faceplate off, you can short it out," he whispered under his breath.

A second later, the metal faceplate of the thumbprint reader was off, exposing a tangle of yellow and white wires. The man fumbled with them for just over a minute, at which point he shook his head. "I can't get this open, not without tearing the door apart." He checked the time on his watch, "We gotta go."

"What about the implant?"

"They're going to have to figure out another way to get it or get us another way to breach this room. They knew about everything else. Someone screwed up. We should have known about the scanner."

It only took a second for the men to reassemble the thumbprint reader and put it back exactly the way that it had been, sliding the black bookshelves back into place against the wall and exiting the house. As they ran from Travis's log cabin, one of the men looked over his shoulder to see the barn fully engulfed in flames, the red spinning lights of the fire department approaching down the long driveway. They had plenty of distraction for their escape, he thought, running back into the woods and getting on the ATV.

It was just a shame they hadn't been able to get what they'd come for.

## 21

"Only time is gonna tell at this point, Travis. We'll have to see how she does..."

Travis, Ellie, and Dr. Wiley were standing outside of Scarlett's stall in the new barn watching the mare, who was laying down in a fresh pile of pine shavings Ellie had arranged around her. The horse was asleep, her eyes droopy, her muzzle resting on the ground as if it was simply too heavy to keep up. Every now and again she'd struggle in her sleep, her breath raspy, as if she was running from the fire in her dreams.

"I've given her a pretty heavy dose of sedatives, plus the first load of steroids, a loading dose of antibiotics, and filled her up with a bunch of fluids. Now, all we can do is wait."

Travis crossed his arms in front of his chest, staring at the ground and then back at Dr. Wiley, "There's nothing more you can tell me?"

Dr. Wiley sighed, shoving his thick hands into the front pockets of his beige coveralls, "I wish I could. The only way to know much more about what happened is for you to pack her up and get her to the vet school at Texas A & M where they can run more tests, but that's hours on the road from here, and honestly, I'm not sure they'd do anything different than I've done. I'll give them a call when they open up in the morning and run it by the head of Equine Veterinary Medicine. He's a personal friend. I think if you give her some time and go slow, we might be able to get her out of the woods. Can't say that for sure though."

Dr. Wiley's last comment sent a knot of dread into Travis's stomach. Being that Scarlett was so close to where the fire started, Dr. Wiley felt like the trauma and the smoke inhalation had injured her more severely than any of the others. He'd asked Travis if he wanted to put the mare down, but after hearing there were options available to treat her, Travis had shaken his head no. Ellie had spent the last two hours sitting with Scarlett on a fresh pile of bedding in her stall, monitoring the IVs and making sure she was comfortable.

"Other than being traumatized, the rest of the horses look okay. I'm gonna leave you a bottle of tranquilizers for them. There's enough for each of them to have a couple of doses each if you feel like they need it. If you need more, let me know. The only one I think you're really going to have any trouble with is Joker."

Travis cocked his head to the side, "He's kind of a wildcard anyway," he said, trying to smile.

Dr. Wiley unwrapped the stethoscope from around his neck and shoved it in his back pocket. "Good to see you are at least trying to get your sense of humor back." Laying a hand on Travis's shoulder, he said, "I'm sorry this happened to you. I'll give you a call about mid-morning to check in on Scarlett. I think I've got some appointments out this direction in the afternoon anyway. I'll probably stop by and give all the horses another once over after I talk to my buddy."

Travis gave a curt nod, "Thanks, Doc. I appreciate you coming out."

"No problem," Dr. Wiley said, turning and walking out of the barn and into the shadows.

A second later, Travis heard Dr. Wiley's truck pull away, the tires grinding against the gravel driveway. Ellie, who had been fidgeting with her blonde ponytail, stared at Travis, "I'm gonna stay down here with the horses."

Travis narrowed his eyes, "You don't have to. Why don't you go home and get some sleep? We've been up all night long."

Ellie shrugged. "The sun's just about to come up. I can't sleep during the day for nothing. I've got a blanket and pillow in my truck. I'll curl up on a couple of bales of hay and hang out here in case the horses need anything. It'll be like we're at a horse show."

Travis chewed his lip. At the horse shows, they alternated spending the night with the animals, sleeping in the extra stall they rented for the tack. It was a common practice, one designed to prevent anyone from walking off with their show saddles, which could run in the thousands of dollars each, and also to keep an eye on their equine athletes. Horses, even with their massive body weight tended to have sensitive systems, especially when traveling. "All right. I'm gonna go up to the house and get cleaned up and then I'll be back down." Travis checked his watch. "The fire marshal is due here in a couple of hours according to Captain Burke. I want to be here for that."

"Of course. You still think this was arson?"

Travis shot a look at Ellie. How could she even ask that? He was exhausted, filthy, and worried about the horses. Every inch of him was covered in smoke and soot, other than the two patches where the paramedics had wiped his eyes off. His lungs still stung and his mouth felt dry and gritty. The last thing he needed was her questioning him. "What else could it be?"

"I don't know," she shrugged. "Maybe a loose wire? Like an electrical fire?"

Travis closed his eyes for a moment. He loved Ellie like she was his younger sister. She'd gone through a lot, just like he had, and had served in the military and struggled with her own version of PTSD. The one thing she was missing was sense. Horse sense she had in spades. People, not so much.

"It wasn't. I can promise you that," he growled, shutting down the conversation. Turning on his heel, he glanced over his shoulder, leaving Ellie in the barn, "Thanks for your help. I'll be back."

# 22

Although Travis had smashed his truck into the side of the barn not once, but twice, in order to get Scarlett and Joker out of their stalls while the barn burned, luckily, the truck was still drivable. When the fire department arrived, they'd pulled it away from the barn, leaving it on the other side of the parking area near the trailers. Travis slid inside after surveying the damage on the exterior. The airbags hadn't gone off, which meant it was likely the truck could be repaired, but there was a significant amount of damage to the front end of the vehicle — the windshield was filled with cracks in a spiderweb pattern, there were dents and scrapes all over the front bumper, part of which was now hanging off of its moorings on the frame. Travis made a mental note to call his insurance agent about the barn and the truck as soon as he could clear his head.

Walking into the house, Travis went directly to the laundry room, stripping off all his smoke and soot-filled dirty clothes and throwing them into the washing machine, turning it on hot. As he heard the machine click on, he strode to the bathroom and started the shower, not waiting for the water to heat up. As the water touched his skin, he realized that it stung. Ignoring the pain, he held his head under the water. For the most part, it felt like he'd gotten a good sunburn, which he hadn't had since his time in the Middle East, stuck in the remote areas of Afghanistan. He scrubbed his body from head to toe, the smell of smoke hanging on the humidity in the shower and then quickly dissipating as the smell of the soap took over.

After a few minutes, he shut the water off, drying himself and wrapping a towel around his waist. He walked toward the bathroom sink and brushed his teeth, rinsing the soot out of his mouth. Drying off his lips with a nearby towel, Travis stopped to stare in the mirror. There were deep black circles under his eyes, the rims edged in red, his normally clear eyes irritated from the smoke. He had a couple of cuts and scrapes on his upper body, but nothing that warranted any type of medical attention. He'd been lucky, that was for sure.

Walking into the bedroom, Travis pulled on a clean set of clothes — a fresh pair of worn denim jeans, a white T-shirt with a faded logo from a horse show on it, and a leather belt. He swung a torn flannel shirt over top. After combing his dark hair, he went to the kitchen and started a pot of coffee, his mind starting to run after the shower.

Thoughts pushed and shoved their way through his mind. There was no way the fire had been an accident, but the question was, who had set it and why?

As the coffee perked, Travis walked towards the war room. He kept all of his critical papers locked in the safe there, including the insurance policies for the house and farm. Hearing the coffee burble behind him, he stuck his finger in the hole of the bookshelf, touching the release for the door. As he did, he frowned. One of the trophies on the shelves had been nudged out of place. It was sitting cockeyed from where it had been earlier. Travis narrowed his eyes, pressing his lips together. Something didn't seem right. Travis felt his chest tighten.

Pulling the bookshelf away, Travis was about to key in the code for the war room when he stopped. The door was painted in a dark, gunmetal gray, the paint rolled on in long strokes, leaving a perfectly smooth surface. Travis bent over, staring at the lock. Despite his careful paint job, there were scratches around the lock, particularly in the area of the thumb reader. Travis glanced back over his shoulder and stared at the scratches again. Quickly keying in the code for the lock and running his thumb over the fingerprint reader, the lock popped open.

In his concern about the horses in the barn, Travis hadn't taken the time to arm the system at the house before he'd run to the fire. A knot formed in his stomach and he shook his head, a surge of anger running through his system. He only had himself to blame. "Are you kidding me?" he muttered under his breath. Travis walked to the computers and pulled up the surveillance from the hour before he'd gotten the alarm on his phone. He stood, watching the surveillance video run at double speed, his arms crossed in front of his chest until ten minutes before the alarm had gone on his phone. Gritting his teeth, he watched two black clothed men enter the barn from the rear. He paused the feed and studied it. Unfortunately, there would be no way to determine their identity. They were covered from head to toe in black clothing, including gloves and ski masks that left only their eyes visible. His surveillance systems were good, but not that good. Facial recognition would be useless without a face to compare it to. Travis watched as they lit the fire in the barn, his hands balling up, his knuckles white, tension filling his chest. It had been arson. "I knew it," he hissed.

Switching to the surveillance feeds for the house, Travis watched to see if his suspicions about damage to the war room door were right. Seven minutes and fifty-two seconds into the recording, he saw what he'd been waiting for – the same black clothed men had entered his house, quickly finding the entrance to the war room, but not being able to get past the thumbprint reader. He shook his head slowly, his mouth dropping open. How did these men know about his war room? And more importantly, what were they looking for?

Travis sat down at the computer, pulling a flash drive out of his desk drawer and copying the files of the barn and house video to it. He had no need for the fire marshal, and the fire marshal didn't need to waste his time at the farm. With the video in hand, he probably wouldn't. That was better. The fewer people on his property, the better. Travis stood up from the desk, the plastic cover of the flash drive warming in his grip. He closed the war room door behind him, heading to the kitchen.

Leaning on the counter, Travis dialed Sheriff Burnett. "We've got a problem."

## 23

"It's mighty early for a phone call, Travis," Sheriff Burnett said, sounding like his mouth was full. "I haven't even finished my oatmeal yet."

"Like I said, we've got a problem."

"What kind of problem?"

"The kind that tries to burn my barn down and kill all my horses."

In other parts of the country, fueled by Big Tech, manufacturing, and finance, the importance of farm life might be hard to understand. But that wasn't the world Travis lived in. He'd chosen to live farther out, away from the chaos of the city. But somehow, chaos had found him.

The sheriff sucked in a sharp breath, "What? What are you talking about?"

"Did you get a message from Captain Burke yet?"

"Burke? No."

"Well, if it's not at your office you're going to be getting one soon. Somebody decided to torch my barn in the middle of the night. I nearly got killed trying to rescue the horses."

"Are they okay?"

"Dr. Wiley just left. Most of them are okay, only trauma-tized. But Scarlett, that's another thing entirely."

Sheriff Burnett's voice hardened, "That's awful. You think it's arson or an accident? What are you saying?"

"Oh no. It's definitely arson. I have the video to prove it. Somebody started a fire in the barn so they could break into my house."

"And you think this has something to do with the Jake West case?"

"Don't you?"

A moment of heavy silence hung between the two men; as if a challenge had been issued. It was clear to him that Jake's missing body and the arson job on his barn were linked, even if Sheriff Burnett wasn't willing to move that fast.

"Well, seeing as you just told me about all this a couple of minutes ago," Sheriff Burnett stammered, "I guess, but I can't be sure. You working on anything else that would've gotten you in trouble?"

Travis fought the anger that was rising up inside of him. If Sheriff Burnett had been in front of him he was sure he would've punched the man straight in his face and gotten an immense amount of satisfaction watching his body crumple onto the ground. "No," Travis barked without explanation. The other skip tracing cases he was fiddling with — finding a guy's girlfriend who had run off leaving him with back due rent, locating a missing shipment that was supposed to be delivered to the local feed store that seemed to have evaporated into thin air, and tracking down a man who his wife thought was cheating – wasn't serious enough to warrant burning his barn to the ground. "No, there's nothing else going on in my skip tracing business that would cause this much of a stir. The only thing is that implant you gave me yesterday."

As the words came out of his mouth, it was hard to believe that nearly a whole day had passed since Sheriff Burnett and

Dr. Scott had found Travis at the barbecue place and dragged him into their mess. Waiting for the Sheriff to respond, Travis's phone beeped. It was Ellie.

"Listen, I gotta go." Travis hung up without saying goodbye. He didn't care what the Sheriff thought.

Pacing in the kitchen, Travis called Ellie back. "You gotta get down here. Scarlett's not good."

"On my way." Travis ran to the back door, grabbing the keys for the Jeep that was parked in the garage. He slid his boots on and jumped in the car, tromping on the gas and leaving a thick trail of dust and grime behind him as he sped to the barn.

The drive couldn't have seemed longer although it was probably not more than a minute in total in the Jeep. The sun had come up over the horizon, only a few wispy clouds floating across the bright blue Texas sky. With the windows open, Travis could hear the morning birds calling loudly from the trees as he passed, their calm was a sharp contrast to the tight knot he felt in his chest. As he got closer to the barn, he could still smell the hint of acrid smoke hanging in the air from the night before. Travis wrinkled his nose, wondering if the smell would ever go away.

Pulling in front of the new barn, the tires skidding on the gravel, Jake threw the Jeep into park and turned it off, leaving the keys inside. He ran from the vehicle into the barn, stopping short as Ellie stood in the aisle. Tears were running down her face. "She's gone, Travis. I'm so sorry."

Travis stood completely still, his mouth open. He glanced inside the stall, the door open. Kira's beautiful mare had her head lolled off to the side, her eyes half-closed, her normally pricked ears drooping. He searched her sides for any sign of movement, watching her nostrils for any flicker of life. "What happened? When I left she was just resting. Dr. Wiley said..." He couldn't get the rest of the words out with the size of the lump in his throat.

Ellie shook her head. "It must've been too much for her, Travis." Ellie looked down at the ground, her shoulders hunched forward, her arms crossed across her chest. She turned on her heel and walked away, disappearing into the tack room. From where he stood, Travis could hear muffled sobs. Ellie loved the horses. Losing one was like losing a family member. Maybe worse.

Travis glanced down the aisle wondering if he should chase after Ellie, but decided to give her a minute to collect herself. She was proud. She wouldn't want him to see her fall apart. It wasn't the way Ellie was tuned up. He understood. Neither was he.

Looking inside the stall at Scarlett, he took a couple of steps forward slowly as if he might wake the mare up from a deep sleep. Squatting near her head, Travis stroked her smooth coat. Her body was already cooling to the touch. As he stroked her, his life flashed before his eyes – falling in love with Kira, their plans to start their own performance horse program, buying the ranch, and surprising her with the pretty filly she named Scarlett – all of it before he knew Kira was a traitor not only to her country but to him. And now this. Now both Kira and Scarlett were dead. His last connection to her was gone and any hopes he'd had of anything of a normal future.

Travis stared at the ground for a moment and then stood up. He gritted his teeth staring at the horse he'd just lost in a fire that should have never happened.

Whoever had burned his barn would pay, and pay dearly.

# 24

It took Travis another hour using the tractor to dig a hole for Scarlett's body on the back of the property and drag her out of the stall. It was an ugly affair. Travis had to use a chain around the dead horse's neck to drag her from where she'd died against the wall of her temporary stall, her tongue sticking out purple and black, the grotesqueness of death already setting in. He got her body into the bucket of the tractor and drove it out to the hole he dug, dropping her in as gently as possible, pouring bucket load after bucket load of loose, sandy dirt over top of her body so the coyotes and raccoons wouldn't get to her.

The entire time, Travis felt sick to his stomach.

Driving back to the barn, his mind cycled through the memories of the fire, the flames, trying to rescue the horses, and now Scarlett's dead carcass. Whoever had burned the barn had broken a code, a code Travis had tried to live by his whole life and was common to those who were in the military and in espionage. He didn't make it personal. Whoever had ordered the fire had made it just that. They'd crossed the line from Travis's professional life into his personal. Sure, the barn was his business, but it was more than that and had nothing to do with his past. The horses were innocent victims. The innocent should never be involved. Whoever had sent the men to torch the barn had forgotten that. They needed to be reminded.

By the time Travis got back to the barn, a darkness had settled over him, his face frozen into a tense mask. Anger was burning in his chest. As he got off the tractor, he walked past the entrance new barn. Ellie was in Scarlett's stall, raking it out. She hadn't appeared until Scarlett's body was gone. And that was okay.

The rest of it wasn't.

Travis walked across the parking lot to the burned-out hulk of what was left of the original stable. Stopping outside, he surveyed the damage. Pretty much the entire interior of the structure was gone, though the attached arena was untouched. He stepped inside the charred remains, stepping over a few beams that had fallen from the roof as it caved in. A few of the stall doors were still in place, left open from when he had rescued the horses, the wood charred and still smelling like smoke, the polyurethane carefully painted on the doors cracked and bubbled on the surface from the heat of the flames.

Travis walked down the aisle, or at least what was left of it, to the tack room. Inside, he could see the line of bridles and saddles sitting. It looked like some of them were damaged, but a few of them might be salvageable. He pulled an armload of bridles off of the wall and walked toward the opening where he'd come in, laying the equipment down on the ground outside. Taking things out of the structure might infuriate the fire marshal or his insurance agent who hadn't had a look yet, but Travis didn't care. He was done playing by the rules. Going back into the building, Travis salvaged three of the five saddles they had. He'd send Ellie to get the rest out and get them cleaned up.

Standing in the sunshine, Travis didn't feel his mood brighten, not one bit. As he looked off in the distance, he saw a cloud of dust as someone made their way down the driveway. He narrowed his eyes and checked his watch. It was early for the fire marshal. Was Dr. Wiley back yet? He glanced toward the barn, wondering if Ellie had already called him to tell him about Scarlett. If she hadn't, he would need to. He swallowed, wondering if he could make the words come out of his mouth. Or, he could just wait until Dr. Wiley showed up that afternoon to check on the rest of the horses.

Travis stared at the car approaching. He strode over to the Jeep, getting a shotgun out from a locked box in the back, pumping the stock to make sure it was loaded. He laid it on the passenger side as he got in and started the engine. He was done playing games. No more taking chances. No more playing nice. Everyone would be treated like a trespasser. Everyone. Travis drove back up to the house in his own cloud of dust, waiting and watching for whoever decided to show up on his property.

Three minutes later, as Travis stood facing the vehicle approaching his cabin, the shotgun dangling from his right hand, he realized it was a police car. Specifically, Sheriff Burnett's. Part of him should have been relieved. But part of him wasn't. The sheriff was the one who had brought the trouble to his house in the first place.

If it actually was the sheriff behind the wheel...

Travis looked over his shoulder toward the sound of hooves crossing dry ground. A couple of the horses that had survived the fire were trotting around one of the paddocks as though the memory of the night before was far away, lost in a part of their minds that couldn't be accessed, their muzzles high in the air as they played in the warm breeze. Scanning the remainder of the ranch, Travis's eye caught on the black rubble of what was left of the barn. A tingle ran down his spine. Something inside of him had broken. The bubble he'd built for himself around the ranch — the idea that it was impenetrable from trouble – had been burst a few too many times. It was bad enough when Uri Bazarov showed up and Travis had to stop a couple of his Russian goons from killing Elena, but losing one of his horses took things to an entirely new level. Now, things were personal.

As the Sheriff's white cruiser got closer, Travis could hear the grinding of the tires of the gravel driveway, the billow of dust behind the car overtaking it as the car slowed down and pulled up in front. Travis narrowed his gaze, staring at the driver. Sheriff Burnett's round face came into view. Travis felt his shoulders slump a little, as if the tension had melted out of them, or at least as much as it could, given what he'd been through in the last couple of days.

"Ready for a fight?" Sheriff Burnett grunted as he got out of the cruiser, using his hands to wedge himself out of the narrow door frame, nodding at the shotgun in Travis's hand. As he slammed the door behind him he frowned, "Probably should've taken the SUV. These cruisers are so low to the ground they're hard to get out of."

Travis pressed his lips together. The cruiser being close to the ground had nothing to do with Sheriff Burnett's issues with getting out of it. "Didn't expect you to be making a house call this morning."

The sheriff took off his hat and mopped his brow with an off-white handkerchief, tinged yellow from years of use. "Well, can't say I expected your barn to turn into a tinderbox overnight either."

Travis licked his lips. His mind flashed to the flames and the heat. He swallowed, remembering how he dragged the horses out of their stalls as he ran through the billows of smoke to get to them. "Yeah, can't exactly say I expected that," he said, looking at the ground.

Sheriff Burnett cocked his head to the side, as if he was

searching Travis for an answer he couldn't find. A moment later, he looked away. "Mind if we sit?"

Travis gave a curt nod and followed Sheriff Burnett up the wide-planked wooden steps of the front porch, still toting the shotgun in his hand. He took a chair next to the sheriff, leaning the shotgun, the barrel pointed at the sky, next to the rough-hewn logs that made up the walls of the log cabin. "Can I get you a bottle of water or something?"

Sheriff Burnett waved him off. "Naw. I'm good. The wife wants me to drink more water, but all it does is make me have to go to the bathroom all the time. Kinda hard when I'm out on the road."

Travis stared at the ground, wondering how much of either of those statements were true. He could see the Sheriff's wife nagging him to take better care of his health. Travis had met her one summer day a few years before at a fundraiser in town for a children's charity. She was a tiny bird of a woman, filled with energy, her face framed by a sharp nose and a high-pitched voice. It was an ideal event for the Sheriff. While Travis didn't know how much Sheriff Burnett was actually out of the office on calls, Travis had seen him around town a whole bunch, spending his time glad-handing people and kissing babies as if he was up for reelection. He wasn't and even if he was, with his easygoing, affable personality, he'd win by a land-slide. As far as dealing with daily accidents, speeding tickets, and drunken domestic issues after a late night at a bar, Travis couldn't imagine the sheriff was actually all that involved in any of those situations.

"Did you come out here to take a look at the barn?" Travis picked at a cuticle, staring off in the distance.

"Yeah, but I'll get to that in a minute. Just wanted to have a sit first."

Travis nodded. He felt like whatever the sheriff wanted to say was gonna take a minute. Maybe Sheriff Burnett was working up his nerve. A lot of people had the same careful reaction around Travis. They had for his whole life. For some reason, they seemed to be intimidated. He folded his hands in his lap, glancing at the shotgun out of the corner of his eye, then turned his head to look at the Sheriff, who was staring off into nothing. Why people were intimidated around him, he was never sure. Whether it was because he was quiet and didn't say much, or the evidence of hard work he'd put in by the sinewy muscles of his body, or whether people had heard rumors around town about him and what happened at his ranch, he didn't know. And at that moment, it didn't matter except for the fact that he wanted to get back to doing what he was doing and stop wasting time.

"You're welcome to sit here all day long if you like, Sheriff, but I've got horses to attend to. If you want my attention, you're gonna have to tell me exactly what you're here for."

The sheriff pulled the handkerchief out of his pocket and dabbed at his forehead again. "I feel bad about the barn, Travis. And I feel like it's kinda my fault. Dr. Scott feels the same way."

Travis narrowed his eyes, "Are you saying you feel bad because of the fire or are you saying you feel bad for some other reason?"

Sheriff Burnett glanced at Travis and then looked away, shuffling his feet on the wood deck of the porch, his boots making a scuffling noise as they slid across the rough wood. "Both, I guess." Sheriff Burnett stared at the ground again and then caught Travis's eye, "Look, something is clearly going on here. Going after a man's livestock — that's kinda out of bounds the way we live."

"True."

Sheriff Burnett leveled his gaze at Travis, his watery blue eyes staring at him, "I can't help but think that if Dr. Scott and I hadn't told you about Jake West, none of this would have happened."

Travis looked away, in the opposite direction from Sheriff Burnett, towards the two barns on the property. They stood in stark contrast to each other, one of them charred and black, the occasional whiff of smoke still hanging in the air from the night before, the other one pristine and white, its outline crisp against the bright Texas sky, filled with hope and new life. Travis swallowed, realizing that for better or for worse, there would shortly be two brand-new barns on the property that was, if he decided to rebuild the first one. His stomach fluttered, thinking about the decision he'd need to make. It should be an easy one. Simply replace the old barn with a brand-new one. Newer and better. And he knew in the end, that would be the decision he would make.

In a few hours, he'd have a conversation with his insurance agent and then one with the contractor who was completing the finishing touches on the new barn. That afternoon, or the next day, or the day after, the contractor would roll down his driveway in his white pickup truck, the ladder rails attached to the bed, the equipment in the back clanging as he hit every pothole on the driveway. The two of them would look at the barn. The contractor would cluck about what a shame it was and then start walking around the project, writing down details. And then, in a few weeks, when Travis got the insurance payout, the contractor would arrive again in his white pickup truck, making the same clanking noise with the equipment bouncing in the bed of his truck, only this time, he would be followed by a line of heavy equipment and dumpsters to demolish what was left of the barn and haul it away. The next day, other trucks carrying laborers and carpenters and piles of material would arrive. Within a few days after that, the skeleton of the new barn would be raised to the sky to match the old one. And then the cycle would be over. Things would be right again.

Or would they?

Travis glanced back at Sheriff Burnett who was alternately staring at him and looking at the ground like a child who had gotten caught stealing from the local candy store and felt guilty about it.

Travis cocked his head to the side, "You don't know that."

Sheriff Burnett nodded slowly, "I think I do. Whatever happened to the body, we don't see that kind of thing out here in Washington County. You know that. Dr. Scott has spent her career dealing with mostly natural deaths and a whole host of crazy agricultural accidents, but nothing like what happened to Jake West. I've never seen it before, not in my entire career..."

## 25

It wasn't hard to imagine that Sheriff Burnett hadn't seen a burned, mangled carcass of a man with a strange implant at any other time in his career. Washington County was a nice place to live for exactly that reason. Things like what happened to Jake West just didn't happen in Sheriff Burnett's jurisdiction. They weren't in Shanghai or Hong Kong where high-tech dripped off of every person that walked by, and they weren't in the urban, cutting-edge life of New York or Los Angeles either. In any of those places, the seedy underbelly of the city might offer up burned bodies from time to time, but this was Texas. And it wasn't the hustle and bustle highbrow parts of Fort Worth or Dallas, either. Travis knew that Washington County was outside of all of that, stranded somewhere between Austin and Houston, nothing more than a footnote in Texas history.

And he liked it that way.

Travis stared at the bottom of the roof eave above him, seeing a tangle of spiderwebs on the finished space under the lip of the porch. He glanced back at the deck planking again. There were a few worn spots on the wood and a few others where the pale-yellow dust from the driveway had collected. When he had a minute, the whole front porch would need to be power washed and re-stained. He glanced back at the charred-out barn. The porch would have to wait until after he figured out what happened.

"So what are you saying, Sheriff?"

The sheriff cleared his throat and pushed himself up off the chair using both arms, his hips leading his ascent to standing, his back bowed as he grunted. "Let's go take a look at that barn."

TRAVIS DROVE the Jeep back down the barn, following Sheriff Burnett in his cruiser, the shotgun riding on the passenger seat. By the time he got out, Sheriff Burnett was already walking toward the building, his arms folded across his chest. Travis sniffed the air, another puff of burning lumber carried on the breeze. Sheriff Burnett shook his head, "What a mess."

Barely able to look at the barn, Travis stared at the ground, kicking at a couple of pieces of gravel. "Like I told you. It's a total loss." As the words came out of his mouth, Ellie emerged from the rubble, carrying a couple of buckets of grooming supplies from inside. Travis furrowed his eyebrows. The plastic bucket was warped from the heat. He nodded at Ellie, "If the stuff is destroyed, you can leave it in there."

Ellie stopped for a second, seemingly surprised to see Travis with someone else. She blinked, then said, "Hello, Sheriff."

"Ellie."

Ellie looked back at Travis, "This is the last of it. I got the rest of the equipment out." She glanced down at the two buckets suspended between her hands, "The buckets are warped, but it looks like the stuff inside is okay. I'm gonna head out behind the barn and get everything cleaned up and put away in the new tack room. Looks like we lost a saddle and a couple of saddle pads, but other than that, everything else just seems to be covered with soot. We got lucky."

At least that was one piece of good news. Travis gave a single nod, "Sounds good. Thanks. I'll be around as soon as the sheriff and I finish our business."

As Ellie walked off, Travis bit the inside of his lip. He and Sheriff Burnett still hadn't finished their conversation. Now, he'd seen the burned-out barn. What else did he want?

Travis felt his jaw tighten. As much as he appreciated the slow pace of living in Texas after being with Delta Force and the CIA, there were times he needed people to move along. This was one of them. "Sheriff? I gotta ask you — why are you here? You said it was more than to see the barn. Now, you've seen it. What's up?" The words came out clipped and strained. Travis had lost his patience. He had things to attend to and they didn't include waiting for the sheriff to find the words he needed.

"And now seeing this — it's above my pay grade, Travis. This is unlike anything I've ever seen in my entire career when you pair it up with the video you sent me. Yeah, sure, we've seen houses and barns burned before. Lost livestock and kids and grandmas and grandpas. And it's all a shock and a shame, but whoever these men are that came and lit your barn on fire, there is no doubt in my mind that they are linked somehow to that charred body we lost and that implant we gave you." Sheriff Burnett looked at the ground and then looked at Travis again, searching his face, "And I feel bad that Dr. Scott and I brought trouble to your house. The thing is..."

Travis narrowed his eyes. The way Sheriff Burnett paused told him good news wasn't coming. He braced himself.

"The reality is I don't have any idea how to help you. Listen, with your background, you know more about dealing with these kinds of problems in your pinky finger than I do with my entire department. Dr. Scott and I will be here to back you, but I don't think low and slow, the way we do things here in Texas, is gonna cut the mustard this time."

"What are you saying?" Travis said, furrowing his eyebrows.

Sheriff Burnett shook his head and then stared at Travis, "I'm saying that I can't protect you or your ranch. You are on your own."

———————

## 26

Travis almost laughed. The idea that Sheriff Burnett thought that he'd have any success at protecting Travis and the ranch from people who'd wanted to do him harm was beyond ridiculous. Travis shook his head slowly from left to right. The sheriff was a nice guy, but he'd admitted he was out of his depth like it was going to carry the shock of the San Andreas fault finally erupting into a massive land shaking earthquake that dropped California off the face of the planet. The news wasn't earth-shattering. It barely registered in Travis's mind.

But Sheriff Burnett was right about one thing — Travis did have more experience in dealing with these kinds of issues than probably anyone in the county. And that wasn't bragging, that was a fact.

"I appreciate you saying that," Travis said slowly, trying his best not to sound sarcastic, "but, I kinda know that already."

Sheriff Burnett blinked, "The thing is, like I said, this is way above my pay grade. I don't want to leave you out on your own, but I think the only way to get the pressure off is if we take that implant and make it known that it's been turned over to another agency."

Travis narrowed his eyes. The sheriff had finally gotten to the point. It was bad enough that Sheriff Burnett was dipping out of his own responsibility in dealing with the missing body and the implant, but now he wanted to throw the pressure off on another agency.

"Are you kidding me? Who are you going to give it to?"

"The FBI. I thought that maybe —"

Travis cut him off. "The FBI?" Travis threw his hands in the air, pointing to the barn. "Do you see what's right in front of you? These people came to my property, burned down a barn with horses in it, killed one of them, and left me with the mess to clean up. And now you want to call in a bunch of federal agents to handle the implant? No sir. That's not happening."

"But Travis..."

Travis pivoted, the blood rushing to his face, the anger from losing the barn and Scarlett exacerbated by the fact that he hadn't slept and had barely eaten since he'd stopped for barbecue. He poked his finger into Sheriff Burnett's meaty chest. "No, sir. You're going to give me time to figure out who these people are so I can get my pound of flesh."

"But..." The sheriff stammered, "I already made the call, Travis. I told him what was going on."

Travis balled his hands into fists, "Then tell them to stand down. You tell them you need time. I'll let you know when I need help and I haven't even begun to scratch the surface." He stared at the barn, his stomach in a knot, fury rising through him, "I've been a little busy dealing with this." He pointed at the charred skeleton of the barn. "And burying one of my horses."

"I know, Travis. Again, I'm sorry, but, I think..."

"I don't care what you think," Travis growled. "You brought me into this. Now, like you said, the trouble has come to my doorstep. I'm gonna handle it. But I'm going to do it in my way and in my time. Tell the Feds to stay away from me. They are not welcome on my property and you aren't either."

Travis wheeled away, striding toward the new barn. He thought he heard the sheriff call after him, but the rush of blood in his ears was so loud, he couldn't hear anything else other than that and the breath in his chest. How dare the sheriff come out to his property, inspect the damage and then tell him to stand down. Who did he think he was?

But the sheriff was right about one thing — he and Dr. Scott had brought the trouble to Travis's house. If they hadn't approached him at Sarah's Barbecue about Jake West's missing body, he'd probably be arguing about the final trim pieces in the new barn with the contractor that morning, not having to deal with a disaster on his own property.

Travis gritted his teeth. He would fix it. He just didn't know how; at least not yet.

## 27

B y the time Travis came back from checking on Ellie, the sheriff was gone. Travis stared down the driveway, but there was no dust cloud, no evidence that the sheriff had come to duck out of the problems in his department, tossing them off to the local FBI as though it was nothing more than a heap of garbage he didn't feel like dealing with.

In reality, Travis knew the sheriff was well-intentioned. He was likely embarrassed they'd lost the body and was trying to help Travis after the two black camouflaged men had torched the barn. From Sheriff Burnett's perspective, Travis could understand what he was thinking. Certainly, the FBI offices had more access to resources than the Washington County Sheriff's Department. That was for sure.

But the one thing that Travis knew about the alphabet agencies — whether it was the CIA, the FBI, the DCA, DIA, and ATF, or any of them for that matter – was that once they took over they'd give only a cursory look to what had happened at his farm, tell him to hand over the implant, cluck a few times about the damage, and promise to take care of the issue.

And Travis would likely never hear from them again.

Having worked in espionage, that wasn't acceptable. At least not to Travis, especially when things had become personal.

Travis had checked in with Ellie when he was done with the sheriff. She was working quietly, humming to herself as she scrubbed and hosed off all of the equipment and supplies they used for the horses. The smell of leather conditioner and lemon soap hung in the air around her. She seemed so peaceful after what happened the night before that Travis didn't disturb her. He walked out to the Jeep and drove back up to the house, leaving it out front.

Walking slowly from the Jeep to the porch, Travis straightened the chairs where he and the sheriff had sat and then sat down himself, putting his feet up on one of the footstools.

With the fire, he had to regroup again. He knew that Sheriff Burnett said he'd help. But questions ran through Travis's mind as a flock of butterflies gathered themselves in his stomach, their wings beating against the inside of his body. Would Sheriff Burnett actually give him a hand? Or when Travis asked, would Sheriff Burnett politely, in the most hospitable Texan way, refer him to some no-name agent with the FBI who'd taken over the case, but buried it below a backlog of other files?

The reality was, that Travis was alone. Alone with the damage to his ranch. Alone with the question of what had happened to Jake West's body and the importance of the implant. The damaged lock on his war room told him that the people who'd come looking for it were connected, and heavily so.

Travis swallowed, staring out at the acres in front of him, his eyes unfocused, his lips pressed together, his fists balled. It was only a question of time before the people came looking again.

He would be ready.

## 28

Keaton Callahan had spent the entire flight from Miami to New Orleans with his eyes locked onto his laptop. He was alone on the Cessna he'd chartered to take the short hop, save for the pilot, an attractive red-haired stewardess with extraordinarily long legs and bright green eyes, and two bodyguards, the names of which he always had trouble remembering.

One of the reasons he preferred the Cessna to other corporate jets was its in-flight Wi-Fi capabilities. While many commercial airliners had just started offering at least semi-decent connectivity to their passengers while in flight, the fleet of Cessna's owned by the FlightLeap Aviation Center was outfitted with not only the best security measures, but the best Wi-Fi in the business. They specialized in transporting businessmen and women who had important work to do that couldn't be interrupted.

And Keaton, the CEO of Explority Biotech, was one of those people.

Exactly two minutes after arriving and checking in at the reservation desk, a red-haired flight attendant made her way through the concourse and addressed him, welcoming him to the plane, "Mr. Callahan, I'm Carmen. I'll be your flight attendant for today. Your plane is ready if you'd like to follow me?" The sentence ended with a slight lift to it, her voice smooth and pleasant.

Keaton strode out onto the tarmac, carrying nothing except his wallet and his cell phone. His bodyguards brought his luggage and the backpack that carried his laptop and his work files. As he made his way to the gleaming white Cessna parked on the other side of the terminal entrance, the wind caught in the lapel of his sports coat, lifting it off to the side, exposing the light blue starched shirt he wore underneath and the sleek black Louis Vuitton belt that prevented his custom-made gray pants from hanging too low on his narrow hips.

As Keaton boarded the aircraft, he squinted through his mirrored sunglasses, watching to make sure his luggage was loaded correctly on board. It was one thing to have people carry it for him, but it was something else entirely to make sure it ended up where it needed to go. And on this trip, there could be no errors. Not one. "I'll take the backpack up here," he barked at one of his bodyguards, a man wearing a pressed black suit with an off-white shirt underneath, the bulge of his gun evident near his waist. Part of Keaton wanted to tell the man that he would have been better off with a gray shirt. Off-white always looked dirty to him somehow, as if the color couldn't decide whether it was white or beige and chose the middle ground, a muddle of yellowish tones.

The man had no tie on. None of his bodyguards did. Keaton didn't require it and the security firm he'd hired recommended they not wear them. If they did, they would be clip-on. It was far too easy for an attacker to grab a tie and use it to choke out one of the bodyguards. They could get hung by their own necks without ever realizing what happened. But the idea of clip-on ties was abhorrent to Keaton. They somehow always stunk of cheap leisure suits and a lack of effort, not to mention no attention to detail.

That's not what Keaton was about. Especially not on this trip.

As soon as Keaton was seated, the pilot came out of the cockpit, a dark-haired man with a thick wave of hair gelled into place on his head, wearing a starched white shirt with black bars and four stripes on each shoulder. "Good morning, sir. My name is Captain Ranker. I'll be flying you to New Orleans. We are ready to depart if you are."

One thing Keaton loved most about flying privately is how deferential the staff was. When he used to fly commercial, even in first class, it seemed the flight attendants were simply annoyed by everyone all the time. The smallest request came with a look of impatience no matter how much you paid for your seat. And no one ever saw the cockpit crew until after the flight was over. That wasn't the case flying private. It was a luxurious customer experience from the minute you rolled up to the terminal to the moment you got off the plane. Efficient. Responsive. Well-designed.

Just the way Keaton designed his products.

Keaton gave a single nod to Captain Ranker, "Let's go."

With that, Carmen closed the gleaming white steps to the fuselage and Keaton settled back in his seat. He glanced around, looking at his home for the next few hours. The Cessna was appointed with wood paneling, finished to a bright gloss that reminded him of the interior of a luxury yacht, with brown leather seats in a variety of configurations. A few of them were facing forward with two facing each other with a small conference table in the middle for in-flight meetings. Keaton had taken one of the seats at the conference table so he had plenty of room for his laptop and Carmen's service, which he was sure would be impeccable. Keaton's two bodyguards had taken up positions in the back of the plane. Luckily, the security company provided him with guards that were pretty much mute. They only spoke when spoken to unless there was an imminent threat. Keaton liked it that way. It never failed that he would be in the middle of solving a major problem or on the verge of a cutting-edge product innovation when some unknowing person would interrupt his train of thought, sending it off the rails and twisting it in a way that couldn't be replicated, like the cars from a maimed commuter train.

As Keaton put on his seatbelt, he felt the Cessna nudge forward and then began rolling slowly towards the airstrip. Since they were on the other side of the city from Miami's enormous international airport, it didn't take as long to taxi and for the sleek plane to jump into the air. As the plane took off, Keaton leaned back in his seat, feeling the cushioned leather hug his back and shoulders, his fingers resting in front of his chest, fingertip to fingertip, his eyes closed as they ascended.

As the plane leveled off, Keaton dropped his hands into his lap and opened his eyes. He sighed. Going to New Orleans represented the last phase of Raashid's project. The whole thing had taken far too long and had taken too much of his energy. He felt his upper lip curl thinking about the amount of time he put into Raashid's demands. It had taken his focus away from the work he'd been doing for Explority Biotech. His lack of attention to his own company had become noticeable. In the last few weeks, he'd started to get calls from board members, wondering what the slowdown in development was and when they could expect the new products they had been promised to be ready for the market, or at least for testing. The calls were painful and humiliating, each one of them subtly suggesting that maybe Keaton was in over his head, that maybe he didn't have what it took to take the company to the next level. Keaton was highly offended by each one of those suggestions and had made mental notes of everyone who had doubted him. He would take care of every single one of their insults, but he had to finalize his business with Raashid first. Keaton swallowed. Raashid wouldn't accept being second place.

Sighing, Keaton reached into his backpack, which he had placed next to him on the floor, and pulled out his laptop, setting it up on the table in front of him. His seat had automatic controls, like the kind that could be found in a high-end vehicle. Keaton adjusted the back so he was sitting straight up and got the computer running, connected to the onboard Wi-Fi. He checked his watch. Without Captain Ranker telling him, he knew that flight would take just over two hours as the little jet sprinted over the turquoise blue waters of the Gulf of Mexico and into New Orleans. Keaton licked his lips as he stared at the screen.

As much as he wanted to relax on the flight, there was work to do.

## 29

By the time the Cessna touched down in New Orleans, Carmen had served Keaton a wide variety of snacks and drinks, most of them left untouched, including the filet mignon with roasted red skin potatoes and asparagus drizzled in extra-virgin olive oil, balsamic vinegar, and finished with pink Himalayan Sea salt. He'd taken two bites and then pushed it off to the side, focused on the final configurations for Raashid's project. Even when Carmen plied him with a flourless chocolate torte served with a side of amaretto laced whipped cream and a double espresso, Keaton only managed a nod of acknowledgment, the coffee quickly getting cold as it sat on the conference table.

The moment the Cessna stopped, Keaton stood up from his seat and grabbed his backpack. He didn't bother looking behind him. He knew the bodyguards were on the move. One of them stepped in front of him as they went down the steps, checking for threats. He gave Keaton a nod, letting him know it was safe to come out of the airplane. Keaton grimaced. Part of him hated the fact that he needed protection, but the board insisted on it. He'd had a wide range of threats from other governments to other companies, every single one of them wanting to get a close and personal look at what was on his laptop. It wasn't surprising to him. Keaton thought of himself as the Leonardo da Vinci of biotech developers — far more creative than someone like Bill Gates or Steve Jobs. Some people thought he had an overinflated view of his abilities. He did not share that opinion.

Stepping off the plane in New Orleans, Captain Ranker gave him a handshake as he departed. "Hope you enjoyed your flight," he said, his eyes wide as if he was waiting for a compliment.

"It was fine. Thanks." Keaton said without stopping, pulling his sunglasses down onto his face.

Waiting for him was a sleek black SUV with tinted windows. The rental company had left it at the airstrip in New Orleans for them. Keaton got in the backseat, letting his body-guards take the front seats.

The drive to the hotel didn't take long. Hotel Montefiore was on the outskirts of New Orleans proper, on the edge of the parade route that was used for one of the most famous celebrations every spring, the Mardi Gras parade.

Leading up to Fat Tuesday every year, the parade itself featured all sorts of music and dancers in various levels of clothing and makeup, some of them looking like they had just walked out of the local PTO meeting slinging candy at the bystanders, others barely dressed, wearing colorful body makeup and tossing beads to the people lining the streets.

The concierge met them at the door. "Welcome to Hotel Montefiore, Mr. Callahan. It's a pleasure to meet you. My name is Samuel and I will be your personal concierge during your stay. Your room is ready."

"Music to my ears," Keaton mumbled, pulling off the mirrored sunglasses and putting them on the top of his head. "Lead the way."

Samuel made pleasant chatter about the weather and the upcoming Mardi Gras celebration as Keaton followed him into an elevator flanked by brass doors. Only one bodyguard followed; the other one was busy parking the car and bringing up the luggage. "Is this your first time staying at Hotel Montefiore?" Samuel asked. Keaton stared at him. He was a thick man, but not very tall. The seams on the shoulders of his jacket seemed to be stretching past what they were designed to handle, but then again, Samuel was built like a fireplug — short and squat with a naturally curled upper lip and narrow eyes topped by a fluff of brown hair that seemed to point perpetually to the right.

"It is."

"And are you here to enjoy the Mardi Gras celebration?"

"You could say that." Keaton's stomach clutched into a knot, the reminder of Raashid's project landing on him.

Keaton ignored the rest of Samuel's commentary. It sounded rehearsed. He chatted through the many options that were available in New Orleans, things to see, the best restaurants, that he simply had to try beignets while he was there with a strong, hot cup of chicory roasted coffee first thing in the morning, and though the ones downstairs at the hotel were good, there was a café half a block to the east that was worth the walk. Samuel hardly took a breath.

When there was finally a pause, Keaton grunted, "I'm sure it is." Keaton followed Samuel as he led them down a burgundy carpeted hallway flanked in matching wall paint with gold filigreed sconces mounted on either side of each of the rooms. As Samuel opened the door, he stepped aside, as if he was revealing a hidden national treasure to Keaton, "May I present to you the Presidential Suite," Samuel said with a flourish.

As Keaton stepped inside, he scanned the room. Unlike the heavy dark burgundy decor of the hallway, the Presidential Suite was lighter. The carpet was a rich navy blue, the walls painted in a subtle shade of gray, sleek leather furniture scattered throughout with modern art decorating the walls. Based on the traditional architecture of the hallway, it wasn't what Keaton expected. Samuel walked over to the windows, pulling open breezy gauze curtains. "And you'll see that you have a lovely view of the parade route. You'll be able to sit out here and watch to your heart's content without having to deal with the crowds. And, we have a wonderful in-house chef who I'm sure would be more than happy to bring up a wide array of foods for you to enjoy while you watch. And our bar service is second to none throughout the city."

As Samuel turned back toward Keaton, the concierge pursed his lips, "Is there anything else I can get for you right now, sir?"

Keaton grimaced. He wanted to be left alone. "No." He spun away from Samuel, "If you'll excuse me, I have work to do."

"Certainly, sir," Samuel said from somewhere behind Keaton.

As Keaton heard the door click closed behind him, he walked over to the windows and stared outside, giving a little shudder. The last thing he wanted to do was watch the parade. That was the whole reason he was here, and it wasn't to be entertained.

Turning back toward the suite, he noticed it had a large glass table, round, encircled by four chrome and leather chairs. Keaton sat down in one of them and pulled out his backpack, opening an instant messaging app he had stored on his computer. "Just arrived."

"Do you like the suite?"

"It's nice."

"How is work progressing on our project?" Raashid wrote back.

Keaton pulled up a program, typing in a password that was twenty-six characters long, from memory. A map loaded on the screen, dots moving in different areas of the city, each of them highlighted in green with a registration number floating next to it. "It looks like our people are working."

"Good. That's what I want to hear."

Keaton clicked on one of the first numbers on the map. The man's profile popped up on the screen, providing the registration information of the implant, the date it was added to the man's body, and his current location given in longitude and latitude, the numbers adjusting with every movement of the man's body. The location data was good within three feet. That was something Keaton was proud of. At the bottom of the screen was a camera icon. Being able to integrate multiple platforms into his tracking software was something it had taken him two months of nearly nonstop work to accomplish. Clicking on it, the program accessed any surveillance cameras in the area that were near the implanted device, hacking into each one automatically. As the cameras came online, Keaton could see a man wearing a pair of jeans and a black T-shirt working at a table, a variety of wires and parts scattered in front of him, putting the finishing touches on a set of bombs. Another man worked behind him, wearing the same outfit. Keaton shuddered. He zoomed in on the man's wrist, seeing the thin white scar against his dark skin. It had been much easier to get people to agree to the implant than he ever suspected.

Another message came in from Raashid, "Are we on schedule?"

Keaton blinked and then pressed his lips together. Raashid had far too many questions and most of them insinuated that Keaton wasn't doing what he was supposed to be doing. "Yes."

"Good. If we weren't, I'd have to show you something like this."

Keaton watched for a moment as the second man in the image stopped moving, his eyes wide. White foam dripped from his mouth as he fell to the ground. The man working on the bomb ran to the man's side, but Keaton could tell by his expression it was too late. The man was dead.

"What did you do?!"

"I had our scientists add a kill switch to the implant. Cyanide."

"What? What do you mean?" Keaton leaped up from the chair and started pacing, his heart tight in his chest. "You don't have any right to make changes to the design. It's mine!"

"I don't? Are you sure?" The cursor on the messaging program blinked, then a video feed popped up in the messenger box. Keaton drew in a sharp breath.

The feed was from a hospital room at the Solomon Oaks Rehabilitation Facility just outside of Miami. A shriveled man lay in the bed, his mouth contorted, one of his hands bent at the wrist at an unnatural angle lying on his chest. An IV pole was next to the bed, two bags of liquids pumping into the man, and an oxygen cannula poking into his nose. The man's lifeless eyes looked half-open or half-closed depending on the angle. No one was in the room with him. He was alone.

"I heard your father's rehabilitation is going well." Raashid wrote cryptically.

Keaton gritted his teeth together. The year before, Keaton's father had a devastating stroke, the right side of his brain flooded with blood that wasn't meant to be there, causing him to lose the ability to speak and the use of the left side of his body. At the time, the doctors did everything they could to reverse the damage, administering TPA, a tissue plasmogenic activating drug that was known to have clot-busting effects that could reverse stroke damage, but it didn't work for Keaton's father. He'd spent nearly a week in ICU, Keaton dragging his laptop to the hospital every single day, suffering through the incessant chatter of doctors and the semi-consoling words of the nurses, while attempting to keep working. After a two-week stay in the hospital, the doctors said that the only thing they could do for Keaton's father at that point was to send him to a rehab hospital and hope for the best.

Although Keaton had chosen the finest unit in the area, the damage done to his father's mind seemed to be irreparable. He had days where he was a little bit better and could mumble a few words, or at least sit up on the side of the bed, but for the most part, he was mute, curled up, living in whatever world was left in his mind. Keaton went to go see him when he could, at least once a week, sitting by his dad's bedside, but was unable to reach out and hold his hand or have a conversation. Keaton's dad couldn't respond, and the idea of holding his father's hand made him nauseous. Why, he still wasn't sure. They had been close at one time, his father his biggest cheerleader when he'd gone to college while his peers were still in high school. They'd lost touch after that, Keaton busy with school and building his career. His dad was a proud man, not one to beg for attention.

"What about him?" Keaton typed, his fingers pounding noisily on the keyboard.

"You know our deal."

Keaton sucked in a sharp breath. When Raashid had approached him about investing in Explority Biotech the year before, Keaton had no idea Raashid was putting himself in a position to control not only Keaton but the company. At the time, the infusion of capital had been a godsend to their bottom-line expenses and had allowed new staff to be hired.

But all of that had gone to the wayside as Raashid had exposed his plan to Keaton. As if bombing New Orleans wasn't bad enough, now, he held his father's life in his hands and had just watched Raashid kill a man unnecessarily.

Keaton had tried to get out of their deal, looking for investors who could replace Raashid's money. Seven months before, when Keaton was on the verge of securing a loan to buy out Raashid, his father had mysteriously had a massive setback, a second stroke that the doctors simply couldn't explain. There was a lot of headshaking, a wide variety of MRIs and CAT scans and consults with two different neurologists, until Raashid mysteriously provided Keaton with the results of a blood test Keaton hadn't been told about by the hospital. It showed that he had a high dose of blood thinners in his body, something that would never be prescribed for a stroke patient with already thinning vascular structures in their cerebrum.

Keaton was furious at the time and started off blaming the hospital until Raashid followed the delivery of the blood test results with a cryptic comment, "It's amazing how quickly someone will deteriorate with too much blood thinner in their system. Did you know warfarin is used to kill rodents?"

At that moment, Keaton knew Raashid had him.

Keaton replayed the moment in his head as he stared at the feed of his father, a lump forming in his throat. Yes, his dad had made progress before the second stroke, but a third would be devastating. He knew if he didn't do exactly what Raashid told him to, not only would he lose his company, but he'd lose the only family he had left.

# 30

After sitting on the porch for what seemed like an eternity, Travis got out of his seat and went into the house. He checked his watch. Only a half-hour had gone by since he'd gotten into it with Sheriff Burnett. Unlocking the door to the war room, he closed it behind him, frowning at the set of scratches in the gray paint on the door.

Inside, Travis went directly to the end cabinet on the work-table, lifting the bookshelves out of the way and keying in the code for the safe. From inside, he pulled out Jake West's autopsy file and the implant that went with it. Staring at it, he realized there was absolutely nothing else in that room that those men could have been interested in. Sure, there were plenty of guns and ammunition stored against the wall, case files from Travis's skip tracing cases, and his personal information and records, but nothing from his time with Delta Force or the CIA. The only thing of any interest in the war room was the implant. How did they know the implant was there and the location of the war room?

And if the implant was the key to understanding what was going on, then he had to unlock it and figure it out.

As he did the day before, he plugged the implant into his laptop and retrieved the information from it. The result was the same. It was garbled, with every other line missing. Travis frowned at the screen. He'd seen plenty of lines of code in his career, the CIA utilizing encrypted documents almost exclusively. But he'd never seen one that had entire lines of information missing.

As the thought landed in his mind, he realized he'd stumbled upon something. What if he had only half the information? Frowning, he cocked his head, staring at the screen, as if he had just arrived in front of a priceless painting and was studying the brushwork. He nodded slowly to himself, realizing that whatever information was on the implant was likely only a piece of the puzzle. Travis shook his head and took the implant back to the worktable, setting it under the magnifying glass again. There was a white substance at the other end of the pod. It looked to be a ground-up powder, but as he moved the implant around, the white powder didn't change positions inside the capsule, almost as if it was vacuum-packed inside. He narrowed his eyes, wondering what it was.

Shaking his head, Travis had a sinking feeling in his stomach. Whoever wanted this implant back wanted it for one of two reasons — they either wanted it for the design, or they wanted it for the information that it held. But if his suspicions were correct, that particular implant only told half the story.

Realizing he wasn't making any progress, Travis quickly locked up the case file and the implant again, securing the war room on his way out. He had thinking to do.

Outside, the afternoon had warmed considerably. Travis got in the Jeep and drove down to the new barn, parking outside. He found Ellie in the tack room, organizing what was left from the fire. Travis grabbed a saddle pad and his favorite saddle, freshly cleaned from the fire, smelling of leather cleaner. Ellie narrowed her eyes, "Where are you going?"

"For a ride. Need to clear my head."

For a second, Travis wondered if Ellie would ask if she could come. Luckily she didn't.

Travis carried his saddle and pad down the aisle, set the two pieces of equipment down on the fresh white concrete, and pulled Gambler, a black gelding, out of his stall, using the hardware on his halter to attach him to the cross ties in the aisle. Walking back to the tack room, Travis grabbed a bridle and a brush.

After sweeping the pine shavings off of Gambler that had stuck to his back and pulling a few out of his long tail, Travis set the saddle pad on his withers. It was still a little damp from Ellie hosing it off, but the bright Texas sunshine had taken care of most of the moisture. Travis swung his saddle up on top of Gambler's back, the horse flinching for a second as the saddle landed, then relaxing. For a horse that had been through a fire, Gambler seemed relatively calm.

Travis adjusted the pad, making sure it was positioned correctly before letting down the girth and tightening it with the strap. Satisfied the saddle was secure, Travis undid the cross ties and slowly put the bit into Gambler's mouth, the big black gelding licking at it as he got it settled. It was time to go.

Travis clucked to Gambler as he walked outside into the sunshine, "Come on. Let's go for a ride," he said, double-checking the cinch and then easing his way up into the saddle. Travis adjusted himself in the seat and bumped Gambler's sides with the heels of his boots, then turned Gambler back toward the new barn, walking down a side road the construction team had cut in to build the new barn.

Travis tugged on the baseball cap on his forehead, lowering it, cutting some of the glare from the afternoon sunshine. Travis took a couple of deep breaths as Gambler lumbered past the new barn, giving a wave to Ellie as she emerged outside, bringing in the last bit of tack and equipment she'd cleaned from the fire the night before.

The motion of Gambler's easy stride relaxed Travis. He looked around as they walked beyond the barn, turning onto a trail Travis had found when he and Kira bought the property.

Kira. Everything seemed to come back to her.

As Gambler walked along, Travis wondered if any of this would've happened if Kira had still been alive. Or what if they had never gotten together in the first place? What if the first spark of attraction had gotten pushed aside in favor of a more professional relationship?

From the underbrush, Travis heard some rustling and saw Gambler tilt his head taking two steps off to the side, avoiding whatever was making the noise. From the edge of the trail, a squirrel sat staring at them before giving a loud squeak and then running up the side of a tree.

Travis shook his head as he rode along on Gambler, pushing the memories away as he absentmindedly flipped the horse's coarse black mane back to one side of his neck. Travis pressed his lips together and sighed. He liked order. Whether it came from his days in Delta Force or not, he wasn't sure. Probably part of it was his upbringing or lack of it. Mostly raised by abusive foster parents, the rigors of the military soothed something inside of him. He always knew what to expect. There were clear consequences, clear outcomes, and clear expectations from the moment he woke up until he went to bed. And even in the murky world of the CIA, Travis had managed to find systems and processes that made sense. That's the way he still tried to live his life to that day. But the barn burning down told him there were people in the world that chose to violate those rules of order.

And somehow the implant was in the middle of this newest bit of chaos.

At the back of his property, there was a stream. Travis

guided Gambler down the bank and turned him toward the water, giving the horse a chance to drink, loosening the reins and sitting relaxed on top of his back. He could feel the warmth of Gambler's body radiating through the saddle. It was subtle with the thick saddle pad and the leather between the two of them, but it was there nonetheless. The air smelled fresh, the last bits of dampness in the woods finally evaporating. Not that they had much of a winter where he lived in Texas, but it was at least more moderate than the hot, dry baking sun of the summer that would send him sweating from his first foot out the door.

Gambler finished drinking, raising his head out of the water. Travis turned him around and started back to the barn. He picked up the pace a little bit, walking faster as he knew he was going home, his big black head swinging gently from side to side.

As Travis saw the barn in the distance, he sighed. Going on a ride was a nice distraction, but he knew it was only temporary. Part of him wanted to keep going forever, never to return to the burned-out barn, the implant, and the missing body. But his gut told him he'd have no peace until he figured out what happened to Jake West.

## 31

T he minute Travis rode up to the barn, he found Ellie outside. Dismounting from the gelding's thick, broad back, Travis handed the reins off to her, "He could use a bath. Smells like smoke."

Ellie nodded, "Yeah, I noticed that. Already took care of Smokey and Joker. Gambler was next on my list," she said, running a hand down Gambler's forehead, straightening his forelock. Ellie glanced at Travis, "Where are you off to?"

"I gotta take care of something," Travis muttered, the muscles in his jaw rippling.

Travis walked away from Ellie without saying anything else, leaving her to handle Gambler. He slid into the Jeep, started up, and headed back up to the house. The data he'd found from the implant was on his mind, the images of the encrypted mess rolling over and over again in his head. He had some tech skills, but what he was looking at was far beyond anything he could decipher in the war room.

Getting out of the Jeep, he walked into the house, kicking off his boots by the back door. As he did, he looked through the contacts on his phone, dialing a number he hadn't used in a while.

Elena Lobranova picked up after the third ring. "This is a nice surprise."

"I wouldn't be so sure until I have a chance to tell you why I'm calling."

There was silence between them for a minute. After the incident in the Oval Office a few months before, Elena had disappeared, recalled to Langley. Travis hadn't heard from his former colleague at the CIA since. But then again, he hadn't reached out to her either. "How've you been?"

"Good."

"How are things at the office?" Travis was intentionally vague, following the training he'd gotten on using unsecured lines.

"Fine. I got a promotion."

Travis raised his eyebrows, "About time.."

Elena grunted. "Maybe. You know how it is here. You're only as good as your last get."

Travis glanced at the floor, "Hey, I need some help with something."

"The kind of help that requires a secured line?"

"Probably."

"Give me a second. I'll call you back."

"Okay." As Travis ended the call, he started to pace from where he was standing in the kitchen and then quickly turned, striding toward the family room, opening the bookshelf, and putting in the code and his thumbprint for the war room. Everything he needed to talk to Elena about was in there. He wanted to be ready.

By the time he got the safe open, retrieved Jake West's file and the implant, his phone was ringing again, the screen reading "Unknown number." "Hello?"

"I'm back. What you got going?"

Travis took off his baseball cap, set it on the work table, and ran his hand through his hair. He closed his eyes for a second, "Honestly, I'm not sure." He spent the next couple of minutes explaining to Elena what had happened — the visit from Sheriff Burnett and Dr. Scott, the attack on the barn, and the data he couldn't decipher sitting on his computer. "It's like I only have half of it. And because it's encrypted, there's no way for me to tell exactly what it is."

"Can you send it to me?"

"Sure." Travis stared at the computer for a moment, wondering why he'd agreed to turn what he had over to Elena so quickly. Once she got her hands on it, it would, for all intents and purposes, be property of the CIA. Travis felt the muscles in the back of his neck tighten. But did he have a choice? He had to trust someone. It might as well be Elena.

Her voice interrupted the cascade of thoughts. "I'll email you a link. Give me a second."

Travis sat down at his computer, putting the phone on speaker next to him. By the time he'd logged into his email, an encrypted link had come from Elena. The address where the link had come from, as well as the one he was supposed to send the data to, was simply a mash-up of letters and numbers that made no logical sense. He hadn't seen one of the computer-generated proxy emails the CIA used in a long time, probably not since he left the Agency five years before. He clicked on the link, uploaded the data from the implant, sending it to Elena, along with a picture of the implant itself.

The line on the call between him and Elena was still open. He could hear some tapping from her end as if Elena was sitting at her desk. "You in the office?"

"Sort of. I'm in the parking lot. Have a briefing in a little while."

Travis's curiosity was piqued, "Anything interesting I should know about?"

Elena chuckled, "Plenty, but last I checked, you don't work for the Agency anymore. Are you telling me you want to come back?"

The question hung in the air for a moment. Travis narrowed his eyes, trying to decide if Elena was being serious or not. Part of him knew she was. They had worked together successfully on a bunch of different operations in the past, their language skills complementary, both of them fluent in Russian, and each of them knowing languages and dialects the other one didn't, which gave them good access to most of the countries left in the Eastern Bloc. For as many people as wanted to be CIA agents, trying to find ones that were a good fit for the Agency was a bit challenging.

"I think I'm good here..."

"Uh-huh. Sounds like it," Elena said sarcastically. "Except for the fact that trouble seems to keep arriving at your door."

"Yeah, there's that."

Travis heard Elena sigh on the other end of the line, "I just got the file. What have you gotten yourself into, Travis?" she said, her voice barely audible above a whisper. "I can tell you right now, you've tripped into something that's way bigger than you think."

Travis grunted, "Clearly. What am I looking at?"

"Honestly, I'm not sure. What I can tell you is when I ran the decryption program, only part of the information is coming back. Are you sure there wasn't another implant somewhere with the rest of it?"

"No idea."

"Well, the reality is whatever this message is, it's been effectively chopped in half. I'm gonna send it back to you so you can see it. Give me a sec."

A moment later, a new email from yet another randomly generated email address popped up on Travis's screen. He opened it and scowled. Elena was right. "This is worse than a redacted document. I can't make heads or tails of this."

"And that's bad, considering the fact that you specialize in heads and tails now."

"Very funny."

"And there's something else, Travis. Can you scroll down to the bottom of the screen?"

"Sure." Travis moved to the bottom of the document as Elena had suggested. There was scrawled writing at the bottom of the screen, whether it was Arabic or Persian, Travis couldn't tell. "What is that?"

"It's Arabic. The Rising Sun."

"What the heck is that?" It'd been a while since Travis had touched on anything that was outside of Texas. He'd had his fill of the Middle East, particularly Israel, while he was with the Agency. The CIA used Tel Aviv and the surrounding areas as a jumping off point for their agents going into the field east of the small country. With the Mossad's blessing, the CIA had a fleet of safe houses and support personnel positioned in the area — everyone from physicians to psychologists to operational specialists and analysts.

"It's the codename for a terrorist organization that we think is led by Raashid Sharjah, an Egyptian billionaire."

"Can you fill me in?"

"Not without a clearance, but I know someone who can."

# 32

"What are you saying?" Travis shot up from his position sitting at his computer in the war room. He glanced toward the surveillance monitors. He could see Ellie riding Joker in the arena, trotting him in tight circles in both directions. That was good. At least Ellie could handle business with the horses while he figured out the rest of the mess he'd gotten himself into.

"I'm saying that I've heard chatter that the Israelis have been tracking these kinds of implants."

"The Israelis?" Travis's mind started to churn as the words came out of his mouth. For the two decades prior, Israel had become one of the leading technological development countries around the globe. With such a small footprint, they needed industries that didn't take up a lot of land. With the arid climate and the limited space the country had, extensive agriculture was out. Tourism was certainly a big part of their economy, but what they had really become known for was their ability to quickly develop and bring to market innovative engineered solutions for weapons and biotech.

A few months before, Travis had read an article online

about new, high-tech weapons Israel was developing – weapons systems and armoring for their Merkava series of tanks, new guns that had the range of a rifle, but were small and easy to maneuver like a pistol, and improvements to their Iron Dome system that had been given to them by the United States to intercept missiles that were launched from the Gaza Strip.

The threats to Israel were real and constant. Innovation was the one thing that kept them one step ahead of their enemies.

"You're thinking that the implant was Israeli-made?"

"I have no idea. But I think it's a place to start." Elena lowered her voice on the other end of the line, "Travis, whatever this is, it's dangerous."

Travis grunted, glancing at the security feed which was panning across the burned-out hulk of his barn at that very moment. It wasn't like Elena to shy away from a threat. "I know."

"Listen, I know you're no stranger to danger, but really, you're going to have to be careful. This is some next-level stuff that's going on. Sharjah is no joke. If you give me a second, I'm gonna send you some contact information for a guy I know. He should be able to help."

"Who is he?"

"A friend." Elena paused for a moment. "I just sent him a message. He's usually pretty fast at getting back to me. I also sent him a picture of the implant."

Travis shook his head, pressing his lips together, "That should get his attention."

"You bet it will."

Travis heard rustling on the other end of the line. "Listen, I have to get to that briefing. You'll stay in touch? Let me know what's going on?"

"I will. And Elena..."

"Thanks."

## 33

T ravis had just set his cell phone down on the desk next to the computers in the war room when it chirped. It was from a number he didn't recognize. "Elena said you might like to meet up?"

Travis stared at the phone for a second. It had to be Elena's friend. "Yes."

"Sunrise Café. One hour." Attached to the text message was an address.

Clicking on the link, Travis saw that it was in Austin. He frowned. What were the chances that Elena's friend happened to be in Texas right now? Part of Travis wondered if Elena's friend was already tracking the implant. But either way, Travis was hoping that Elena's contact could shed some light on what Travis had gotten himself into.

Knowing the drive to Austin would take an hour, Travis shoved the implant and Jake West's autopsy file in a black backpack he had in one of the cabinets in the war room and walked out the door.

An hour later, Travis pulled up in front of the Sunrise Café after circling the block in multiple directions a few times. Based on what Elena had said, Travis guessed her friend was Israeli, probably Mossad. Travis glanced in the rear-view mirror of the Jeep. As far as he could tell, he hadn't been tailed, although if there was one active Mossad agent in the area, he probably wasn't alone. They worked most of the time in small cells, each person in the group having specific responsibilities. And the Mossad worked fast. Travis was sure that in the last hour, if he was meeting a Mossad agent, they had pulled a full background on him and knew more about him than he knew about himself. Even though Elena had vouched for Travis, that wouldn't be enough. The Mossad was notoriously suspicious, as they should be. Having traveled to the region on multiple occasions, the way Travis had explained it to people who had asked, was telling them to imagine they lived in Austin and the people in Dallas wanted to wipe them off the face of the earth.

Israel wasn't a country with boundaries, only agreed-upon treaty lines after years of skirmishes. Active minefields still peppered the countryside, cordoned off by yellow and black warning signs and barbed wire, which only served as a reminder of the tumultuous past of the small, isolated country. Driving along the winding, narrow roads to the north, it was possible to see the UN outpost that occupied a flimsy barrier between the massive radar arrays perched at the top of the Golan Heights and the outskirts of Damascus. No, the Israelis were not people to be trifled with. While they might seem generally upbeat, their positive demeanor camouflaged people who were fearlessly loyal to each other and to their country.

Travis pulled into a parking spot at the Sunrise Café and walked in the front door, still wearing the T-shirt, baseball hat, worn jeans, and cowboy boots that he'd had on when he took Gambler for a ride a few hours earlier. There hadn't been time to change. There was no real need to. He'd fit in just fine wearing what he had on, even though he was in one of the nicer areas in the outskirts of Austin.

Travis glanced around the café, trying to spot the person he was meant to meet. He had no name and no description. The café itself was largely empty that late in the day, only a couple of older women laughing in the corner and two men working on their laptops, chunky earphones over their ears. A single barista was working behind the counter, refilling the trays of muffins and scones, her back covered by a black t-shirt, cut through by the green strings of her apron. Soft music played in the background. It sounded like bluegrass. Instrumental. Sitting alone was an older man with a head full of gray hair. He seemed to be crouched over a cup of something hot, the tendrils of steam curling up from inside the white mug, his wrinkled hands circling it. As he glanced up at Travis he gave the slightest lift of his chin, acknowledging his arrival. Travis licked his lips and walked toward the man, trying to fight off the urge to check over his shoulder. The prickle at the back of his neck told him he was being watched. He didn't argue with his gut. It had protected him more than once. He just hoped his luck would hold out through this meeting.

As Travis slid into the booth, the man lifted his gaze, his gaze meeting Travis's eyes slowly. "Hello, Travis. It's nice to meet you."

Travis blinked, sliding the backpack toward the corner of the booth. "Thanks for making the time."

The man looked down at his coffee and then took a sip. "I'm in town for a conference, so your timing was good."

Travis raised his eyebrows. The conference was a nice cover story, but if Travis had to guess, he guessed that the man was stationed in the United States as a liaison with one of the alphabet agencies, or even working undercover on another project that no one knew about. Travis glanced down at the table, wondering what kind of operation the man in front of him could possibly be running right in Travis's backyard.

From out of the pocket of his wrinkled gray button-down

shirt, the man pulled out a pack of gum, "My name is Eli Segal." He nodded at Travis, extending the pack of gum toward him. "Would you like some?"

"No, thanks."

Eli shoved the piece of gum in his mouth, balling up the wrapper and dropping it on the table. He shook his head, "I quit smoking a few months back. The only thing that seems to get rid of the craving is chewing this blasted gum. I go through a pack a day, can you imagine that?"

"No, I can't."

"Well, you didn't drive all the way here at breakneck speed from your ranch in order to have me tell me about my issues with my cravings, now did you?"

Travis narrowed his eyes. The fact that Eli mentioned the ranch and his travel time told Travis everything he needed to know. The request to meet so quickly was no accident. It was intentional, a way to force Travis to move quickly. It was Espionage 101 — don't give your contact enough time to prepare so you can see what they're really up to.

"Not exactly," Travis said, shifting in the seat. "My friend said you might have some information."

Eli raised his eyebrows, "Not much for pleasantries, are you, Travis? You're the kind of man that likes to get to the point."

Travis felt the muscles in his jaw tighten, "You could say that. There's no reason to beat around the bush."

"This is a phrase I haven't heard before, but I think I understand what you're saying."

Travis set his hand on the black backpack. "I have a couple of things in my backpack I'd like to show you, but I don't want to get myself shot." He raised his eyebrows, as if he was letting Eli know he knew the Mossad agent was likely not alone, and likely not unarmed, "Is that satisfactory?"

Eli gave a long slow nod, the fluff of his gray hair moving as he did, "Certainly. I love a good show and tell."

As Travis pulled the file out of his bag, he saw Eli glance around the café, as if he was sending someone a silent signal. Travis looked over his shoulder to see another man with dark hair and tanned skin sitting by himself, wearing headphones staring at a laptop. He glanced at Eli and then right back at his work. Travis caught Eli's eye. "You have the surveillance jammed yet?"

Eli let out a belly laugh, "You are the real deal, as they say, my friend," he smiled, reaching across the table and clapping a hand on Travis's forearm. "Yes, we are good to go, as you Americans say. Young David has it handled."

The Mossad had done their job. Travis pulled the file out of his backpack first and slid it towards Eli across the wood table. Eli nodded, "I'm so sorry. I completely forgot my manners. Would you like a coffee?"

Travis narrowed his eyes. Coffee was the last thing he was thinking about. "No thanks."

Travis stared at Eli. With a wrinkled hand, Eli flipped the cover open and quickly thumbed through the images. He pushed the file back to Travis not more than a few seconds later at which point Travis jammed the file back down deep inside of his dark backpack. Chewing on his gum, Eli furrowed his eyebrows, "Why do you show me this?"

Travis blinked, "For two reasons. First, the body in that file is missing. Stolen right out of the Washington County Coroner's Office. And second," Travis reached into his backpack, "this was found inside the body."

As Travis pushed the bag across the surface of the table toward Eli, the man caught it under his folded hands, only separating them after glancing around the café and getting another affirmative look from his watcher. Eli narrowed his eyes as he looked up at Travis, "Are you sure this was taken from the body?"

Travis gave a single nod. "According to the medical examiner, it was implanted in the man's right wrist, in the flesh just above the joint."

Eli glanced again at the implant, his face becoming ashen. He pushed it back towards Travis who grabbed the bag and stuck it back inside of his backpack, zipping it closed.

Travis watched as Eli dipped his head and chewed furiously on his gum, his hands folded in his lap. A moment passed before Eli spoke again. "Elena mentioned you tried to pull the data off of the implant?"

"I did."

"Were you successful?"

Travis chewed his lip. If Eli had talked to Elena, then he knew Travis had seen the first pass of the data, or at least what could be deciphered. But Travis knew if he wanted Eli's help he'd have to play along and answer Eli's questions. "Partially. I was able to download the data from the implant, but it was heavily encrypted and filled with gaps."

"And our mutual friend was able to clean it up for you?"

Travis nodded. "She did, but unfortunately either the data is corrupted and I was only able to download half of it..."

"...Or the implant is missing data."

The way that Eli finished Travis a sentence, Travis knew there was something more to the story and Eli knew what it was. Travis licked his bottom lip and looked down at the table, adjusting the baseball cap on his head, "Look. I appreciate you meeting me, especially since you know I'm no longer active. But the reality is that whoever took Jake West's body and put the implant in him seems to want their property back. If you know something, I'd appreciate the help."

"Yes, Elena told me about your barn. I'm sorry for your loss. Israelis have a great love of all things equine."

Travis nodded, "I appreciate that. Elena said that she thinks whoever is responsible for the implant, the name Sharjah is tied to it."

Eli nodded, re-folding his hands on the table, "Yes. She sent me a copy of the data. I looked it over while you were driving here." From out of his pocket, Eli drew a cell phone. He touched the screen, entering the password and opening it up. After a few seconds, he pushed it toward Travis. "Meet Raashid Sharjah."

Travis stared at the image Eli set in front of him. Raashid Sharjah was a dark wiry-haired man with matching dark eyes. In the picture he was smiling, which revealed a broken front tooth that looked more like he'd been in a bar fight than anything else.

"Sharjah. Yeah, Elena mentioned this guy's a billionaire. What's with the tooth?"

Eli shrugged. "Rumors have it that he got his tooth broken when he was young in a street fight near his home in Egypt. You Americans would call it a turf war. After that day, he decided never to get his tooth fixed so he would have a constant reminder of where he'd come from every time he looked in the mirror."

Travis raised his eyebrows, pushing the phone back toward Eli. "I've heard of crazier reminders. How's he tied to all of this?"

Eli pulled a paper napkin from the dispenser at the end of the table and wrapped up his gum, pulling another piece from the pack and shoving it in his mouth before speaking again. "This nonsense with the gum needs to stop," he mumbled. Clearing his throat, he stared at Travis, "Raashid Sharjah is a true believer."

"Islamic?"

"Definitely. He believes the world would be a better place if we all lived under a global caliphate with their arcane, rigid rules."

"Including the ones how infidels, the ones that refuse to accept their beliefs, should be beheaded?"

"Oh yes, especially that one." Eli paused for a second. "Raashid is a billionaire, as I'm sure our friend shared with you. Made his money in the textile business. Manufactured fabrics near his hometown of Minya in Egypt, expanded to multiple locations throughout the country and then started importing and exporting his products around the globe. Eventually, he used his money to start to buy significant holdings in other companies, building his empire."

"Sounds like the game of Monopoly." Travis raised his eyebrows.

"I'm not familiar with this. You said it's a game?" he asked, cocking his head to the side.

"Yeah. A board game."

"In any event, Raashid was very focused on his business until his younger brother, Sadi, got into trouble."

"What kind of trouble?"

"Big trouble. The kind that gets you snatched up off the street never to be seen again."

## 34

"The kind that gets you taken?" Travis raised his eyebrows. "And I'm assuming you might know where Raashid's brother, Sadi, is?" Travis's mind raced. It was becoming blatantly obvious that the people that had come after him were looking for far more than just the implant. Clearly, Raashid was involved in a bigger plot.

Eli gave a slow nod. "Suspicion of terrorist activities."

Travis swallowed and folded his hands on the table. Suspicion of terrorist activities was Agency speak for the fact that they knew an individual was up to something, even if they weren't sure what. Most of the time that phrase meant their suspicions were dire enough a government was willing to yank the person off the streets and stick them in a black site until interrogators could figure out exactly what they were up to. Travis blinked. The pieces of the puzzle were starting to fall into place.

Eli cleared his throat and used his fingers to push his wispy hair back into place. "Sadi became a concern to us a few years ago. We started watching him, and then because of our joint cooperation agreements, quickly discovered the Americans were too. You cowboys got to him first, though." Eli smiled, his thin lips pulling across his face. He glanced away from the table as if taking stock of who was around him and then looked back at Travis, "After a couple of months, our American counterparts were kind enough to allow Sadi to have a vacation with us."

"And he's been with you ever since?"

Eli nodded.

Travis rubbed his chin, pulling his fingers across the rough stubble of his face. He blinked a couple of times and then looked back at Eli, narrowing his eyes. Eli and Elena must have a good relationship for Eli to be as forthcoming with Travis as he'd been. Travis decided to press his luck. "What's the goal here? Raashid's got a beef with the West. A lot of radical Islamists do. And what's with the implants and dead bodies being stolen?"

Eli pressed his lips together and then leaned forward toward Travis, "Raashid Sharjah is one of the most dangerous masterminds I've bumped up against in my career. And you can tell by looking at me that I've been in this game for more than a minute. I've not been part of the interrogations of the brother, but I can tell you Raashid has been highly offended that we have kept his brother from him, especially since it's Israel that has him. They have a strong family connection. Because of that, any proclivities he had toward harming the West have grown exponentially."

"That's a lot of fancy language to say he's mad."

Eli licked his lips, "Indeed. If you want me to put it plainly, he wants to destroy the United States and then Israel. That's his entire goal. That's why the name of his operation is Rising Sun. It's the direct translation of his last name in Arabic. He wants a new day in our countries, one without the freedoms we enjoy now. He's not likely to stop until he gets it, unless we are able to stop him first. Implants like the one you have could give him a great deal of control over the people."

"So he blames the two countries for what happened to his brother?"

Eli nodded.

"And he doesn't recognize the fact that Sadi is a terrorist?"

"Apparently not."

Travis leaned back against the booth and rubbed the back of his neck with one hand. He was quickly getting a headache. He glanced at Eli who was swapping out his pieces of gum again, the balled-up wrappers lined up neatly on the edge of the table. "And somehow the implant and the missing body are tied into this whole mess. Is that what you're saying?"

Eli nodded, chewing, the smell of peppermint floating across the table. "That would be my guess, yes. I need to do a little more research, though."

"Then let's get started. I have a debt to settle with Raashid."

Eli got up from the table, carrying his mug. He leaned toward Travis. "If you hear anything, keep me in the loop?"

"Sure."

# 35

Keaton had spent the day locked up in the Presidential Suite of Hotel Montefiore. At dinner, the concierge he'd met when he'd arrived, Samuel, arranged for a meal of poached salmon, a baked potato, green beans with truffle oil, a platter of fruit, crudités and a plate of cookies. Keaton stopped briefly to eat, picking at the food, leaving much of it on his plate in the middle of the suite, and taking a single chocolate chip cookie back to his computer, which he finished as he worked. He didn't have much of an appetite.

The plans were coming along nicely to finish Raashid's project, minus the fact that Keaton was missing one important part of the necessary data — the second implant. As he stared at his computer, he pounded his fist on the desk, trying to figure out how he was going to finish the coding without the information. Had Raashid killed the man to make his job impossible or was it something else – like a robbery gone bad? Maybe the guy was working on the side for someone else and Raashid found out. A shiver ran down Keaton's spine. He wasn't afraid of much, but based on what he'd seen, Raashid was worth a measure of fear.

"You haven't made this easy for me have you?" Keaton muttered under his breath, putting his fingers to the keyboard again. Raashid had announced three months before that he'd separated the final detonation sequences into two of the implants. Keaton would have to have access to both of those people in order to complete his work. At the time, Raashid said it was a protection for both of them. Now, trying to finish the project, Keaton wasn't so sure. Finishing the project was the only way to get Raashid to relinquish control of the shares of stock he held in his iron grip on the company, not to mention the threat against Keaton's dad.

But then somehow, one of the people carrying the data he needed had died.

Keaton frowned. It had to be Raashid, but that didn't change things. The bottom line was one of the men trusted with the implant — and specifically, one that carried the other half of the detonation sequence — was dead and when Keaton's people had gone to retrieve the body, the implant had disappeared.

And even though he'd tried every trick he could find to activate the implant again, Keaton had been unable to access the data remotely.

Each of the implants had precise GPS technology that told Keaton exactly where the team was. But something must have happened when the man was killed. The implant had gone offline and hadn't come back on since.

Keaton leaned back at his desk, closing his eyes for a moment, interlacing his fingers behind the back of his head. His stomach had tightened into a tiny knot, enough so that it was threatening to throw up the salmon he'd eaten for dinner. The salmon had been delicious going down, but he wasn't sure exactly how good it would taste coming up again if he couldn't hold it together.

Keaton swallowed, dropping his hands into his lap, his shoulders slumped. He needed to find a solution, and fast. The images Raashid had shown him of the feed from his father's room at the Solomon Oaks Rehabilitation Facility flashed through his mind. If Raashid had paid someone to dose his dad with warfarin and give him a second stroke, everything in Keaton knew Raashid wouldn't hesitate to kill his father off. For all he knew, the first stroke had been a product of Raashid's handiwork as well.

Keaton shook his head and chewed his lip. Perspiration gathered at the back of his neck. He swatted at it with his hand like it was a bug, getting up and going to the thermostat, turning it down a couple more degrees. The pressure was getting to him.

Sitting back down at his makeshift desk, Keaton heard the buzzing of a drone from outside of the balcony. He turned away from his desk slowly, in time to see the black drone hovering just outside the door, the propellers whirring so fast they couldn't be seen. From outside, he could hear a low voice say, "Open the door, Keaton."

Getting up from the table, Keaton walked to the door and slid it open, a blast of the heat from outside entering the room. The drone made its way into the suite, circling three hundred and sixty degrees as if Raashid wanted to see the entirety of the luxury suite Keaton was staying in. Keaton stood stock still, staring at it. "What do you want, Raashid? I'm trying to get my work done."

"I certainly hope that's the case," Raashid's voice announced through the speakers on the drone.

Keaton shook his head and glanced away. Part of him still couldn't believe he was having a conversation with a drone. For all he knew, a fully automated robot in human form might knock on his door next. Raashid seemed to have access to technology that went far beyond what Keaton could have ever expected. If their relationship wasn't so coerced, Keaton might have been curious about Raashid's supplier, but he wasn't.

Sucking in a deep breath, Keaton crossed his arms across his chest, straightening up. He knew the drone had cameras on it. He couldn't let Raashid see he was nervous. Raashid knew the implant was missing, but Keaton still had time to come up with a solution. Maybe...

"Like I said, Raashid. I've got work to do. What do you need?"

"An update."

Everything in Keaton wanted to pick up one of the chairs from around the table and swing wildly at the drone, knocking it out of the air, but Keaton stood still, trying to keep his composure. Sighing, he started to pace, "The teams have been working all day pretty much. Everything is set. We're just waiting on the final placements and uploading the last bit of coding."

"And when will that happen?"

"Soon." Keaton skipped the part about how it wouldn't happen at all if he couldn't access the other half of the detonation coding for the bombs. The last thing he needed was for Raashid to become irate and do something rash, whether that meant killing him or killing his father. Keaton needed time.

Keaton shook his head ever so slightly, thinking. He realized it didn't really matter if Raashid killed him or not. He just hoped if he did it would be fast. Living the way he'd been living was no good. Being in jail would probably be better. The constant pressure of having to perform for Raashid was taking its toll. He wanted his company and his life back. He'd finish the project and then figure out a way to get things back to normal, no matter what it took.

But he had no choice. Raashid controlled his company and held the life of Keaton's father in his hand. Other than his dad and his work, Keaton didn't have anything.

Keaton turned and faced the drone, speaking loudly, forcing himself to sound optimistic. "Actually, you should be pretty happy with our progress. Everything is set. We've acquired all of the vehicles and all of the locations. The team has been working nonstop without breaks. I think your plan is going to come together nicely."

"And why do you say that?" The voice from the drone sounded suspicious.

Keaton felt like he was suddenly part of a sales pitch, "The target is a good one. New Orleans is nothing more than a backward city more worried about another Hurricane Katrina than anything else. There will be no shortage of targets. I found out an estimated ten million people flood into the city for Mardi Gras every single year."

"And all of them are infidels," Raashid growled.

Keaton shuddered. Raashid had shared with Keaton his desire to bring an Islamic caliphate to the United States. Mardi Gras was the perfect opportunity to publicly punish the United States in one of its most open party forums. It was like the Super Bowl, only it lasted for weeks rather than just one evening and was spread out over miles and miles of roadway in the city. The fact that Mardi Gras was a parade and not simply a singular event at a venue made security nearly impossible. That was to their advantage.

"I think you're going to get exactly what you want out of this, Raashid. You'll see people on their knees. Your message will be loud and clear."

"I hope you're right, Keaton. But we must stay humble. The Koran says, 'And the slaves of God are those who walk on the earth in humility and calmness.' I just hope you can stay humble and calm while we finish the job."

"And then you'll give me my company back?"

"We'll see," the voice from the drone said as it buzzed out of the room and into the darkness.

## 36

Travis had taken the first sip of his morning coffee when his phone rang. He hadn't heard from Eli since the day before. Staring at the screen, he half expected it to be another unknown number. It wasn't. It was the Washington County Coroner's Office. "Hello?"

"Travis? This is Dr. Scott."

Travis furrowed his eyebrows and licked his lip. "Dr. Scott? I didn't expect to hear from you today. Everything all right?"

"I know you've got a lot going on at your ranch. I'm very sorry about your barn. Sheriff Burnett told me about that, but I need to have you come to my office immediately."

Travis froze in place, a tingle running down his spine. "And why is that?"

"Jake West is here."

## 37

Travis left his still hot coffee sitting on the counter, scooping up his cell phone, wallet, and keys to the Jeep as he ran for the door. Sliding on his boots, he jogged outside to the Jeep and got in, taking off down the driveway, leaving a cloud of dust and grit in the pale morning light behind him. In the rearview mirror, he saw the burned-out barn getting smaller and smaller as he pulled away.

Exactly twenty-two minutes later, Travis pulled into the Washington County Coroner's Office, which was housed at the back of the Sheriff's Department. He parked the Jeep in visitor parking and then stormed into the lobby, startling the officer on duty. "I'm here to see Dr. Scott."

The officer at the desk furrowed his eyebrows as if not sure whether to let Travis in or to pull his gun. "And you are?"

"Travis Bishop. She called me. Told me to come down here."

"Right. Yeah, she's expecting you. You can come on in."

The moment the door buzzed, the automatic lock releasing, Travis gave the door a jerk, striding down the hallway past Sheriff Burnett's office. The door was closed. Where the sheriff was, Travis wasn't exactly sure. Glancing at it, he felt bad that he and the sheriff had left things the way they did. Up until then, they'd had a good working relationship. How it would be going forward, Travis wasn't sure. But that wasn't something he could worry about at the moment.

Passing a few more offices, Travis wove his way through the maze of hallways at the back of the building and finally found Dr. Scott's office. The door was closed. Without knocking, he turned the knob and pushed the door open, standing in the doorway.

As he scanned the room, Travis saw Dr. Scott sitting behind her desk, her eyes wide at his sudden entrance. Sheriff Burnett was perched in a chair off to the right, and a man with dark eyes and sallow skin stood off to the left in front of Dr. Scott's bookcases, his hands jammed in his pockets.

As soon as Travis barged into her office, Dr. Scott stood up, coming around from behind. "Travis, thanks for coming. This is Jake West."

Travis ignored Sheriff Burnett's presence. He took two long steps over to Jake and stood square in front of him, sizing him up. Jake was in his early thirties, Travis guessed, and a few inches shorter than him. He had a distinctly Middle Eastern look; as if he was Lebanese. Travis didn't bother introducing himself. "I thought you were dead."

Jake raised his eyebrows, "Seems like that's been a common concern."

Travis scanned the room, looking at Dr. Scott and Sheriff Burnett, crossing his arms across his chest, "Somebody mind telling me what in the Sam Hill is going on here?"

Sheriff Burnett shook his head, his hands folded across his belly, staring down as if there was something very interesting on his belt buckle. He muttered under his breath, "Heck if I know."

Travis stared at Dr. Scott, "You? Do you have any explanation?"

"There must have been a mistake when I sent the registration information from the rod from the body into the company. It must've had a typo. I'm so sorry, Travis. I don't know what to say."

Travis turned his anger onto Jake West, "And how did you end up here?

Before Jake could answer, Sheriff Burnett stood up, hooking his thumbs into his gun belt, "Now, Travis. Let's try to calm down here. Why don't you pull up a chair and we'll see what we can figure out?"

"Figure out?" Travis bellowed, "You all have had me running for the last couple of days, put my life in danger, all over someone who's not actually dead, who has the same name as the person that got turned into charcoal. How do you account for that?"

"I can't," Dr. Scott sniffed, her voice trailing off.

## 38

"You can't explain what's going on? That's obvious," Travis grunted, flopping down into a chair at the back of Dr. Scott's office. He glanced at Jake West, who seemed to somehow be detached from the drama that was ensuing between Dr. Scott, Sheriff Burnett, and Travis. A smirk tugged at his cheek as if he was vaguely amused by the fact that everyone had thought he was dead when he wasn't.

Travis shot Jake a look, "How did you end up here?"

Before he could answer, Dr. Scott cleared her voice, her fingers wrapped around her mug, "That was my fault, I suppose. I couldn't find any of Jake's family, so per our procedures, we put an ad out in the paper. They have an online edition. Apparently, someone that knows Jake told him about it."

Travis stared at Jake, "That's how you ended up here?"

Jake nodded. "That's right. A buddy of mine texted me last night. He scours the local papers for stuff he can salvage to sell online. Saw the death notice and request for relatives. Thought it was funny."

Travis raised his eyebrows, "Do you?"

Jake shrugged, "Sorta. Doesn't seem like the rest of you think it's all that funny, though."

Travis looked away from Jake. He was probably a nice guy, but his lighthearted outlook on what had happened was grating at Travis. Part of Travis wanted to pull Jake off of his chair and throw him through the plate glass window at the back of Dr. Scott's office right out into the parking lot and then run over him with his truck. His presence, or lack thereof, is what had started the whole cycle. Travis pressed his lips together. He should be back at the ranch, dealing with the skip tracing clients and training horses, not chasing the undead.

"Do we have any explanation for this? Anything better than it was a mistake? Any idea who the body actually was?" Travis said. He knew his words sounded impatient, but he didn't care. He stared at Dr. Scott and Sheriff Burnett. Dr. Scott stared down at her mug but didn't say anything. Maybe he shouldn't ask questions in front of Jake West, but Travis didn't care.

Sheriff Burnett cleared his throat, "Well, Travis, as Ava said, it's a case of misidentification."

"But it's not like you can go back and fix your mistake, can you, Dr. Scott? You've got no body to double-check the serial numbers on the rods and plates, do you?"

"That's true," Dr. said, her voice barely above a whisper.

"And that doesn't eliminate the fact that there was a dead body here with an implant in it and now it's gone. It also doesn't solve the problem that somebody burned my barn down, took the life of one of my horses, and nearly killed me in the process in order to get the implant back, now does it?"

Travis shot up out of his seat and started pacing. He could feel the heat rising to his cheeks, the fury inside of him building. If only Dr. Scott and Sheriff Burnett had left him alone, he wouldn't be sitting where he was, facing down a man who was supposed to be dead, but wasn't. And it did nothing to solve the problem of who the dead body was and what the implant was for.

"Did you say implant?" Jake's voice came out barely above a whisper.

Travis wheeled around, his arms still folded across his chest. He narrowed his eyes at Jake. "I did. Why?"

"It might be nothing." He glanced at the floor, "A few months ago, I got a text from my sister. We're fraternal twins. She'd been looking for a new job and had found one, something to do with supply chain issues. She's on some sort of special project having to do with supply chains. It was only supposed to take a couple of months, but she thought it would pay enough to give her a chance to figure out what she really wanted to do with her life. She has always been like that. Always flitting off to the next best thing. It's like she's got a bad case of shiny object syndrome. Whatever glitters she wants to go after."

"Get to the point," Travis growled.

Jake glanced at Travis, "Sorry. Yeah, so she texted me and said she'd been hired by a company. They were gonna pay her a hundred thousand dollars for two months of work. The only thing was, they were going to implant a tracking device in her wrist. She wanted to know what I thought about that."

As the words came out of Jake's mouth, a shiver ran down Travis's back. An implant placed in the wrist sounded a little too familiar. That couldn't be a coincidence, not after everything Travis had seen and what he'd learned from Eli. "Was it the right wrist?"

Jake nodded. "Yeah. The reason she was worried about it is we have matching tattoos. She was afraid the scar would mess up the ink and I'd be mad." Jake pulled up the sleeve of his shirt and held it in front of Travis. The word fidelity had been written across his wrist. "Like I said, we're twins. Were loyal to each other. Gia didn't want me to be mad."

Travis narrowed his eyes. There was a matching scar on Jake's wrist on one side of the tattoo. Travis reached for Jake's other arm and pushed his sleeve up, checking for scars. He glanced back at Sheriff Burnett and Dr. Scott, "Do you have an implant?"

"Yeah. That was the other reason Gia was reaching out to me. She knew I'd gotten one for my job. She was planning on working for the same company."

Travis narrowed his eyes. He couldn't imagine allowing himself to be tracked twenty-four-seven for anyone. Right before he left the CIA, he'd heard some whispers from his former Delta Force buddies that the military was considering an RFID project for combat personnel as a way to better track where assets were and make split-second tactical decisions. His buddies were concerned about the invasion of their privacy.

"Who do you work for?"

"A biotech firm based out of Miami called Explority Biotech. They hire people all over the country. I'm based here. Work in the IT division"

Dr. Scott got up from her desk and walked with tiny steps toward Jake, holding out her hands as if she was expecting him to lay something precious into them. Jake lifted his right wrist and held it out for her to see. Travis watched as Dr. Scott carefully probed the space between the bones and the muscles, feeling for the lump under his skin. "It feels the same as the one I took out of the dead body." She glanced at Jake. "Any chance you'd let me remove the one in your arm so I can compare it to the other one I found?"

Jake frowned, his face becoming pale. "I thought you only worked on dead people."

Dr. Scott smiled, "Yes, that's true, but I have the same

medical degree as any doctor that works with live people. I actually have more experience than most surgeons do. And I promise it won't hurt."

"Okay."

"Let's go."

## 39

The decision to take the implant out of Jake's very much alive wrist seemed like a good one to Travis. At least they could see if it was the same design as the one they'd taken out of the dead body – whoever that was.

As Jake and Dr. Scott walked down the hallway out of her office toward the lab, Travis and Sheriff Burnett followed. Travis tapped Jake on the shoulder. "Jake, do you know anything about the project your sister is working on?"

Jake shook his head, "Not much. I haven't heard from her in a while. She said not to be concerned if I didn't hear from her until after Mardi Gras. Told me not to call her. Said she'd be tied up until then and things were ramping up." He pulled a cell phone out of his pocket and thumbed through his texts. He glanced back at Travis, "Yeah, it's been a couple of months. The last message she sent told me not to worry, but that the project was highly confidential and she was going quiet until after it was over. She promised to come back into town and take me for a big steak dinner once she got paid."

"What about this Explority Biotech that you work for? Tell

me again why they wanted to put an implant in you?" Travis wanted to follow up with the question, and why you agreed?

"Like I said, they're a biotech company. They're working on a protocol to help people who are noncompliant with their medications."

"Like who? What are you talking about?" Travis put his hand on Jake's shoulder as they walked down the hallway to get his attention as they followed Dr. Scott into the autopsy room.

Jake shrugged, "You know, like people who have to take medication every single day and maybe they don't want to. What the researcher said to me was that it was for people who had mental conditions. Things like schizophrenia, or bipolar disorder. A lot of times they don't like how the medication makes them feel even though they need it. They'd rather live with the consequences of their disease — hallucinations and huge mood swings and stuff — rather than take the drugs they are supposed to take. The implant was supposed to solve that problem."

Travis paused in the middle of the hallway as Jake, Dr. Scott and Sheriff Burnett disappeared around the corner. He stopped and looked at the floor, thinking to himself. He certainly knew a lot of people, both men and women, that had come back from the Middle East with problems, issues with PTSD, depression, anxiety, and a whole host of other issues. It was one of the major reasons why so many highly decorated, heroic veterans were living homeless once they became civilians again. Travis had seen people like that on his few trips to the VA. He'd been one of the lucky ones. Although he'd gone through his battles, he hadn't come away with any of the mental scarring from his work with Delta Force or the CIA, or at least nothing that he would admit to.

By the time Travis glanced up, he was the only one left in the white painted hallway, the hum from an overhead bank of fluorescent lights the only noise anywhere near him. He looked in both directions realizing he was alone, lost in his thoughts. He blinked a couple of times, getting his bearings, and then headed in the same direction that Jake, Dr. Scott, and Sheriff Burnett had before they left him.

As Travis walked into the autopsy room, he saw Jake seated on the edge of the autopsy table. Jake grinned, "Dr. Scott wanted me to lay down on this cold steel table. I told her I'd already had one brush with death. Didn't need another," he smirked.

Travis nodded but didn't say anything. He scanned the autopsy room. The bright surgical light above the table where Jake sat was on. It cast a sharp shadow over the rest of the room, although there were lights on everywhere. It was like being part of an eclipse, one light brighter than the next. On the stainless-steel tables, the equipment stationed against the wall whirred and hummed, waiting for the next request to come from the coroner. A screen saver on one of the computers displayed the Washington County Courthouse clock tower with a black log-in box hovering in the middle of the screen, ready for Dr. Scott's password. Travis wrinkled his nose. The faint odor of bleach hung in the air, tinged with something that smelled like citrus, probably from one of the many cleaners Dr. Scott used to keep the autopsy room sanitary. A faint puff of air floated over Travis's skin as he glanced toward the bank of cold storage units against the wall, their doors securely latched and closed, the vibration of the cold air compressors keeping the bodies in stasis humming from somewhere on the other side of the wall.

"Ow!" Jake yelled.

Travis shot him a look. He was smiling again. "Just kidding."

"I'm putting the numbing agent in, that's all." Dr. Scott mumbled. "There's a reason I prefer dead bodies."

Curious, Travis walked toward Dr. Scott, standing over her shoulder to get a better glimpse of what was going on with

Jake's arm. Over Jake's leg, Dr. Scott had draped a blue surgical cloth, his tanned arm laying in stark contrast against the bright color. Dr. Scott sat on a rolling stool and had a stainless-steel tray to her right side. The tray was draped in the same blue surgical cloth that Jake's leg was, filled with an array of different implements. Next to Dr. Scott on the tray was a small vial and a clear syringe with a needle attached. Travis blinked, staring at the label on the vial. Dr. Scott met his eyes as he looked at it. "Lidocaine. It'll numb the area enough so I can get the implant out without causing Jake any discomfort. She glanced up at Jake. "Now, the only bad thing is the only sutures I have in the lab won't dissolve. That's not exactly an issue for dead bodies. I'm gonna have to put a couple of stitches in to hold the incision closed. Once we're done, you'll have to wait a week or so and then you can take them out, or you can come back and I'll take them out for you. Sound like a plan?"

Jake nodded. "Yeah. Let's get this over with."

Dr. Scott gave a nod, the blue gloves on her fingers probing his wrist once again for the location of the implant. "Tell me, can you feel that?"

Jake balled his hand into a fist, moving his fingers. "No. I can't feel anything. My whole hand is asleep."

"That's fine. It'll wear off in a little while. I used the same drug on you that they use in the dentist's office when you have a filling. The numbness is only temporary."

Travis watched as Dr. Scott reached over and picked up the scalpel. She held it with a strange level of comfort; as if it was another part of her body. Watching her wield it surprised Travis a little. He knew that the blades on a medical scalpel were insanely sharp, meant to slice through flesh with the smallest amount of damage to the surrounding tissue possible. Dr. Scott held it as if it was an extension of her hand, cocking her head to the left as she pressed the blade into Jake's skin. Travis glanced at Jake's face. He'd watched as the first trickle of blood came from his wrist and then looked away, staring at something on the wall of the autopsy room. Travis kept his eyes glued to the incision. He was fascinated by the process. Dr. Scott looked over her shoulder. "Mind handing me some gauze, Travis?"

"Sure," Travis said, handing Dr. Scott a short stack of the white squares. "Where's your assistant?"

She dabbed at the blood on Jake's arm. "Edward? The new guy? That's a good question. Called and left me a message this morning. Quit. Just like that. No explanation."

As Travis listened, he glanced around the room. Sheriff Burnett had taken up a position on the other side of the room, sitting in Dr. Scott's desk chair, leaning back, his thumbs hooked in his gun belt. He was looking in the other direction as if his eyes couldn't stand the sight of blood. Travis narrowed his eyes, realizing they'd come to an uncomfortable truce. A knot formed in his stomach. It wasn't from seeing the blood, it was from the way he and Sheriff Burnett had left things after their last conversation. "What are you doing, Sheriff?"

"Just sitting. That's all."

A half-smile pulled at Dr. Scott's face. She whispered, "The sheriff isn't too comfortable around blood."

Travis refocused on the incision in Jake's arm, pushing the memories of his conversation with the Sheriff away. As much as Travis didn't like the idea of the FBI being involved, if the Sheriff already called them, there was nothing he could do about it.

Dr. Scott picked up the scalpel again and was carefully nipping at the edges of the tissue, widening the incision. Pressing her lips together, she dropped the scalpel back on the surgical tray, swapping it out for a pair of forceps. Travis watched as she bit her lip. "I want to be careful I don't crush this as I pull it out. Trying to retrieve all the broken parts would make for a lot more work."

"I don't like the sound of that," Jake grimaced.

Taking the forceps in her right hand, Dr. Scott leaned over the incision, dabbing at it with a fresh piece of gauze as it oozed with blood. Travis could see the glint of something inside Jake's arm. In one smooth movement, Dr. Scott hovered the forceps over the implant, sending them into Jake's flesh and then pulling it out, quickly covering the fresh wound with another piece of gauze. She dropped the implant and the forceps down on the surgical tray, reaching for a clear bottle of liquid with what appeared to be a bent straw on the top. "Jake, I need you to move your arm and hold it over the table while I flush this for you."

Jake did as asked, extending his arm toward what would've been the head of the stainless-steel bed, near where there was a drain. Dr. Scott held Jake's arm lightly, her hand open, as she squeezed a gentle stream of the clear liquid to flush out the wound she'd put into Jake's arm in order to retrieve the implant. She gazed down inside his arm. "This is just saline, a little saltwater that matches the composition of the water in your body. I just want to rinse out the incision and double-check it before I stitch you up." A second later, Travis saw a few drops of blood-tinged saline running down the drain. Dr. Scott dabbed at the incision again. "All set. You can rest your arm back on your leg and I'll get you stitched up."

## 40

Travis stared at the implant as it sat on the surgical tray between the scalpel and the forceps. At first glance, it seemed to be exactly the same design as the one Dr. Scott had retrieved from the missing dead body. A shiver ran through Travis's back. The odds of them ever locating the body or figuring out who it was were getting smaller by the hour. The value of the body, not that there wasn't inherent value to every single human life, might have dissipated to almost nil as well. If Travis had to bet his own life, whoever had stolen the body away from the lab was interested not in the death of the human being, but in the retrieval of the technology.

"You said whoever your boss was at Explority Biotech said this was for helping people with managing medications?" Travis said to Jake, a scowl pulling across his face.

Jake nodded, looking down at his arm for a second. Dr. Scott was fishing black suture lines through his flesh, her fingers quickly tying perfect knots, the process looking a lot like she was repairing the hole in a piece of fabric rather than stitching Jake's arm together. "Yeah. The guy that runs the company — his name is Keaton Callahan — said the idea was they could track the implant. It's got some sort of a GPS locator in it. Not only that, but each one of the implants had some sort of placebo. He said we'd be periodically dosed with it just to make sure the mechanism was working correctly."

Travis crossed his arms across his chest and started to pace. If what Jake was telling him was true, then the white compound at the end of each one of the implants Travis had seen, which was now two to be exact, was probably nothing more than a crystallized version of sugar, probably remanufactured out of its common forms to resemble something closer to the way medication would be presented to the body. He frowned, "Part of this doesn't make sense to me, Jake. I mean, this is a small implant. It can't contain enough medication for somebody to use for a long period of time. What's with that?"

Dr. Scott unwrapped a bandage, the crinkling noise of the paper the only sound in the room. She laid it across Jake's wrist, pressing the adhesive on the edges down and then stripping off her blue gloves, tossing the wrinkled latex onto the surgical tray. She stood up, stretching her neck. "I see what you mean Travis. I read recently some labs are working on high potency medications — really just reformulations of things that we normally take. They concentrate them so highly that an implant like this one might last for a year or so. But, if I had to guess, I would suspect they're coming up with a longer-term plan, maybe an implant that would last for anywhere from one to five years. Some of those types of technologies are already on the market."

Travis frowned, shaking his head. "What are you talking about?"

Dr. Scott walked over to a sink, washed her hands, and then retrieved an evidence bag from a drawer nearby, using her wrinkled gloves to pick up the implant and drop it inside. She waved for Travis to follow her. Sheriff Burnett heaved himself out of her desk chair and got out of the way as she walked over to the medical equipment. "Technology like this has been on the market for a while now, I think. Not only do we have transdermal delivery systems for medications, things that look like a Band-Aid, laced with a particular type of medication that's absorbed through the skin, but there are subcutaneous implants. The most common one I can think of is for contraception. It's ideal for people that don't want to have children and don't want to take a risk. Honestly, although I'm not sure how I feel about it, I did read a controversial case where a parole judge was requiring some of his female inmates to have the transdermal contraception implant put in before they were released from jail. I guess in his way of thinking, it would prevent the woman from having more children they might not be able to take care of."

Travis shrugged. He wasn't the least bit interested in issues like that. Especially not since he'd left the CIA five years before. Large social and legal issues seemed unwieldy, like an octopus that needed to be wrestled to the ground. People would come up with what they thought to be the answer and then very quickly realize there was yet another tentacle ready to wrap around their neck. "So, you're saying that you feel like these implants could be a long-term solution?"

Dr. Scott shrugged. "Anything is possible, especially in biotech research. These guys that run these companies are super imaginative. They take the common problems that medical doctors have and try to come up with new and innovative ways to solve them. An implant like this, if used correctly, could be helpful. Like Jake said, people with mental illness have a high level of noncompliance. Jake was absolutely right. They don't like to take their medication. It makes them feel funny, or they lose what they perceive to be their edge. I had a sister like that."

"You had a sister with mental illness?" Travis glanced at Sheriff Burnett who shrugged as if he didn't know.

Dr. Scott nodded, pressing her lips together. For a moment she looked like she was far away, then she refocused on Travis. "Bipolar disorder. It's characterized by periods of major depression and periods of major elation called a manic state. It's like being on a seesaw. One day, my sister was higher than high and the next, she couldn't even crawl out of bed."

Travis crossed his arms across his chest, cocking his head to the side. His gut told him there was more to the story. "What happened to her?"

Dr. Scott blinked, looking at the ground and then leveled her gaze at Travis, "Ten years ago, she went through a period of time when her manic state was out of control. She wouldn't sleep, wouldn't eat, and ended up using markers and paint to write and draw every thought in her head all over the walls of her apartment. She said it was the best she'd ever felt. Her mind was filled with new ideas and she told me she felt like she had been sitting at the edge of the universe learning all day and all night."

Travis raised his eyebrows, "And she was off her medication?"

Dr. Scott nodded, "She'd been seeing a new psychiatrist and they were trying to rebalance the drugs. Bipolar disorder is one of the most difficult mental illnesses to manage. Trying to find the balance between bringing someone up when they are depressed and bringing them down when they're manic is nearly impossible. The brain is a more complex organ than anyone could have ever imagined. And even now, with all the medical developments we have, they've only barely scraped to the surface of what goes on between somebody's ears. Anyway, they tried a new medication on her..."

"What was your sister's name?"

"Kathy." Dr. Scott cleared her throat, "Kathy didn't like the side effects. Said the medication upset her stomach and made her edgy. I kept calling her and calling her. I went to her apartment to try to get her to take her medication. I got her old medications refilled, thinking that maybe if she went back on medication she was familiar with that she'd feel better about the situation, but when I saw the state of her apartment, I knew that she'd slipped over into a world I wasn't sure I could follow her to. The last time I saw her, I left her in her apartment, thinking she'd do exactly what she had been doing — stay up all night long, paint more gibberish on her walls. I had a call in to her psychiatrist to try to get her some inpatient treatment the next morning, but it was too late..." Dr. Scott stared at the floor.

Travis frowned, "What happened to her?"

"That night, she reached a new level in her mania. From the writings I found on the walls, she thought that God told her she could fly. She lived on the fourth floor of an apartment building. She went out on the balcony, stood on the edge, and jumped to her death. I got a call in the middle of the night telling me she was dead."

Travis shuddered. "I'm so sorry about that, Ava. I can't imagine."

Ava straightened up, her voice changing back to a more professional demeanor, "So, as you can imagine, I can see a definite use for these implants. If my sister had one, with a highly concentrated, timed dose of her medications, even if she had to have it replaced once a year, or every five years or ten years, it would be worth it. I might still have my sister."

"And you think that's what these guys were working on?"

She shrugged. "I can only go by what Jake has said." She glanced down at the implant on her desk. "I am curious about what they are using to test for the medications. I didn't have a chance to check the other one before I handed it off to you, but I'm gonna crack this one open and see what this white powder is. Hopefully, it's something inert."

"You think it might not be?" Sheriff Burnett frowned.

Dr. Scott shook her head. "I have no idea."

## 41

D r. Scott ushered Travis, Jake, and Sheriff Burnett back to her office while she ran the chemical tests on the implant, sending them away clucking like she was a mother hen and they were three little chicks. "The last thing I need is one of you distracting me while I crack this thing open. Give me ten minutes and unless it's some sort of compound I'm not expecting, I'll be right back with you and we can figure out the next steps."

Sheriff Burnett led the way back to Dr. Scott's office. The three men sat in relative silence, Jake picking at the edge of the adhesive bandage Dr. Scott had put on his arm while they waited. Sheriff Burnett started a conversation with them about baseball, asking both of them how they felt about the Texas Rangers. Travis didn't respond. He couldn't be less interested.

Staring at the ground, Travis's mind drifted back to the fire. He could still smell the burning timbers in his nostrils, the image of Scarlett's dead body in her stall delivering him a gut punch. To an outsider, it probably appeared as if he was cold by the way that he'd dragged her body out of the stall, calmly using the tractor to dig a hole and drop her body inside, leaving mother nature to do what it wanted with her carcass away from the hungry eyes of raccoons and coyotes in the area.

But that couldn't be farther from the truth. The life he'd built for himself, the few skip tracing clients he had, the reining horses, the ranch out in the country away from the hustle and bustle — it was all carefully designed to help him stay in balance. As much as he would have liked to pretend he didn't understand what Dr. Scott meant about her sister and the varying moods she experienced, that wasn't the case.

During his career in Delta Force and with the CIA, Travis had seen things, things that were seared into his memory and couldn't be erased, no matter how many times he sat astride a horse, or how many times he carefully checked all the weapons in the war room to make sure they were ready just in case.

And, not that he'd been wrong to be prepared. A few months before, Uri Bazarov had shown up at the ranch, forcing Travis to use his skills to protect Elena, leaving bodies in his wake. Only that time, he didn't feel bad about using the tractor to bury Uri's henchmen on his neighbor's property. That wasn't personal. It was business.

But burning his barn down, that was personal.

Travis stared at the ceiling, stretching his neck from side to side. And here he was, sitting in the Washington County Coroner's Office with not much more information about what was going on than he'd started with. He ran through what he knew — a body had been stolen from the refrigerated units down the hallway from where he was sitting. That body held an implant. After taking the implant back to the ranch, his home had been attacked. And now, the person they thought belonged to the implant was alive, which left the question about who the other man was. Was it a coincidence the two men held the same name? A case of identity theft? With Jake West's arrival that morning, it gave them a connection to a biotech firm and another implant, but no answers, no motive, and no larger picture that Travis could confidently connect, despite the meeting he'd had with Eli Segal, who still hadn't gotten back to him.

Before Travis had a chance to fully sort the thoughts that were building up in his head, Dr. Scott barged through the door, hitting it so hard that the door banged on the wall behind it, leaving a dent in the drywall. "We've got a problem!" she yelled, her eyes wide.

Travis shot up out of his seat, "What's wrong? Are you hurt?"

"No, no. I'm fine. But the implant? It didn't contain highly concentrated sugar or anything like it. That white powder is cyanide."

## 42

"Cyanide?" Travis said, his mouth hanging open. "What are you talking about?"

Dr. Scott nodded and licked her lips, "Yeah. I know. It's crazy. I cracked open the implant. On the one side there is a small circuit board, like something you'd see in a computer, but a miniaturized version. On the other side is a little compartment for a powder. It didn't take me long. I took a sample, dissolved it in some saline, ran it through the mass spectrometer and it came up right away. The machines are all locked down right now. I have to call a biohazard specialist to get the sample out of it. Probably have to call the FBI too."

Travis started pacing, his hands interlaced behind his head. His mouth hung open, slowly swinging his head from left to right, "Are you kidding me? So they weren't micro-dosing with a placebo, then?"

Dr. Scott shook her head, flopping her body down into the chair that Travis had vacated, "No. Whoever has control of these implants can kill people off whenever they'd like."

The words hung over the room for the next few seconds, no one saying anything. Then, as the reality settled, it was like someone lit Jake on fire. He erupted out of his seat, raspy breaths coming from inside of him, "Wait! Are you saying I was carrying cyanide around in my body for the last few months?"

Dr. Scott nodded. "That's exactly the case, Jake. If Keaton Callahan, or whoever else had control of the dosing software had flipped it on, you would have been a dead man in less than a minute."

Travis dropped his hands to his side and kept pacing. He whipped around, staring at Dr. Scott and Sheriff Burnett, "If what you're saying is true, and I don't doubt it is," he said, holding his hands up, "Then we have a far bigger problem than we ever imagined. Any idea how many people have been implanted, Jake?"

Jake shrugged, his face pale, "I have no idea. I still can't believe it." He licked his lips, his eyes going suddenly wide. "What about my sister? Gia. She's got the implant too." He ran his hands through his hair, "Oh my God! They could kill her and I would never know about it. Do you think that's what happened to the other person, the other body that you thought was me?"

All eyes were on Dr. Scott, who was staring at her phone. "Funny you should ask that, Jake." She lifted her head slowly, scanning the room, "I just got the toxicology report back on the John Doe. We have to use an outside lab and it takes a while for the test process, but yes. He died from cyanide poisoning before he was ever shot."

Travis watched as Jake slumped down into the chair that was behind him again; as if the reality of the situation had sucker-punched him. Striding across the room, Travis pulled a chair from against the wall and set it right in front of Jake. As he sat down, the two men were practically knee to knee. It was a technique Travis had used while he was in Delta Force and the CIA, breaking the personal boundaries the people kept between each other. He stared at Jake, "Okay listen, man, you are out of the woods. Dr. Scott got the implant out of you unless there are more in your body you haven't told us about?"

"No." Jake stammered, "That was the only one. They said it was only for testing. I thought I was doing them a favor. They wanted to be able to track me. I didn't think it was a big deal. I was working on the project anyway."

Travis took a deep breath. "Tell me again what your role was on the project." It was a simple question. One that Travis knew Jake would be able to answer without too much stress. That was by design.

Jake swallowed, "Like I told you, I was hired to help with the tech side of the project. They were having issues with the implants communicating back to the main server. I fixed that. I've been working on other updates since then. I don't even work that much. They pay me a full-time salary. When a request comes in, I take care of it."

"So you're sort of on-call for Keaton Callahan?" Another easy question.

Jake shrugged, "I guess. Yeah. You could say that. The requests come in at crazy times. That seems to be his only expectation — that I work on it as soon as it comes in."

"Have you ever met him?"

"No. I saw him one time through a videoconferencing call when I was first hired, but that's it. I get emails."

"Ever talk to him on the phone?"

"No."

All of the softball questions had a purpose. Travis had been trained to start with easy, obvious questions to get someone talking, to help loosen up their vocal cords and their memories, giving them confidence as the questions got harder. It wasn't Travis's intention to try to break Jake. He didn't need breaking. Jake seemed more than willing to share with Travis, Dr. Scott, and Sheriff Burnett whatever he knew. It was simply a question of asking for more information, information that would help him figure out the next step. Travis's mind swam, thinking about the conversation he'd had with Eli Segal about Raashid Sharjah. His thoughts raced. How was all of this linked together? He pressed his lips together. Maybe it was. Maybe it wasn't. Travis still wasn't able to see the bigger picture, but he knew he'd have to if he wanted to avoid another attack on his ranch.

Travis searched Jake's face. "So, you'd make tweaks to their software and you were asked to test out an implant that was supposed to microdose critical medications. That sounds simple and straightforward. Anything else? Is there anything else you can think of that seemed out of character? Any unusual requests?"

Jake blinked, looking up at the ceiling and then quickly dropping his head to stare at Travis. His eyes darted to Sheriff Burnett and Dr. Scott as well, "There was one thing. They asked me to memorize a sequence of numbers and letters. Didn't tell me what it was for. I thought maybe it was some sort of cognitive test. You know, companies are all into that stuff right now. They told me that no matter what, I had to remember the sequence throughout the entire time I was employed by them. They told me I needed to set up a special time each day to practice so I didn't forget. But they didn't give me a copy. They had me memorize it with a woman. She was like a trainer. Like I said, I thought it was part of some psych eval or something."

Travis shook his head, "Letters and numbers?" Travis glanced over his shoulder. Sheriff Burnett was standing a few feet over Travis's right shoulder, his arms crossed across his chest, his bushy eyebrows furrowed together. Dr. Scott was on the other side of the office, her body crumpled into one of the chairs. Their eyes were glued on Jake and what he would say next.

"Yeah. Letters and numbers. But I have no idea what they are for..."

## 43

"How did the interrogation go? Does he know anything?" Eli said quietly into the mouthpiece of his satellite phone.

Eli Segal was pacing in front of a worn wooden bench in a small community park near the apartment the Mossad had secured from him on the outskirts of Austin, Texas. The afternoon had turned balmy, the humidity on the rise, the breeze that kicked up lifting Eli's thinning hair and tousling it on the top of his head.

Around him were only two other people that he could see — a mother with a young boy and a young girl throwing crackers into the duck pond about fifty yards from where he stood and an older gentleman, probably fifteen years Eli's senior sitting on a park bench on the other side of a stand of trees, resting in the shade, his body hunched, a cane laying near his right knee.

"No. He doesn't seem to know anything, at least not any more than he's already given us."

"Nothing on Raashid's next plan?"

"Like I said, nothing," the voice on the other end of the line said. Barry was one of his most trusted Mossad interrogators, calm, clever, and efficient. He had ways of extracting information from prisoners of the state of Israel without them ever realizing they'd given up something important. "The problem is, Eli, we've had Sadi stashed away for the last couple of years. We've kept him in isolation. He's had no contact with the outside world, especially Raashid, so he's got no new intel. But, I do have some information that might be helpful for you."

Eli furrowed his eyebrows. The Mossad was constantly adding individuals, whether by their choice or by coercion, to their intelligence base. As a country, they had no choice. Unlike their larger counterparts like the United States, Russia, and China, with a smaller footprint, they had fewer resources and were flanked on every side by aggressive enemies that would love nothing more than to see the country and her people obliterated. But Eli had realized after decades in espionage that their small stature on the world stage gave Israel certain advantages as well. They were able to be more agile with their techniques, as well as more aggressive in protecting themselves. They didn't have the eyes of the world on them like the United States did. They were just trying to survive, after all. Who could blame the small nation state with the number of enemies that were camped on their borders for being assertive in their right to protect themselves? And what other politicians and organizations didn't like, the government of Israel ignored, preferring to wave off other dignitaries from other countries in the name of self-preservation, rather than make excuses. The Israelis did what they wanted to do, when they wanted to do it, and how they wanted to do it. It was the only way they could survive.

"And what is that?"

Barry cleared his throat. "A couple of weeks ago, we brought in an Egyptian national. Picked him up off the streets of Minya, the town where Raashid and Sadi grew up, on the outskirts of the Nile valley. He's not tied directly to Raashid's organization,

Rising Sun, but he's on the edges of it for sure. Said he'd heard something big was planned, but he wasn't sure what."

Eli narrowed his eyes, "Barry, you've got to give me something more than that. The implant the American showed me, it's highly sophisticated. Looked like it had GPS capabilities and possibly a kill switch on the other end of it."

"And you're thinking we manufactured this?"

"No, I'm not saying that, although I know we are toying with that technology. What I am saying is that if there are people running around the United States with these implants, there's a reason for it. And it's not just research. And you know as well as I do the chatter has been that the Sharjah's Rising Sun organization has been planning something for the last several years, probably on American soil. If we can help the Americans, they will help us."

"Well, that goes to what our new guest told me…"

Prisoners of the Mossad were called "guests" of the state of Israel. It was a euphemistic term. They were for the most part treated well as long as they were agreeable and gave up every shred of information they were asked to provide. Unfortunately for them, many of the guests of the state of Israel couldn't prove they'd given up all of the information they had until people like Barry had shown them the consequences of not doing so.

"Our new guest mentioned that Raashid hasn't been seen anywhere near Minya for the last several months. Rumor has it that he's been jetting back and forth to the United States. The rumor was he had a place in Miami and was working on some kind of a project with a biotech firm. Our guest felt that he was managing a new investment for his company."

"And how did this individual find out about it?"

"He's a chemist. Has a Ph.D. in chemical engineering and has done consulting for Raashid."

Eli frowned, "Why did we pick him up in the first place?"

Barry grunted, "Eh, who knows? His file said he was doing

research on some chemical compounds that were raising a red flag with Tel Aviv. Chemicals plus Raashid could spell trouble."

"Like biological or chemical weapons? That kind of a red flag?" Eli, for the most part, loved working with Barry. Barry's nose for the truth made him excellent at what he did. The challenge with Barry was that he sometimes got so focused on getting the information that he forgot they needed to be able to do something with it.

"I guess. The point is, that Raashid has been MIA for quite a while. This guy I've been meeting with thinks he's in the United States. Says everyone in Minya is all abuzz with this new project that he's on. Rumor has it it's going to change things for the better...for the entire Middle East."

The wheels of Eli's mind clattered like it was a train picking up steam on the tracks. If even half of what Barry had said was true, then Raashid's goal to build a caliphate in the United States might be coming closer to fruition faster than they realized. "Anything else?"

"Nothing more, except that whatever is going to happen is going to happen soon. Very soon."

## 44

After Eli hung up the phone with Barry, he shoved the thick black plastic case of the satellite phone into a briefcase he slung over his shoulders. He needed a minute to think, a moment to process all the information that was coming at him. He interlaced his fingers behind his back and started onto one of the park's walking paths, strolling slowly, listening and watching everything that was around him. There were birds above him in the trees, the dappled sunlight forming ever-changing shapes on the trail in front of him as the sun danced between the branches in the afternoon light. The breeze that had picked up beforehand continued. It was humid, especially by Israeli standards, but it wasn't unpleasant. Overall, he liked America. It wasn't Israel, of course, but as a place to work, it wasn't bad.

The mother and the children laughing and playing at the duck pond had left, leaving a few mallard couples and their babies swimming around in the water quacking and waiting for the next park patrons to bring them something to eat. The old man that had been sitting on the bench was still there, his head lolled off to the side as if he were taking a nap in the middle of the park, the warm afternoon nudging him off to sleep. Part of Eli wondered if the man was still alive, but it was better for a man in his position to not ask those kinds of questions. He needed to stay focused.

As Eli walked, he unlaced his fingers from behind his back and shoved his hands into the front pockets of his rumpled khaki pants. He'd paired with it a wrinkled button-down shirt in a light gray, the same outfit he'd worn to meet Travis the day before. If his wife had been with him, she would've been irritated by both the wrinkles and the gray shirt with the khaki pants. He could almost hear Layla's voice in his ear, "Eli Segal, you must not go out in public looking like that!" But he hadn't heard Layla's voice for seven years, since she died from cancer.

Although he missed his wife dearly and the life they had together it had freed him to do the work he loved without any guilt. He no longer had to worry about leaving his wife alone for long stretches while he traveled at the whims of Tel Aviv. If he was honest with himself, it had never been much of an issue. Layla was fiercely independent and was more than happy to spend her days helping the neighbors and working in their garden in the hills of Tiberias. When he was there, she was happy. When he was gone, she was also happy. She was the perfect Mossad wife, never demanding any answers and never condemning him for missing family time with their girls or holidays with his rigorous travel schedule.

Eli's mind drifted back to the meeting he'd had with Travis Bishop, formerly of the CIA, earlier that day. How Travis had managed to trip his way into the mess with Raashid still was a bit of a mystery. Eli paused for a second, closing his eyes, feeling the Texas sun settle on the side of his face. Was it pure coincidence that someone tied to Raashid's organization had ended up in the same county as Travis Bishop? Eli opened his eyes and started strolling again, resuming his thoughts. He was making assumptions that perhaps weren't there. There was no way to know if the body that had gone missing was tied to Raashid or not. His contacts told him the implants were connected to a biotech company based in Miami. And now, based on what Barry had said, Raashid had been also tied to the Miami area. Coincidence? Possibly. Was it probable? No.

The obvious question floated to the front of Eli's mind as a man on a bike whipped by him, wearing a blue and black helmet, out for his afternoon ride, nearly knocking Eli over. Eli sucked in a breath. Now that Travis Bishop was involved, could he be trusted?

Eli stopped near a park bench and sat down, setting his briefcase next to him. He pulled the black satellite phone out of his bag again, slowly glancing over his shoulder as if he was looking for birds or chipmunks or squirrels. He wasn't. He was looking for anyone who might be watching him, other than people from his own government. David, who had accompanied him to the coffee with Travis, was sitting in a car in the parking lot within sight of Eli, but there was no one else around. Unfortunately with his work with the Mossad, he was never alone. There was always someone nearby. It was meant to be a protection and a comfort, but there were times that Eli wished for a bit more privacy. Although Eli couldn't complain. David did exactly what he was supposed to do. Watch. He left Eli to his own devices other than that.

Dialing a number on his satellite phone, Eli shifted in his seat, crossing his legs, bobbing his foot up and down in the brown crêpe soled shoes that he wore, waiting for the call to connect.

"Eli?"

"Elena. I'm glad you picked up. We need to talk."

"Is everything okay?" Elena asked.

On Eli's end of the phone, it sounded like papers were shuffling in the background. "Yes, of course. Did I catch you at a bad time?"

"No. Just busy, like usual."

It seemed every American Eli spoke to said they were busy. It had to be a national epidemic. "Langley have you on the run?"

"Of course. What else is new?"

There was silence between the two of them for a moment. Eli had met Elena nearly a decade before when she'd come through Tel Aviv on a break between operations in the Eastern Bloc. As part of the arrangements with the United States, CIA agents made themselves available for debriefing by the Mossad if the Israelis determined there was a critical need for information the CIA might have. Most of the time, the exchanges were friendly, unless, of course, Langley decided the information the Mossad wanted was better off left unsaid. The problem was the Mossad only liked one kind of secret — their own. They had little patience for other countries keeping important information from them. Elena had been one of the agents Eli had debriefed over coffee and pastries one afternoon. The exchange had been pleasant. His experience with Elena was that despite her petite size and porcelain features, she was a powerful agent. And her physical attributes worked to her advantage. A former gymnast, not only was she well-built and athletic, but many of America's enemies would never suspect that a petite blonde with short-cropped hair and ruby red lips could be coming after them for important information. Men would always be men, Eli remembered thinking at the time.

"Were you able to meet with Travis?" Elena asked.

"Yes."

"I'm assuming that's why you're calling?"

"Yes." Eli looked down at the ground, his eyes following a crack in the pockmarked concrete in front of the worn wooden park bench. A few strands of scraggly grass were attempting to grow in between. What most people didn't realize about grass is how powerful its root system was. Over time, it could crack and crumble even the most well-constructed concrete. It might take years to do so, but eventually, the grass would win.

And that's how the espionage game was won.

Governments like America or Israel would get a small piece of information, the first blade of grass breaking through the concrete barrier of an enemy's organization, exposing their plans. The Mossad or CIA would build their roots from there, working to destroy what seemed like an opportunity to their enemies. But as Eli sat on the phone with Elena, he wondered if she would be part of the solution or part of the problem. Whether he liked it or not, he had to trust someone. If there was a disaster on American soil, it would impact the entire globe, including Israel.

"I need to ask you a blunt question, Elena. And I need an honest answer."

"Of course, Eli. I think we've always had a good relationship." The answer sounded more like a question than a confirmation.

"We have. And I want that to continue. Israel and the United States need to work together. But if you have any hesitancy about what I'm about to ask you then I do need you to be honest. Lives may depend on it." Eli's mind ran through the information he had in front of him – the fact that Raashid had been missing and tied to a biotech firm in Miami, his anger at the fact that Mossad still had Sadi, Raashid's desire to bring a caliphate to the world, and the implant that Travis had shown him just a few hours earlier.

"Can Travis Bishop be trusted?"

"Travis?" Elena chuckled. "Are you kidding me? I've worked with him for years, Eli."

"But he's no longer active with the CIA, correct?"

There was a pause; as if Elena was deciding how much to say. "No. He's not. He left the Agency five years ago. He and one of our other agents, Kira Pozreva, were engaged. They bought the ranch he has now in Texas and then she left for her last mission. She supposedly got killed in Ecuador. But the thing was she didn't."

"And he helped you recently, didn't he?" Eli pretended to not have heard much of this story before, but he kept tabs on all of his contacts in other governments.

"Keeping an eye on me, are you, Eli?"

"Well, you know..."

"I know..." Elena sucked in a breath, "A few months ago, I got myself into a jam. I found information that certain people didn't want to get out. They tried to paint me as a traitor. All of it happened in Travis's backyard. He helped unravel the entire issue and ended up killing a couple of our agents who'd flipped and were trying to unsettle our government."

"Yes, yes. I remember this now." The details of what had happened in the Oval Office emerged as if they came out of a fog in Eli's mind. He'd received a briefing from the director of the Mossad the next day based on his relationship with Elena. The director reported that she'd discovered a Russian plot to kill the President and the Joint Chiefs, creating a Constitutional crisis and in effect, a coup in the United States, replacing the president with a more pro-Russia VP. But it never happened.

Travis and Elena had figured out the plan and used contacts of theirs to gain access to the White House, Travis arriving just in the nick of time to prevent the death of the President.

"Which brings me back to my original question. Can he be trusted?"

## 46

"Why are you asking me this, Eli?

Eli shifted on the park bench, re-crossing his legs, and shoving a stick of gum into his mouth. He discovered in his years of espionage work that approaching things slowly, as if everyone was a spooky horse ready to bolt, usually got him answers. Their own impatience would usually move them exactly where he needed them without him having to lift a finger. And although he didn't want to do that to Elena, that's exactly what was happening. "Things are evolving. And I have concerns..."

"Concerns about what?" Elena's voice hardened; as if she was offended by his assertion.

"Eh, well, you know with Travis no longer being an active agent, it does call things into question."

"Okay, Eli. Enough!" Elena snapped. "Listen, I know you Mossad guys like to go over and over the same points again to see if people will change your stories. I'm not going to change my story. If you're looking for someone to trust, Travis Bishop is it. And no, I don't think he put himself in the situation on purpose. Knowing him the way I do, he just wants to be left alone. He'll serve if called upon, but at this point, I think he just wants to stay on his ranch, ride his reining horses and do a little skip tracing work on the side. That's it."

Eli narrowed his eyes, "And you don't think he'll want revenge for what was done to his barn and the loss of his horse?"

"Of course, he will. He wouldn't be Travis Bishop if he didn't."

Eli smiled to himself, "Good. That's exactly what I wanted to hear."

## 47

E
dward blinked a few times, staring at the monitor in front of him. He stood up, rolling his neck from side to side. He'd been watching the team deploy the series of bombs Raashid wanted to be detonated throughout New Orleans for the last several hours. Most of the people working on the project had absolutely no idea what they were doing. They'd been told to deliver packages to certain locations and leave them there. And, as part of their employment contract, not only were they required to have an implant placed in their wrist so their location could be tracked at all times, but they were also required to wear name badges that had surveillance cameras embedded in them. The workers had no idea the cameras were there, and the badges weren't personalized. They'd been told that the company was using name badges as opposed to uniforms and that they should be happy about the situation.

At least Edward was.

After escaping the doldrums of the Washington County Coroner's Office, sent there to work as a sub for a few days while they secured the body of the traitor they'd killed and then burned for threatening to reach out to the FBI, Edward had sent a polite but terse text to Dr. Ava Scott, the sniveling woman who'd ruined their plans, telling her that he would no longer be able to work for her.

The fact that they had been unable to retrieve that first implant had thrown Keaton into a fury. Edward glanced down at his wrist, noticing the thin white scar where his implant was. When Keaton found out the implant was gone and that Edward had been unable to retrieve it even after trying to break into Travis Bishop's war room, he remembered feeling cold sweat gather on his forehead, absolutely sure that Keaton would flip the kill switch on his implant and he'd be dead any moment.

But it hadn't happened.

Instead, a few hours after the bad news, he'd gotten a call from Raashid, who told him to get on the next flight to New Orleans and be prepared to coordinate the bombs. It was a promotion of sorts, at least the way Edward looked at it. Why it happened that way, he wasn't exactly sure. Maybe Keaton hadn't told Raashid about the missing implant? For all intents and purposes, Edward had failed, not able to get it back, but at least he had coordinated the retrieval of the body. The hope was that law enforcement in Washington County would be so busy focusing on what happened to the missing body and their identity that they would give up on the mysterious piece of technology.

And that seemed like a logical plan until Sheriff Burnett and Dr. Scott decided to get Travis Bishop involved.

Despite his concerns, Edward kept his mouth shut, trying to do his job for Keaton, even though his loyalty was to Raashid. He'd worked for Raashid for years, starting as a runner in Minya, Egypt where Raashid controlled all of the textile mills. He worked his way up in Raashid's organization, eventually becoming one of Raashid's most important confidants. Raashid trusting him with the deployment of the bombs was a new level of respect and authority. He owed his life to Raashid, as well as his prosperity. As Edward grew within Raashid's organization, his wealth grew as well. He didn't have money the same way Raashid did, though. No one did. Raashid was a billionaire, living high above everyone else. But Raashid paid Edward well, so well in fact that he'd been able to move his family out of the town and into a protected compound with three houses inside the walled property, one for his wife and children, one for her parents, and another for his. They were well provided for and had nothing to worry about.

And neither would Edward, if they could pull off Raashid's plan.

Edward focused on the screens again, watching as one of the rented delivery trucks pulled up in front of the Academy of the Sacred Heart on St. Charles Avenue in New Orleans. He stared as the surveillance cameras across the street captured the box truck parking near the service entrance, the name badge camera following the driver as he wheeled a dolly inside of the truck, retrieving three large cardboard boxes sealed with multiple layers of packing tape. Each one was addressed to the Director of Curriculum at the all-girls Catholic school. He smiled. If he didn't know better, Edward would have guessed it was a load of textbooks.

Staring at the feed from across the street, Edward shook his head, realizing that within a day, the beautiful, historic school constructed in the late 1800s with its elaborate decor and its rambling southern architecture would be leveled to the ground, bodies taken with it, hopefully many. When Raashid first told him of the target, something inside of Edward shuddered, thinking about the children of the school being maimed, dismembered, and killed, their blood oozing onto the debris near them, but then he remembered that sacrifices must be made in order to accomplish their purpose.

Edward stared at the screen, watching as the delivery

person wheeled the dolly with three heavy boxes up a ramp next to the loading dock. He'd been instructed to take the boxes into the basement and leave them there. Edward narrowed his eyes, his heart tightening in his chest. Their tech team had allowed them to breach the signal of the surveillance cameras in all of the buildings where they were placing the bombs. Edward watched as the doors of the freight elevator opened in the basement. The man stopped, checking the clipboard resting on top of the boxes. He'd been told that his bonus payment of five thousand dollars for making a successful delivery depended upon getting the boxes to the basement into the precise location where they needed to be delivered. Like all of the people they'd recruited, the man asked no questions, only interested in doing what he needed to do to get his extra payment.

A second later, Edward saw the name tag camera bobble again as the dolly surged forward, taking the boxes to the back corner of the basement, directly under the elementary wing of the school, and placing them next to one of the support beams.

"One down, four to go," Edward muttered under his breath.

It wasn't true, or at least not really. Of the five bombs Raashid had commissioned for his project, only two of them were going into buildings. Edward changed the surveillance feed on the monitor over to the other location. They'd managed to acquire access to a camera across from Gallier Hall, the original city administration building for New Orleans. He cocked his head to the side, staring at the image in front of him. The building itself was garish, at least in his estimation, reminiscent of Greek architecture with towering stone pillars in the front balanced off by a capstone of figures carved inside of a towering triangle, as if the Acropolis had arrived smack dab in the middle of the bayou. It reeked of Greek conquest, but somehow managed to fit in among the eclectic architecture that was all over New Orleans. The only thing that the buildings

Edward had seen had in common was the more flamboyant and ornate they were, the more they would fit in. It was like a mishmash of buildings all in poor taste.

Running his fingers across the computer keyboard in front of him, he made a few adjustments to the view and was able to access the feed for the second truck. The driver had been given a similar box truck to the one that had been used at the Sacred Heart Academy, bright orange with black and white lettering along the side, a roll-up door on the back allowing for easy access to the cargo inside.

Edward had given each one of the drivers multiple stops to make, unloading boxes at each one of the locations. Raashid had wanted to simply send each driver with the delivery of the bombs, but Edward convinced him that they needed to make things look as normal as possible. Sending a large truck out with only one delivery didn't make sense, not given the story they'd told each of the delivery people when they were hired. The last thing they needed was someone to get curious, start opening boxes and then call the police. Their entire operation, a year in the making, would fall apart with the full weight of the American law enforcement system chasing them down. Edward shook his head. That was the last thing they needed. The plan had to go off without a hitch, all five bombs simultaneously exploding in different areas of New Orleans during the raucous festivities of Mardi Gras. It was meant to create chaos.

And it would...

# 48

The philosophy behind the mission Raashid had created was simple – bombs going off simultaneously in any area of the world would spread law enforcement and first responders thin, so thin that it would give not only Raashid and his men time to escape, but create the most chaos and devastation. Chaos and disorder were what they were after. Trauma surgeons referred to the first hour after an injury as "The Golden Hour." During that hour, they had the most likelihood of being able to save a life. After that, the odds declined radically.

Setting five bombs off at one time would do exactly that.

Edward licked his lips, watching as the driver of the truck in front of Gallier Hall loaded three boxes onto the dolly he'd been provided with. Edward had been waiting for this moment. He felt the muscles tighten in his chest. He'd watched the driver stop at the New Orleans Passenger Bus Terminal, a warehouse on St. Claiborne Avenue, a refined southern fusion restaurant on Magazine Street, and now the former City Hall of New Orleans, the historic building constructed in 1845. Not all of the deliveries had bombs, but the ones for Gallier Hall did.

Attacking the City Hall had been his idea, taking out one of the most historic icons of the city. It seemed fitting somehow...

In addition to Gallier Hall and the Academy of the Sacred Heart School, their team had been wiring bombs into rental cars that would be parked in front of three other targets along the parade route.

Edward wanted to laugh. The whole idea that they could pull this off was preposterous, and yet somehow it was within reach. Time was ticking. Mardi Gras had already started, the fourteen days of revelry before Ash Wednesday sending bands and marchers down nearly every side street in New Orleans, or at least it seemed that way, snarling traffic. And all of that fun would come to a screeching halt the next day.

Edward closed his eyes for a second and leaned back in the chair, lacing his fingers behind his head. In his mind's eye, he imagined what the moments after the bombs went off would be like. A shudder ran through his spine as he remembered a bomb going off in Cairo when he was a teenager, the acrid smell of the smoke and the fumes filling the air, the choking, burning sensation in his lungs. Edward opened his eyes and glanced down at his left arm, looking at the scars that were left behind. He'd been fifty feet away from the explosion at the market set off by radical separatists, ones that were not fans of the current Egyptian government. Glass rained down everywhere, the concussion of the explosion deafening him for what felt like hours. As his hearing came back, his mind was filled with the screams of women and children, mothers crying as they held their dying babies, the yells and grunts of people begging for help in the ensuing fires. The memory had never left him. And then there was the wail of the sirens as the Army was deployed, Egyptian police scattered all over the city, and ambulances carrying those who could survive away. His wounds had been survivable, but he knew what they were planning on doing the next day in New Orleans wouldn't be.

Edward gritted his teeth. Sometimes violence was the only path to change.

His phone rang. Raashid. "Status?"

Edward straightened in his seat, getting a message that Raashid was already in New Orleans from one of Raashid's bodyguards. Raashid had taken a position on the outskirts of the city, near the Gulf of Mexico after renting an ocean-side mansion that came complete with a speed boat ready and waiting at the dock. The estate had been rented by one of his shell corporations, of which Raashid had dozens, buried in legal jargon and fake holding companies. "All is well. Going to plan."

Raashid grunted, "Give me the details."

"The delivery was just made at Sacred Heart. The curriculum director should be thrilled with her new books."

"Excellent. And our other donations?"

Talking in code was a necessary evil. Intelligence services around the world had deployed scanning technology that looked for keywords in nearly everyone's conversations, whether voice, text, or on their Internet searches. Some of the words were obvious — bomb, missile, attack — while others were more subtle, code words for operations or assets that might be in play. Even with encrypted technology they had to be careful. Privacy, or what little people had left, had nearly completely evaporated. "Yes, I think the Greeks are going to be very happy. I just got a message from the driver that delivery will be completed momentarily." Although Edward hadn't gotten any such message, Raashid would understand what he was trying to say, referring to the architecture of Gallier Hall.

"And our other projects? How are they faring?"

Edward narrowed his eyes. People always seem to be surprised when they met Raashid in person. Edward had been when he met him the first time. He said very little, and for how committed he was to bringing a caliphate to the world, he camouflaged it well, wearing Western clothes, usually a pair of jeans or pressed pants, and a button-down shirt. He was well-spoken and well-mannered in every single situation. He could easily have tea with the Queen of England and then turn around and talk about global domination with the Taliban somewhere in their hidden caves in Afghanistan and manage to offend neither party. And although Raashid was determined, he wasn't without a more dangerous side. Edward had seen it himself, but only once. And that one time had been enough.

"It's all good news. Ready to begin on time and on schedule."

"Excellent. Keep me posted with any updates."

"Of course." Edward licked his lips, "One question, if you don't mind."

"Certainly. What's on your mind?"

"The inventor."

Ever since Raashid had decided to take a controlling stake in Explority Biotech, effectively forcing Keaton Callahan to work for him, Edward had been nervous. There was something about Callahan that seemed skittish and untrustworthy. Coercion, of course, would make anyone a little unsteady. Raashid had told Edward about what he'd done to Callahan's father, effectively debilitating him with a series of strokes. That was the side of Raashid Edward was most afraid of. Raashid could be cool and calculating, brutal without remorse when he needed to be. Lately, it seemed his more aggressive side was coming out.

"What about him?"

"How does the outlook for his company seem?"

"I'm uncertain about that..." Raashid's voice trailed off as if he was lost in thought.

"And what about the ranch?" The men on the team had been unable to get the implant from Travis Bishop's ranch. It was locked in a war room behind a thick steel door that the men were unprepared to breach.

"I am working on a plan to take care of that as well."

Edward swallowed. Everything in him wanted to ask for more information. Was Raashid planning on killing Keaton Callahan and Travis Bishop? Was that part of the mop-up? Or perhaps it didn't matter. Maybe the damage done to the city of New Orleans would be sufficient. Although it could take months, Edward knew that the FBI would ultimately figure out Keaton Callahan's role in what they were preparing to do. Would they look that closely at Travis Bishop? It was hard to tell.

Edward swallowed again. "If you'd like me to tie up any extra loose ends, please let me know."

"I will."

The call ended. Edward blinked a couple of times, that knot that formed in his gut while he spoke to Raashid easing just a little. Edward glanced down at the scar on his arm. Part of him had an urge to find a sharp knife and cut the implant out of his wrist, eliminating the possibility that he could be killed by Raashid's invention, but he knew he couldn't. If Raashid found out he'd removed his implant, Raashid would probably take a machete to Edward's neck, seeing it as a sign of disloyalty, a threat to the organization he'd built, and the chance to get his brother back.

And as much as Raashid wanted to leave a legacy of a global caliphate around the world, Edward knew his entire focus was his brother. He wanted him back. Whether blowing holes in the city of New Orleans would accomplish that goal, persuading the Israelis and Americans to release him, Edward wasn't sure.

## 49

E lena ran down the hallway after leaving Director
Stewart's office, nearly crashing into two other agents
who were turning the corner at the same time as she
was, "Sorry!" she yelled in passing as she darted by them.

Skidding to a stop outside her office door, she shoved it
open and slammed it closed behind her. She'd just gotten done
relaying the fact that Eli Segal had called her asking for information about Travis Bishop. Although the conversation itself
seemed as mundane as a melting scoop of vanilla ice cream, to
anyone working in the CIA, it was anything but. If the Mossad
was sneaking around, particularly putting a senior case officer
like Eli in play, something was happening. Something big.

And it had to have something to do with that blasted
implant Travis had found.

Throwing herself down in her desk chair, Elena shook her
head. How Travis ended up getting in the middle of these cases,
she had no idea. The only good news was that Travis was
known to the Agency. As a former CIA agent, Director Stewart
had worked with him personally. His loyalty was unquestioned.
But, Elena knew the reality of Travis and the way he thought.

When he'd been given a job to do, the odds of him leaving it unfinished were zero.

That meant that whatever Eli was sniffing around in, Travis was involved in as well. Elena shook her head, mumbling to herself, "Why did I connect the two of them? What was I thinking?"

After meeting with the director, Elena's perspective shifted. The Middle East desk had sent over a set of eyes-only files that Director Stewart had shared with her, chatter about an impending attack somewhere on American soil. The reports seemed to circle around exactly the same man that Eli Segal had mentioned — Raashid Sharjah, the Egyptian billionaire whose brother was currently being held by the Mossad.

Before leaving Director Stewart's office, they had sent a coded message to one of their outposts in Egypt. Elena tapped on her desk, looking at the time. If it was midafternoon at Langley, it was night in Egypt, as they were seven hours ahead. But that was no excuse for not getting back to her. The CIA didn't run on bankers' hours. They ran all day and all night every single day of the year, day, after day, after day.

Elena decided to distract herself by checking her email, glancing at her phone every few seconds. Exactly three minutes later, it rang from an unknown number. "Agent Lobranova?"

"Yes."

"This is Barnaby. You called asking for information about Raashid Sharjah?"

Elena pulled her phone away from her face for a second, double-checking that the encrypted icon was on her screen. The little red blinking lock was flashing, meaning she could speak freely. She pressed her ear to her phone again. Elena had never met the man who was calling himself Barnaby. That might be his real name, or it might not be. It didn't matter. He was likely the intelligence officer on duty manning the Egyptian outpost. Working in the CIA meant that people came in and out like waves crashing on the beach. Elena would bump into someone like two ships passing in the night and then hear from them again two or three years later. Relationships went one of two ways in the CIA – either they were ride-or-die relationships with someone, or they flitted in and out like watching hummingbirds jump from blossom to blossom. "Yes. We've heard some concerning chatter."

"So have we."

"What do you know?"

Barnaby sighed, "Well, I've spent the last couple of weeks talking to my contacts in Minya. That's where Raashid's major holdings are. He's taken over pretty much all the textile manufacturing up and down the Nile Valley."

"He's expanded his operations?" Although Elena had cursory information about Raashid based on what she could access on her own and what Director Stewart had shared with her, getting first-hand reports from someone on the ground was critical.

"Yes. Raashid is a serial entrepreneur. He specializes in mergers and acquisitions. The legitimate side of his business is to go into different industries, find either companies that are doing really poorly or companies that are thriving and take them over."

"Like a hostile takeover?" Elena scowled. The way Barnaby pronounced the word "poorly" made her wonder if he was British, or had been educated there.

"In some cases. In others, it's friendly. He's got holdings in a wide range of industries, everything from textiles, which you know about, to construction, gambling, hotels, and even biotech. And that's just the legitimate side of his business."

Elena furrowed her eyebrows, "Gambling? I thought this guy was a religious zealot?"

Barnaby grunted, "He is. But what better way for him to take down an industry than to control it?"

The answer landed hard on Elena. Barnaby was absolutely right. Raashid was calculated. Playing the long game. "And what about his other businesses?"

Chuckling, Barnaby said, "You mean his hobbies? The ones like arms trafficking, terrorism, and assassinations? Those?"

"Uh-huh. What do you have on those?"

"Well, that's where things start to get a little interesting. Apparently, Raashid hasn't been seen much in Egypt over the last few months. Rumor has it he's been working on a project out of Miami."

Elena nodded. That matched what she had heard from Eli. "Anything else?"

"Yeah, the most significant thing is about eight months ago, I guess a group of mercenaries for hire, led by Raashid himself, tried to break into the black site where his brother, Sadi was being held."

"What?" Elena frowned. "How is that even possible?"

"Honestly, I have no idea. From what we've heard, and the sources are good, he assembled a team and went to Syria."

"Syria? Is that where Sadi's being held?"

"Yeah, apparently so. The Mossad's got black sites all over the world. They seem to be particularly fond of Syria right now."

Elena frowned, "Why's that?"

"Because of the chaos. With the war that's been going on there, Syria has been bombed into smithereens. Their borders are porous, their government is in shambles. It makes it easy for outside governments to travel onto their land with no concern about interference."

"Why don't they have Sadi in Israel?"

"That's a good question, one I'm not sure I can answer. You'd probably have to ask the Israelis. If I had to guess, it's because they don't want any kind of attacks on their own land from Hamas or Hezbollah. Holding a prisoner like Sadi

Sharjah would bring exactly that kind of trouble to their doorstep. It'd be a real black eye."

Elena nodded. What Barnaby was saying made sense. Except that he hadn't finished the story about Sadi's jailbreak. "From what you're saying, I gather the raid was unsuccessful?"

"Correct. Sadi's still holed up with the Israelis. From what I hear, Raashid is furious."

## 50

Pausing for a moment, Elena processed what Barnaby was saying, tapping her fingernail on the edge of her desk. "Let me see if I've got this straight — Raashid gets a strike team together, finds out his brother is in Syria and makes a move on an Israeli black site. Is that about right?"

"Yep. That's about the size of it."

"Then what happened?"

Elena heard typing in the background. "Give me a sec," Barnaby mumbled. "I have all the details logged in my report. Want to pull it up so I can give it to you straight."

"Yeah, sure."

"Here it is." Barnaby sucked in a breath, "According to our sources on the ground, Raashid showed up at an old warehouse about seventy miles outside of Damascus. Not much in the area except for the warehouse. Couple of crumbling old buildings, some houses, that sort of thing. His strike team had ten members, including himself."

Elena raised her eyebrows, "He was willing to get his hands dirty?"

"To rescue his brother? Absolutely. Seems like other than

building his empire, getting his brother back is his main focus in life. That and punishing our government since we took him in the first place. Since Sadi was taken, the guy's practically venerated like a saint around here. As a matter of fact, a couple of guys here in the office call him Saint Sadi." Barnaby chuckled, "Get it? When he's a saint already?"

"Yeah. Can you finish the story?" Elena didn't find Barnaby's joke amusing.

"Sorry, guess you have to be here in order for it to be funny. Anyways, Raashid shows up with his strike force at this dilapidated old warehouse a good chunk of distance away from the mess in Damascus. They arrive in the middle of the night, heavily armored, you know the drill. Armored cars, lots of gunfire. They break into the building but don't get far. Israeli snipers start picking them off. Raashid and a couple of other guys make it into the building, searching for Sadi, but there is one thing they don't realize."

"What's that?"

"There's an empty missile silo beneath the warehouse. It was built that way, to camouflage the fact that the Syrians were hiding weapons in the middle of housing areas."

"The black site is on top of a missile?"

"Not exactly. The UN had come in about five years before everything erupted in Syria and made the Syrians remove all of the missiles, but the silo itself was still there."

"And that's where the Israelis were hiding Sadi?"

"Correct. By the time Raashid and the rest of his guys realized they couldn't get to Sadi since he was being held hundreds of feet below the building, they'd taken heavy casualties. Out of the ten guys on the strike team, only Raashid and two more made it out."

"And I'm assuming the Mossad moved Sadi after that?"

"That's correct," Barnaby sighed. "Where he is now, we have

no idea. Honestly, I don't want to know. The guy's trouble. Let the Mossad deal with him."

Elena shook her head. She understood what Barnaby was saying, but she didn't like it. Dangerous terrorists like Sadi Sharjah needed to be contained and someone had to take responsibility for it. Sometimes it was the United States, sometimes it was Israel, and sometimes other countries stepped in to give them a hand. Even the Canadians had upped their intelligence game, getting their squeaky-clean fingers dirty in a couple of cases that their media would have loved to know about, but had been carefully hidden.

"What happened after the Mossad moved Sadi?"

"That's the thing, we don't really know. Sadi is off the radar again. The Mossad has him hidden away in the far reaches of the globe. He's probably in Antarctica by now."

Elena shook her head, "If anyone was going to have a black site in Antarctica, it would be the Mossad."

"True that! As far as where Raashid goes after that, that's where things get interesting. As far as we can tell, he came back to Egypt for a while, appeared to be settling down and running his businesses again, and then starts jetting off to the United States."

"And was this a recent change? Like just after the rescue attempt?"

"Sort of. He'd been going to the US a lot, but it just increased in frequency. Listen, when you're a billionaire, air travel is nothing like it is for you and me. These guys have their own planes and pilots. They can go whenever they want to go, wherever they want to go. Raashid's trips into the United States had been increasing in frequency starting about eighteen months ago. We've gotten word that he'd started buying into biotech firms in the United States."

A shiver ran down Elena's spine. The implant. "And he's been spending more time in the US ever since?"

"As far as we can tell. He's got people in his organization running the businesses here, it seems, particularly the legitimate ones. What he's doing in the United States, I have no idea. You got something on him?"

Elena spent the next couple of minutes updating Barnaby on the information she had — about the call she had gotten from Travis, the missing corpse, the implant, and how she'd connected Travis with Eli Segal, as well as the mysterious call she'd gotten from Eli a few hours earlier. "The thing is, if the Mossad's calling, you know something's going on."

Barnaby snorted, "Especially if Eli Segal's the one that's making the call. He's a legend around here." There was a pause for a moment, voices behind Barnaby, "Listen, I gotta go. Something else is popping. Whatever you do, you gotta warn Travis Bishop that this is no joke. If they've come for him once, they will come again. This Raashid is for real and he'll do whatever he has to get what he wants."

The hair stood up on the back of Elena's neck, "I will. Thanks, Barnaby."

"You bet."

Elena sat at her desk for a moment, staring at the ceiling. The information Barnaby had provided was helpful, clarifying even. It was as though she had all of the materials to paint a beautiful portrait, the paints, the canvas, the brushes, but no subject. Now the picture was forming in her head.

And Travis was square in the middle of it and had no idea a target was about to be on his back.

Elena wiped sweaty palms on her pants and sucked in a deep breath. A knot formed in her throat. What Barnaby said balanced the information she'd gotten from Director Stewart and Eli, but not in a direction she expected. Her assumption was that this was about terror. Maybe it was and maybe it wasn't. What had become clear was that as much as Raashid wanted a caliphate as part of his legacy, he wanted his brother back more and he wanted to punish America for taking him. Blood was always thicker than water. Somehow Raashid thought he could leverage the Mossad into giving Sadi back. How exactly, Elena didn't know.

Before Elena could do anything else, she heard her phone ping. A text. It was an unknown number. "What's this?" she scowled.

"New intel just arrived. The target's in New Orleans. Meet me there for a beignet and a chicory coffee. Bring your friend. Eli."

## 51

"I was just about to call you."

Elena scowled into the phone. After Eli's mysterious text, her next move had been to call Travis. Luckily, he picked up on the first ring. "You were? What about?"

Travis cleared his throat, "There've been some developments here. Ones that go along with the questions I asked you before. Can we talk freely?"

Elena glanced at her phone, confirming her encryption was on. "Yes."

As she waited for Travis to speak, a young woman walked into her office with a printout. Elena mouthed, "Thank you," as the woman handed it to her. It was a boarding pass for a flight that was leaving out of Reagan National, headed to New Orleans. Elena blinked and looked at the time. The plane departed in four hours. With Washington, DC traffic, she had about an hour left in the office before she had to go. Luckily, there was a go-bag stashed in the back of her car, filled with everything she would need for a seventy-two-hour jaunt. Pressing her lips together, she wasn't sure if she had the right clothes for New Orleans in the early spring, but what she had would have to do. She chewed her lip for a second, realizing once she got on the ground she could reassess. "What's going on?"

"You know the body I told you was missing?" Travis's voice was low, barely audible.

"Yes."

"It's not anymore."

"What do you mean?" The words came out of Elena's mouth slowly.

"The so-called dead body of Jake West managed to walk itself right into the Washington County Sheriff's office this morning."

"I take it he's not dead?"

"Not even close."

## 52

Travis waited on the other end of the line for Elena to respond. There was quiet between them for a moment. "Elena? Are you still there?"

"I am. I'm thinking."

"Well, don't work too hard. At least not before I fill in the rest of the information."

"All right, hot shot. You think you've still got the stuff? Fill me in."

Travis cracked a smile. If there was one thing he missed from working at the Agency, it was the banter between colleagues. They were work relationships, to be sure, always at an arm's length, unless teams were sent on an operation together. Then, the calculus changed significantly. What started as a professional relationship often grew personal roots, as living and working with the same people closely for weeks or months at a time changed everything. And Langley was notorious for their operational romances. It was strictly frowned upon, of course, but being sent to a foreign nation for months at a time with only a small group of people to protect the team could wear down even the most stalwart prude.

Travis sighed, wishing he could say that had never happened to him, but that's exactly what happened between him and Kira. He licked his lips, pushing her memory aside. "I got a call from Dr. Scott a few hours ago. Jake West strolled into her office."

"How is that even possible?"

"It's a long story, but suffice it to say it's a case of wrong identity. Anyway, the most important thing is that he had intel to share."

Elena sniffed. "Like what?"

Over the next few minutes, Travis updated Elena on how the mistaken identification had happened, the implant Jake had in his arm, his missing sister, Gia, and his ties to Explority Biotech. "And that's not the most interesting thing."

"What is?"

"Three things actually... First, Jake has a sister who is also working for the company. She's been out of pocket. Hasn't talked to her brother in months. Jake's worried about her."

Elena grunted, "He should be."

"The second thing is, Dr. Scott pulled the implant out of Jake's arm. He agreed to it. She decided to take a closer look and discovered the white powder on the one end is a kill switch."

"A kill switch?"

"Cyanide."

"What? So whoever has control over the implants can kill people willy-nilly?"

"Yep. That's my guess. Dr. Scott also said the body that they'd recovered had died before it had been burned. Guess how?"

"Cyanide poisoning."

"You get an A on your exam, Agent Lobranova."

"I thought you said there was a third thing?"

"I did, and this is the most interesting. Jake said the

company forced him to learn a long password or keycode — a series of letters and numbers. Said he's never seen it in writing. Was told to memorize it and never write it down anywhere. At the time, he thought it was some sort of a cognitive test, but I'm not so sure."

Elena twisted in her desk chair, standing up. "What are you thinking?"

"That somehow the code he has is linked to whatever plan Raashid Sharjah has up his sleeve."

"Is that something Eli told you about?" The words came out slowly; as if Elena was having trouble forming them.

"Yes."

"Well, interestingly enough, I just got a message from Eli. He'd like us to join him in New Orleans ASAP. I think you should bring your friend Jake with you. I'll have travel send you airline confirmations."

"Will do. But there's something I need to take care of first."

## 53

A s Travis ended the call, he set his phone down, thinking. He'd left Jake at the coroner's office with Sheriff Burnett. They were going through a debriefing process to try to get information for the report. Travis had told them he needed to head back to the ranch to check on the horses. And that was at least partially true. But now, there was something else he needed to do.

At the next stoplight, he sent a quick text to Ellie, telling her to take care of the horses for the next few days because he needed to make an emergency trip out of town. A few seconds later he got a thumbs up from her. Travis shrugged. At least that was good. She wasn't asking any questions. As the traffic started to move forward away from the city center in Burton, where the sheriff's office was located, Travis listened to his voicemails. There were five in total — two from his insurance agent, one from the contractor wondering if he had any other changes to the new barn and asking what happened to the other one, one from a horse training client that was curious if he'd put together the show schedule for that spring because they wanted to come and watch their horse, and the last one from a potential skip tracing client who had lost track of an adopted child and wanted to know if Travis could help.

As he drove, Travis called back the insurance agent and the contractor, putting them in touch with each other. "Get it done," he said in his message to the insurance agent. "I need the stalls back and I gotta go out of town for a couple of days. Call Ellie if you need anything."

But even as Travis dealt with the mundane phone calls, he wasn't fully concentrating on them. He was more focused on the thoughts running in the back of his head about Jake, the password, and the cyanide-laced implants. When added to the information he'd received from Eli about Raashid, he knew something dire was about to happen. And now, given the fact Eli had requested his presence in New Orleans told him that the case had gone to a whole new level.

What that level was, he wasn't sure.

## 54

As Travis drove the Jeep down the long driveway approaching the log cabin and the barns at Bishop Ranch, he saw vehicles parked out front of the burned-out structure, a couple of men standing with their arms folded in front of their chests. Travis narrowed his eyes. The insurance agent and the contractor. As much as Travis wanted to go down to the burned-out skeleton of the barn and deal with the two of them, he didn't have time.

Pulling the Jeep into the garage, he quickly closed the garage door behind him, not wanting to invite the contractor or the insurance agent to bother him. He went inside, kicking off his boots at the door and heading straight to the bedroom, pulling a black nylon backpack from the top shelf of his closet, next to a stack of baseball hats. He dialed his phone as he did. Dr. Scott picked up after one ring. "Travis?"

"Is Jake still there?"

"Yeah. I was just taking a blood sample from him to make sure none of the cyanide leaked into his system. Why?"

"Put him on the line." The words came out sharp, but Travis

didn't have time for pleasantries, and more importantly, he didn't care.

"Travis? What's up?" Jake's voice sounded serious.

"Stay at the coroner's office. I'll pick you up in thirty minutes."

"Why?"

I'll tell you when I get there." Travis ended the phone call before Jake asked any more questions. Unlike Elena's phone, he knew his line was unsecured and whoever was looking for the implant might be listening. For all he knew, it could be Raashid Sharjah himself. If Raashid was directly involved, it explained what had happened at his ranch. People like Raashid didn't care who they hurt in order to meet their goals. Travis pressed his lips together and shook his head as he threw a few pairs of jeans, a couple of T-shirts, and some toiletries into his backpack. All he wanted was to be left alone, and here he was, dragged into yet another disaster of the CIA's making. Or at least it appeared that way at the moment.

Zipping the bag closed, Travis slung it over his shoulders and then went into the family room, releasing the bookcase from the wall and scanning his thumb over the lock to get into the war room. Inside, he went straight to the cabinet where the safe was hidden, keying in the code and opening it up. He pulled out the implant from inside, leaving it in the evidence bag. He glanced over his shoulder and then darted to a drawer in his desk, pulling out another plastic bag and dropping the implant still inside the evidence bag inside, sealing it shut. Cyanide was deadly, even in small doses, that's what made it so attractive as a poison to foreign governments. He was lucky the seal hadn't broken. If it had, he'd be dead already. The Russians were notorious for their prowess at developing poisons that were impossible to detect and even more deadly. A cyanide derivative, Novichok, had been used on the Joint Chiefs a few months before and almost on the President himself. The last thing Travis wanted to do was accidentally break the seal on the implant and somehow dose himself.

Closing the safe, Travis left the war room, locking the door behind him. He strode out to the garage, getting in the Jeep and starting it before opening the garage door. From his phone, he armed the security system and the cameras for the log cabin, making sure he had running surveillance feeds of the remainder of his property. He might be leaving, but he wasn't going to be unaware if someone else tried something.

And given what had already happened, they just might...

## 55

Twenty-five minutes later, Travis pulled up in front of the Washington County Coroner's Office. Jake was sitting outside on a park bench that someone had installed in front of the door as if it was a place to stop and watch the birds. Why, Travis had no idea. It seemed like a stupid place to put a bench, but then again, people did stupid things all the time.

"What took you so long?" Jake said, standing up.

Travis checked his watch, grimacing. "By my account, I'm two minutes early." Travis had left his backpack in the car. He held the plastic bag in his hand.

Jake glanced at it, "Is that —?"

Travis nodded. "Sure is. Taken from the dead body." He stared at the door, "Come with me."

Striding into the Sheriff's office, Travis looked at the officer behind the desk. It was the same one from earlier that day. "Open up. Gotta go see Dr. Scott."

The officer sat for a second, his eyes widening and his mouth drooping open before clamping his lips shut as if stifling a sharp retort. The door buzzed. Travis pulled it open. He strode down the hallway, pushing the door to Dr. Scott's office open without knocking. She was sitting behind her desk leaning toward her phone. Sheriff Burnett was still perched in the chair in front of her desk. They both appeared to be talking to someone.

"As I said, we have a little bit of a situation down here in Washington County. We need an agency that has broader capabilities than we have here."

"What seems to be the problem?" a male voice said at the other end of the line.

Dr. Scott nodded at Travis and mouthed the words, "FBI."

"We have a missing corpse," she responded.

"I'm not sure that's a sufficient problem for the FBI to get involved in."

"Oh, I think you're gonna want to get involved," Travis said loudly.

"Who's this?" the male voice from the other end of the line said.

Travis narrowed his eyes. "I'll ask you the same question."

"FBI Agent Dustin Richards. Austin office. Again, who is this? Identify yourself."

Travis glanced up in time to see Dr. Scott's eyes go wide and Sheriff Burnett holding up his hand toward her as if telling her to give Travis a moment. Travis wasn't waiting for permission, "Agent Richards, this is Travis Bishop. You need to get your sorry self down here. What Dr. Scott isn't telling you is that not only do we have a dead body, but we've got two high-tech implants with GPS tracking capability and cyanide in them. They may be linked to a bigger terrorist plot that's about to be executed on American soil."

"And how do you know this?"

"Because I used to work for the CIA.".

## 56

As soon as the words came out of Travis's mouth, the pairing of the word cyanide and terrorist seemed to get Agent Richards's attention. "I didn't..."

"No, you didn't. Get a team down here right now. We've got two implants that need to be contained. Dr. Scott and Sheriff Burnett will fill you in on the rest of the information once you get here."

Apparently, Agent Richards hadn't heard the words "former" in Travis's introduction. "Yes, sir. We are on our way."

"Good." Travis slammed the receiver down on Dr. Scott's phone.

Sheriff Burnett raised his eyebrows, "That certainly sped up the process, didn't it?"

Travis glanced at the Sheriff. Part of him was glad Sheriff Burnett was taking a lighthearted approach to Travis's behavior. Maybe there was hope for their relationship once everything got sorted out. But then again, Travis might not be alive to see it.

He dropped the implant on Dr. Scott's desk. "Thought you

should probably have this back. Didn't exactly want cyanide sitting around at my house if you know what I mean."

"I can't blame you," she said, reaching into her drawer and pulling on a pair of latex gloves.

Travis furrowed his eyebrows. It seemed strange to him that anyone would have sets of latex gloves in their desk, but then again, she was a coroner and he'd seen stranger things before. "I bet Agent Dustin Richards is scrambling to get to his SUV as we speak. My guess? He'll have his team here within the hour. Probably more people will arrive within two or three. Be prepared for an onslaught."

"And where will you be?" Dr. Scott asked, standing up from her desk, pinching the top of the bag together as if she was carrying nuclear waste.

"Jake and I are going to take a little trip."

## 57

"Where are we going?" Jake said, following Travis out of the Sheriff's office.

"New Orleans."

Jake stopped on the sidewalk in front of the building and stared at Travis, "New Orleans? I have work. And I don't have any clothes. I can't leave right now. And they are probably gonna be mad I let Dr. Scott take that implant out."

Travis narrowed his eyes. "You wanna be carrying cyanide in your body?"

"No." Jake shoved his hands into his pockets and looked at the ground.

"You have your ID on you?"

Jake nodded.

"That's all you need. We'll take care of the rest when we land. Let's go."

After stammering for a few seconds about his car being left in the parking lot, muttering something about it being towed away, Jake finally got in the Jeep. Travis started the engine and heard the tires squeal as he pulled out of the sheriff's office lot. His phone pinged with an email. Flight confirmations for him and Jake. Travis pressed on the accelerator, hearing the engine roar to life as he headed for the freeway. "We've got just enough time to make it."

A second later, a text came in from Elena. "Get yourself to the airport ASAP. But don't worry, they will hold the plane for you and Jake."

Travis smiled. The CIA was clever. They were able to pull strings that people never saw, like a master puppeteer behind the scenes. How they were managing to delay the plane, he wasn't sure. It could be something as simple as telling the pilot to slow his pre-freight flight checklist, or a direct call from someone at Langley telling air traffic control they couldn't release the plane until they got the green light from someone in Washington. Unknowing travelers, simply trying to go on vacation, escape for a weekend, or visit a loved one, thought their delays were all weather, mechanical, or personnel. That wasn't always the case. The master strategists were moving the pieces on the chessboard, playing a dangerous game that very few people even knew existed.

The thought hung with Travis as he and Jake dropped off the Jeep in long-term parking, the two of them traveling in silence.

Austin-Bergstrom Airport wasn't nearly as big as Dallas's DFW airport, but it still served its purpose as a regional hub, hosting half a dozen airlines. Making their way through the parking garage, Travis could smell the jet fuel fumes hovering in the air, the odor of sweaty bodies as they passed a few people making their way into the terminal at a slower pace than Travis and Jake.

Ignoring the ticket counter, Travis headed directly for the security checkpoint, getting in line behind what looked to be a group of teenagers traveling with their school, all wearing matching red T-shirts, their excited voices talking in rapid-fire as they seemed to check their phones nonstop. Travis glanced down at his phone and then at Jake as he adjusted the baseball hat on his head. "You got your cell phone with you?"

"Of course."

"Give me the number." As Travis looked at Jake, he noticed that the color of his skin had paled a little bit. Travis automatically glanced down at the bandage on Jake's arm, wondering if he'd popped a stitch, but there was no blood seeping through. Travis narrowed his eyes after keying in Jake's phone number. "I sent you a text. You've got my number in case you need it." He forwarded Jake's boarding pass to Jake's phone and then looked at him again. "You've never done anything like this before, have you?"

Jake's head swung left and right slowly, like an owl's would, his eyes just as big. "Can't say I have. I'm in IT, man. I didn't sign up for this."

"None of us ever do. My grandma used to say, 'God doesn't call the equipped, He equips the called.'" Travis said as the security people waved him forward. "Go with the flow. I'll let you know when you need to be worried."

As Travis stepped away from Jake and put his backpack on the conveyor belt that led to the scanner, he glanced back at Jake. Part of him wondered if Jake would bolt out of the airport, turning from the security line and heading in the other direction. Elena wanted both of them there. He was sure it was because she wanted to hear Jake tell his story directly. More likely? She wanted access to whatever the password was that he was asked to memorize. The thing about Elena was that she was disarming. For as intimidating as Travis could be physically, with his trim physique, tanned skin, and square jaw, Elena was equally disarming, with her pixie-cut blonde hair, red lips, and diminutive size.

As Travis passed through the security checkpoint, he waited on the other side, checking to make sure Jake was making his way through. He was. Travis glanced down at his phone, sending a text. "Just cleared security."

"See you in a few hours..." Elena replied.

Boarding the jet offered the customary amount of pushing and shoving by the passengers, people complaining when their oversized luggage wasn't allowed on board, and passengers struggling to lift their bags into the overhead compartment. The CIA had managed to get Travis and Jake in the first row of coach behind first class. As they went to sit down, Travis leaned over and helped an elderly woman who was struggling to lift her flowered suitcase into the compartment above. She looked over her shoulder at him, her gray hair framing her face. "Why, thank you," she said through pink lipstick. Travis blinked, "You're welcome."

Something about the woman reminded him of Catherine, the MI6 agent he'd met at The Sour Lemon, a restaurant friendly to the intelligence community, in Austin. He'd met Catherine years ago. Travis pressed his lips together. Why the memory was surfacing at that moment, he had no idea, other than he'd been summoned by the CIA as he had that day.

As he slid into his seat, tightening the seat belt around his waist and adjusting it underneath the silver belt buckle he was wearing, he chewed the inside of his lip, wondering what the CIA had gotten him into this time...

## 58

The flight Travis and Jake were on between Austin and New Orleans took off ten minutes earlier than expected. As the flight attendant closed the hatch and announced an early departure Travis raised his eyebrows and looked at Jake, who didn't seem to see the significance. Travis muttered under his breath, "Gotta love the CIA."

As they taxied down the runway, Travis nudged Jake, "You might want to take a nap. Things are going to get busy as soon as we hit the ground."

"How do you know that?" Jake said, his eyes wide.

"You can call it gut instinct or experience. Either one will work," Travis said, lowering the brim of his baseball cap down over his eyes. He crossed his arms in front of his chest. "Either way, you should try to sleep."

An hour later, as the flight attendant's voice came on the overhead speakers, telling the passengers that the plane was about to start its descent into New Orleans, Travis woke up. He blinked a couple of times and glanced at Jake, who was out cold next to him. Travis elbowed him, "Time to wake up, Sleeping Beauty. We're just about to land."

"Already?"

"Yeah, already."

As the plane descended, it seemed to hover for a tentative moment over the tarmac before gently touching down, the tires giving a squeal and then sending a roll of thunderous vibrations through the plane as the pilots reversed the thrusters and slowed it down. A ping went off overhead followed by the flight attendant saying "Welcome to New Orleans. We will be at our gate in a moment. Please stay seated with your seat belts fastened until the plane comes to a complete stop."

Travis ignored the announcement. He unclipped his seatbelt, flipping the two sides away from him. He shrugged his shoulders, realizing he felt stiff. He was tired of sitting, even though it had only been just over an hour.

Travis glanced out of the window as the plane stopped at the terminal, seeing the jetway extend itself toward the fuselage, feeling the rush of warm, humid air coming from outside, filtering its way through the dry air in the plane. A man wearing a pair of khaki pants and a bright blue polo shirt stepped onto the plane and spoke to the flight attendant. For a moment, she seemed confused, cocking her head to the side. Travis narrowed his eyes as she pointed to them. The man walked forward a few steps and stopped, leaning over the seats where Travis and Jake were seated. Travis looked up at him. He was young, probably in his early twenties. He was clean-shaven, although Travis doubted whether the young man could even grow a beard. There was a lanyard around his neck, although whatever badge it held was tucked inside his shirt. "Travis Bishop and Jake West?" the young man said, staring at them, a wide grin on his face as if he was just about to tell them they'd won the lottery.

Travis frowned, but gave a nod.

"Come with me."

Jake popped up out of his seat and Travis followed, pulling

his backpack down from the overhead compartment. A few of the first-class passengers glared at them as they walked by, probably wondering why they were allowed to depart the plane before everyone else.

By the time Travis got off the plane after retrieving his bag, Jake and the young man were standing and waiting halfway up the jetway, the two of them engrossed in a deep conversation.

Travis shouldered his backpack and gave the young man a nod, "Who are you?"

The young man pulled the ID badge out from underneath his shirt, showed it to Travis, and then stuck it back inside. "Shields. I'm here to retrieve you."

Travis gave a sharp nod and followed as Shields walked through the concourse. Jake hung back, walking at Travis's shoulder. "Did you know that Shields is an intern? I didn't know they had interns with the CIA."

Everything in Travis wanted to grab Jake, toss him up against a wall, and knock some sense into him. He rolled his eyes instead, "Of course they do. Every government agency has interns."

As they walked, the questions from Jake continued. "How could they? I mean, they're not trained." His loud whisper showed he was clearly nervous.

"How do you think they get their training?" Travis said.

"Don't you CIA agents have to go to someplace? Isn't it called the ranch or something?"

Travis nodded, "Yeah, the Farm. Camp Peary. My guess is our friend Shields is a gopher. Probably a local college student with a political science major. Nothing to be excited about."

Jake stared at Shields, then back at Travis, "Oh. Yeah, I guess that makes sense."

Travis nodded. "Just follow along, Jake. Everything is going to be okay.." Travis hoped the words he said weren't a lie.

## 59

Gia leaned over the sink in the basement bathroom, resting the palms of her hands on the chipped Formica counter next to the sink. Her shoulders were slumped. She stared at a stray hair that had curled itself in what was left of the water at the bottom of the bowl after she'd washed her hands. Gia stared at her reflection in the mirror, one of the lights in the fixture above blinking on and off in a way that threatened to give her a headache.

She'd been working on the project for days. Her position with Explority Biotech had sent her to New Orleans to set up for a conference. Like everything else with Keaton Callahan's company, she wasn't allowed to tell anyone. Why it was a secret, she wasn't sure, but she'd been told she was still unable to reach out to family, not even her brother Jake. It felt like she'd been in New Orleans for weeks, but it hadn't been. She'd only been there five days.

Her work with Explority Biotech had started off relatively interesting. After submitting to a full psychological exam and agreeing to have a GPS implant put in her wrist, Keaton Callahan had asked her to solve some emerging problems he was having with the supply chain, only communicating with her via email. Finding the necessary parts for all of their items already in production at Explority had become a growing issue with slowing exports out of China and backlogs of ships entering ports in the United States. "It's a delay we can't afford, Gia. I hope you understand why this is important." Gia threw herself into the project, trying to find solutions. As she was ready to offer a few ideas, things had abruptly changed.

The week before, she received a text from Keaton telling her to pack up her things in Miami and move out of the long-term corporate housing rental the company had put her up in. His instructions indicated she needed to be ready to move to a new site in four hours. Putting her work aside, she spent the morning packing, rehearsing the series of letters and numbers she'd been told to memorize during her intake interview as she did. It was something she'd gotten in the habit of doing when she was bored or didn't have any other things to think about. The woman who had trained her told her it was critical that she keep the numbers and letters fresh in her mind, but that she didn't write them down. Why, Gia was unsure and she couldn't get a straight answer out of the woman. Seeing there was no point in pressing the issue, Gia gave up, memorized the sequence, and moved on with her life. She hoped it was some sort of psychological test, like a virtual inkblot test, that she could pass.

That afternoon, after stuffing a backpack and a single suitcase with the few things she had with her, Gia arrived in New Orleans where she was met by a driver from the company, who dropped her off at the Old South Hotel. The man was mute for the entire drive to the hotel, only telling Gia to leave her bags in the car and that he would see to having them taken to her room. In exchange, he handed her a key card and told her to report to the basement. She would be given instructions there.

By the time she arrived in the basement, there was a hive of activity, workers bustling all over the space. She stood in the doorway scanning the people until someone interrupted her. "Are you Gia?"

Gia turned to see a thick-bodied man with coarse hair combed over to the side, wearing a black Explority Biotech T-shirt and a name badge. She nodded.

"I'm Edward. Keaton told me to expect you. Let's get to work."

Without much other explanation, Edward handed her a matching black T-shirt and a name tag, telling her to go into the bathroom and change. "Don't forget to wear your name tag at all times. It helps the hotel security to know who we are," he barked as she walked away.

Gia nodded even though it didn't make sense to her. Wouldn't the t-shirt be enough? Gia didn't say anything. Edward didn't seem like the kind of man who wanted to discuss things.

Edward pointed to a pile of boxes in the corner. A single tan folding table with metal legs was set up nearby. "There are three stacks of boxes," he said, pointing. "Folders in one, brochures in the second pile, and inserts in the third. They need to be put together for the conference."

"There's a conference here? I thought I was supposed to be working on supply chain issues" Gia furrowed her eyebrows. No one had mentioned anything to her about a conference. She'd only been told to pack up her stuff and get on a plane.

"Yes. Next week. There are ten thousand to stuff and you are the only one doing them. Now get to work."

Gia watched as Edward walked away, a strange smile on his face that Gia couldn't quite understand. Gia swallowed, not sure what his expression meant.

Hours later, Gia realized she'd barely made a dent in stuffing the folders. Her back and neck hurt from being hunched over the flimsy folding table, and sitting down to work on the project didn't make the aching much better.

And that's all she'd been doing for the last few days.

Her days had grown into a humdrum rhythm. She'd spend the morning stuffing folders with a letter supposedly penned by Keaton Callahan, bragging of the developments he'd brought to Explority Biotech, two pamphlets, and a glossy fact sheet. Pamphlets on one side, the letter on the other. She took the thirty-minute lunch break Edward gave her and then spent the afternoon doing the same, heading outside for fresh air when she could, and picking up dinner and taking it back to her hotel room each night.

Three days into her project and she'd only stuffed about a third of the folders. During one of her breaks, she mentioned her slow progress to Edward who seemed uninterested, as if he was more focused on something else. That was one of the first times she'd seen him that day. Edward stayed cordoned off in a small office at one end of the basement space the company had taken over from the hotel, the door to his office perpetually closed, a man wearing a matching black Explority Biotech T-shirt sitting in a chair right in front of the door, guarding it, as if Edward were reviewing state secrets inside.

That afternoon, Gia stared at the door for a little too long, catching the look of the guard sitting in front of it. She quickly turned away, staring back at the massive folders she was supposed to be stuffing. She had the distinct feeling that what she was doing didn't matter, as if they were simply trying to keep her busy and in their sights. But, if they wanted to pay her a salary for stuffing folders, so be it, she told herself.

On the other end of the space, closer to the office that Edward occupied, there was the nearly constant rattle of the service elevator going up and down as Explority Biotech people moved large square cardboard boxes on chipped yellow dollies out of the basement. On one of her breaks, she walked by the stacks of boxes, running a single finger over the smooth brown cardboard, catching a glimpse of the label. The address she saw was to the Curriculum Director at Sacred Heart Academy. Gia frowned, but kept walking, feeling the eyes of the guard at the door in front of Edward's office boring into her back. Why was Explority shipping boxes to a school? She sighed. Maybe they were samples of their medical devices for classrooms or some other kind of donation. Maybe...

But something didn't make sense. Something was eating at her, but she had no idea what was going on.

Outside, Gia walked slowly down the block toward a local café that was a few storefronts past the hotel's entrance, taking her time. She wasn't all that interested in spending the rest of the afternoon in the damp basement. She pulled the cell phone she'd been given by the company out of her pocket and typed in a number, waiting for it to connect. She walked a little faster away from the hotel as she did, her strides shortening, "Jake, it's Gia. I'm in New Orleans. Something's going on. I'm scared..."

As she sucked in a breath to say the next words, she felt a hand grip her shoulder, spinning her around. She felt a pinch in her neck and grabbed at it with her hand, covering the area that stung. She glanced up, only to see the face of the man who'd been guarding Edward's office grinning at her as everything went black.

## 60

"You got her?" Keaton said into the phone.

"Yeah. We just got to the van. We'll take her to the other side of the city and wait there until you tell us what to do next."

"Good. Just remember. I need her alive. She's the only one with the codes."

"Yes sir. We'll take good care of her."

"See that you do."

Keaton tossed his cell phone on the table he was using as a makeshift desk while he was in New Orleans. On the face of it, the Presidential Suite at the Hotel Montefiore was expansive and luxurious, but after staying in it like a captive for the last few days, it felt more like an overly decorated jail cell than anything else, as though he was under house arrest. Which he was...

Keaton had tried going out a couple of times when he'd first gotten to New Orleans, thinking that taking a break would clear his head. Leaving the hotel, he'd seen a blue sedan parked in front of the main entrance, two men seated inside, both of them with dark hair and beards. Walking down the block, a man trailed him slowly on the other side of the road, not making any effort to try to hide the fact that he was watching Keaton. Keaton had quickly turned back to the hotel and gone back upstairs. It had to be Raashid's men. They were in town to help with the so-called "conference." It was the cover story of why Keaton was in New Orleans in the first place, an elaborate event bringing investors into the city to enjoy Mardi Gras and hear the latest progress from their star CEO Keaton Callahan himself.

It was all a cover.

Keaton pressed his lips together, feeling the skin on his lower lip crack, the metallic taste of blood in his mouth. The cover story of the conference hadn't been his idea. It had all been Raashid, invitations sent out, travel arrangements made, the hotel booked, brochures and folders printed in high gloss navy and silver, all without Keaton's knowledge. By the time Keaton figured out what was going on, there was nothing he could do. He'd never felt so powerless.

And the blood he tasted on his lip wouldn't be the only one spilled.

The Old South Hotel, the venue Raashid had chosen for the conference, was right on the Mardi Gras route. What exactly he had planned for it, he wasn't sure. But that wasn't the problem he was facing now or at least the most immediate one.

He needed the codes.

Grabbing Gia West was at least some semblance of a win, he thought, slumping down behind his desk, staring at the monitors. Raashid had told him that two of his employees had been given codes he would need to access the data stored on two of the implants in order to arm the bombs Raashid's men and unknowing Explority employees were deploying throughout the city.

Keaton swallowed, wondering if that was true. Would Raashid actually take the chance that his carefully planned event wouldn't happen? It didn't seem likely, but that didn't solve the problem of the codes. They only had one person who had the password. Gia.

A trickle of sweat ran down the back of Keaton's neck. He batted it away like an unwanted mosquito. He'd given up everything in order to have his company, and to save his father's life, even if he and his father weren't that close anymore.

And now Raashid had set another barrier in front of him. The codes.

He'd been working on a problem for the last week, and almost had a solution. Raashid had refused to give anyone full access to the configuration of the system that would arm the bombs without both passwords. And now, one of the people Keaton thought had the password had been lost, the body burned, the implant held by Travis Bishop. It had been Keaton's hope that the code would be on the man's implant, but even with Edward's help, they'd been unable to retrieve it.

That only left him with two options. Either the second half of the password had died with the burned body or someone else had it. Raashid hadn't bothered to tell him if the same people that had the implant also had the codes. For all he knew, he could be looking for four people and not two. There was no point in asking Raashid. Keaton knew he'd be punished for the question.

Worse yet, the implant technology he'd spent years developing had failed. Keaton frowned at the screen in front of him, adding a few more lines of code to the program he'd been writing. The implants had been designed to be tracked whether they were in someone's arm or not. But somehow, when the body with the code was burned, the implant had been shut off. Not only could he not find the implant, but there was no way to access it. Even if Raashid had buried the rest of the password inside the implant, the code had died with the man, unless someone else had it.

Keaton swallowed. At that moment, he only had half of what he needed. If Raashid found out, there was no telling what he would do. There was no doubt in Keaton's mind that his father would be a dead man. Keaton would probably be dead too, Raashid deciding that Keaton's inability to acquire both of the passwords was an abject failure of his mission. To make it worse, Keaton didn't even know if he needed the passwords in order to enable the bombs. It didn't make any sense. If Raashid was that committed to his project, wouldn't he have the means to do what he wanted? Keaton chewed the inside of his lip. The more Keaton thought about it, the more finding the passwords sounded like just another exercise in the long line of ones that Raashid wanted him to fulfill to prove his loyalty.

Like he had any choice.

Keaton licked his lips. But at least they had Gia. That was one positive development. He'd told Edward to grab her and keep her sedated. Keaton hadn't bothered to tell Edward why and Edward hadn't bothered to ask.

Keaton blinked a few times at the screen, rubbing his eyes. With any luck, the program he'd written would be a workaround to get through the encryption on the file he needed to open with the last set of instructions instead of waiting for the data from the implants and the codes. Then he wouldn't need Gia, the dead man, or someone else.

Frustrated, Keaton pounded his palm on the table in the Presidential Suite. He got up, throwing his hands in the air as if he was having an argument with someone, but no words came out. Picking up a vase from one of the side tables he threw it against the wall, the blue and silver metallic paint shattering into a million pieces against the pristine white drywall and then dropping to land on a patch of white tile floor, the boom echoing off of the walls. Keaton threw himself down on one of the leather couches and rubbed his forehead. Things were out of control and he knew it.

He'd been in control of every facet of his life for as long as he could remember. Off to college at the age of sixteen, graduating with a Master's Degree in IT by the time he was twenty. Companies clamored to hire him for his ability to innovate and produce. When he discovered working for someone else actually meant doing what they wanted, he started Explority on a single weekend, filing the legal paperwork himself online.

He'd never looked back. And now, Raashid had managed to usurp control of the company from him, and there was no way out...

---

## 61

After winding their way through the airport and out to the parking garage, Travis and Jake jumped in a nondescript gray sedan with Shields behind the wheel. "Where are we going?" Travis said, reaching behind him and handing Jake his backpack.

"I could tell you, but then I'd have to kill you," Shields said in a fake gravelly voice, a grim look on his face. He chuckled, glancing at Travis, who wasn't smiling. "Just kidding. We have an office here. I'm taking you there."

"Is Agent Lobranova on the ground yet?"

Shields shook his head, "I don't know anything about that. All I know is I was given your names and your flight number, told to retrieve you, and bring you back to the office. That's it."

Travis pressed his lips together, staring out of the window. It was typical Agency protocol to limit information. He shook his head. Seems things never changed.

As Shields wove his way onto I-10, Travis watched New Orleans unfold in front of him. The industrial gray buildings of the Louis Armstrong New Orleans Airport faded into the clusters of traffic on the interstate. They could have been in any city in any country around the world. Having traveled as much as he did, Travis realized the only real difference from city to city was the language the green signs were printed in.

After heading northeast away from the airport on I-10 to the Lake Pontchartrain Causeway, Shields got off at the exit for Little Bayou Circle. The stark freeway travel was quickly replaced by a few sets of low office buildings, a doughnut shop with a neon light blinking in the window, stating their beignets were hot and fresh at that very moment, a hair salon across the street and a crawfish shack next to what looked to be a local branch of the post office.

Travis shook his head. New Orleans was a mishmash of business and old southern Bayou traditions brought in by the Cajun folk and the Creoles generations before. As Travis glanced around, he realized they were outside of New Orleans proper.

He narrowed his eyes at Shields, "Where are we, exactly?"

"We're in a suburb pretty far northeast of the city, called Little Bayou. It's nice around here. Quiet. People are friendly, but they kinda stick to themselves too. They don't seem to like strangers very much."

Travis raised his eyebrows, "And I'm guessing you're a stranger?"

"Stranger than most. I'm originally from Michigan. I've learned pretty quick that southerners think anyone from north of the Mason-Dixon line might be a traitor."

Travis nodded but didn't say anything as Shields pulled the charcoal gray sedan over a curb and into the parking lot of a three-story brick building. On the first floor, there were two retail stores — one had a sign in front that said "Willie's Guitar," and the other "Little Bayou Books," the door open, propped with what looked to be a bucket of fake pink and orange plastic flowers.

Shields pulled the sedan around back, parking the nondescript sedan in the middle of a line of other nondescript vehicles. Two cars over from where they parked, a middle-aged man with a potbelly was rummaging around in his truck, pulling out a dirty black guitar case as Travis stepped out of the vehicle, grabbing his backpack from Jake, who followed. The man with the guitar glanced at them for a second and then kept moving. Travis did the same.

At the back of the building, there was only a single door. The man with a guitar case disappeared around the side of the building, as if he were going to use the front entrance for his guitar lesson. Travis and Jake, following Shields, went through the back, entering under an old rusted aluminum awning that had a couple of dents on the lip, as though someone had tried to carry something tall in through the doorway and managed to catch it on the awning before realizing what they'd done. The glass door on the back of the building had a little bell on it that rang as they opened it. It was unlocked. Travis narrowed his eyes. The CIA chose the strangest locations for their offices. That was part of the plan, making sure that their enemies weren't looking for them in all the normal places – near military installations, in sprawling government buildings, or downtown as part of the bustle of major cities, occupying floors and floors of important office space in mile-high office buildings.

No, many of the CIA offices were tucked away in buildings like these, hidden by the normalcy of everyday life.

The musty smell of old paper and dirty carpet filled Travis's nose. He followed Shields to a narrow flight of steps that was covered with cracked pale yellow linoleum, metal edging screwed into the front of each step as if that would protect the flooring. It hadn't. Jake trailed behind Travis. At the top of the flight of steps, Shields turned left, angling for a single door about two-thirds of the way down the hallway. As Travis looked back over his shoulder, he saw the staircase turned and went up another floor. Glancing around, he realized there was only one doorway in the hallway. Narrowing his eyes, he followed Shields as the young man disappeared inside. The placard outside simply read 201. Nothing more.

Standing just inside the door, hearing it click closed behind him, Travis took a second to assess his surroundings. The muscles of his jaw rippled. Directly opposite the door, there was a large open space, with a bank of windows on the other side of the room that faced out to the street. They were covered by a thin film of cheap curtains, the afternoon light threatening to intrude on what was happening inside.

To his left, there were two doors, almost as if the space was originally a large apartment or meant to be a condo. The one on the farthest side of the room was closed, but the one nearest to where he was standing was open. It was dim inside. A man with black hair passed by the doorway, glanced at Travis, giving him a little lift of the chin in acknowledgment, and then kept moving. A knot formed in Travis's stomach. He had no idea who the man was.

To his right, there was a kitchen, two people leaned over steaming cups of coffee, staring at a piece of paper in front of them, one of them holding a pen and making circles on the paper as they talked, the other one holding a sandwich, taking a bite. On the far side of the wall there was another closed door.

By Travis's count, there looked to be at least eight people in the office. All of them were dressed very casually. Shields was the only one wearing a polo shirt. Without exception, everyone else had on some combination of T-shirts and torn jeans. To some, it might have seemed to be unprofessional, but Travis knew it was all about maintaining the Agency's cover. It would seem terribly out of place if people wearing suits and ties and skirts and heels were traipsing up the back staircase of an old building above a guitar studio and a bookstore. The people working at the office were playing the part, as they should.

Travis blinked, watching Shields, who motioned to them, waving them forward to the darkened room near the door where Travis had seen the man a moment before. As they walked in, the man left, his white T-shirt reading "Good Vibes" on the front of it as he twisted to the side to get out of the way. "Welcome to New Orleans," he whispered as Travis went inside. He didn't bother to introduce himself.

Travis turned and watched as the man walked away. The man acted like he knew Travis, but his face didn't seem familiar.

"Travis!" A voice called from across the room, breaking his stare. From behind a table set up against the wall in front of a bank of computers, Elena sprung up from her chair and trotted over to him, giving him a hug. As he looked down at her, he smiled. "Good to see you."

"Good to see you too, Travis!" she said, squeezing his arm. She glanced at Jake, "You must be the famous not dead person. I'm Elena."

Jake laughed, "That's one way to put it."

Travis looked around. Shields had disappeared. So had the other two people that were in the room when Travis and Jake walked in. Clearly, they'd likely been told to give Elena the space when her guests arrived. "Sit down, sit down. Your flight was okay?" she said, waving them to a couple of empty office chairs, sounding more like a long-lost cousin than an Agency asset working a case.

Travis glanced around the room as he pulled a chair out from underneath the table. The room was surprisingly dark, the single window hastily covered in cardboard that had been stapled to the frame. On two of the four walls were long tables like the one where Elena had been sitting when they walked in, filled with computers. In the center of the room, two additional folding tables had been buttressed up against each other, a mishmash of unmatched desk chairs stationed around the periphery. The office reeked of a temporary setup. Travis had seen many of these throughout his years with the CIA. A blandly named shell corporation would approach a landlord with empty space, pay for a set of offices or an entire floor for six months to a year in cash, receive the keys and a moving truck would arrive in the middle of the night, quietly outfitting the office in whatever supplies could be scrounged up in the area. Just as quickly, days or weeks later, the people from the office would disappear, as well as all of the furniture. Months later, the landlord, looking to renew the lease, would arrive to find that the building had been vacated, never really knowing when it had happened.

Travis pulled up a chair in front of the hastily assembled conference table and sat down, tossing his backpack on a chair next to him. Elena plopped down on the other side of the table, adjusting the chair to make her diminutive form more visible. Jake sat to Travis's left at the head of the table, folding his hands on the surface.

Elena's voice became serious, "As much as I'm glad to see you again, Travis, I wish it was under better circumstances. You've gotten yourself into another big mess, haven't you?"

Travis shook his head, "Honestly, trouble seems to find me."

Elena glanced at the surface of the table for a second, her face cast in a sharp shadow from the bulbs of the single overhead light, and then lifted her eyes toward Travis, "I'm sorry about your barn and losing Scarlett. I know how much the horses mean to you."

Travis stared at her for a second then glanced down and swallowed. "How did you find out?"

"You know..." Elena's voice drifted off.

A knot formed in Travis's stomach. No matter how anonymous he tried to stay, it seemed like the CIA always kept tabs on him. He chewed the inside of his lip. For all he knew, they probably even kept a log of what he had for breakfast. He might be out of the CIA, but was he truly? He wondered if he would ever know the answer to that question.

Elena's voice interrupted his thoughts, "Listen, I have some information that neither of you is going to like very much."

Travis narrowed his eyes, "Okay. What's going on?"

Elena looked toward Jake, "I'm sorry, Jake, but your sister has been taken."

## 62

"What?" The words came out as almost a whisper from Jake's mouth. "What are you talking about?"

Elena blinked, glancing at Travis, then settling her gaze on Jake, not actually answering his question. "When was last time you talked to her?"

"It's been a while..."

"As soon as we heard from Travis that you were alive and about the codes you'd been asked to memorize, we put a tail on her. She walked out of the building where she was working and then disappeared."

Travis watched as Jake got up from the table, interlacing his hands on the top of his head as though he had just gotten done sprinting as fast as he could and was out of breath. He dropped them, staring at Elena, his eyes wide. "When did this happen?"

"In the last few hours. I'm sorry, Jake. We're doing what we can to track her." Elena cleared her throat. "You didn't get a ransom demand, no contact with the kidnappers, nothing like that?"

"Can't say I have. We've been in the air and then came

straight here." Travis watched as Jake pulled his phone out. His hands were shaking. "No, there's nothing here. Oh my God! What am I gonna do? What if they hurt her?"

"You're going to sit down. That's what you're going to do," Travis growled. Having Jake freaking out wasn't going to help anyone.

"That's easy for you to say, Travis. It's not your sister."

Travis glared at Jake. He sat back down, closing his eyes. Travis looked at Elena. "What else can you tell us?"

Elena sighed, "Truthfully, not much. I'm actually hoping you guys can fill in some of the blanks. What I know at this moment is that Explority Biotech is planning on having some sort of a conference here over the next couple of days."

"During Mardi Gras?" Travis said, narrowing his eyes.

Elena shrugged. "I know. Doesn't exactly make a lot of sense to me either with how crowded the city is, but whatever. We'll figure that out as we go. They seem to have rented the basement of the Old South Hotel, the same hotel where they're hosting the conference. They've had people down there working for nearly a week. Doing what, we don't know yet."

"How is it that you don't know? You haven't infiltrated them yet?" Travis frowned.

Elena raised her eyebrows, "As you can tell by this hastily constructed office, we've been on the move. Apparently, the New Orleans office beats a hasty retreat out of downtown during Mardi Gras season and holes up in some building on the outskirts to get out of the fray. All the Agency assets in the area have been busy getting this place up and running. And, not to mention all the stuff that's been happening in Texas with you guys we just found out about has set us scrambling."

"But you said Eli wanted us here?"

Elena nodded, blinking. "That's exactly right. We're gonna go and meet him here in a couple of minutes. I wanted to have a chance to chat first."

Elena clearly had an agenda. Travis narrowed his eyes. "What else are you not telling us, Elena?" He could tell something was going on in the mind behind Elena's porcelain skin and red lips.

She looked calmly at Jake. "I need to know about the password. Now."

## 63

J ake spent the next few minutes telling Elena everything that he'd already told Travis about his work with Explority Biotech, the limited contact he'd had with Keaton Callahan, and the requirement to learn the password. Elena narrowed her eyes at him, folding her hands on the table. Travis watched her. It was textbook CIA interview style, right from the Camp Peary playbook. Agents stayed very low-key, very non-confrontational, at least until someone was transferred to a black site. Then all bets were off. "Jake, can you tell me anything about the person that taught you the password?"

Jake shook his head, "Honestly, not that much. It's been a while."

"It was a woman?"

"Yes."

"Did you see her face?"

Jake shook his head, "No. We were on a video call, but she never enabled her camera. I could only hear her voice."

"Was there a name on the screen, anything that identified her?"

"No. It was just a series of numbers, like it was a telephone number or something, but too many digits."

"Okay, can you close your eyes for a second and see if you can see the screen in your head? Was anything else interesting about the numbers that were displayed on the screen?"

Travis watched as Jake closed his eyes for a second. A moment later they popped open. "It was weird," he said, leaning toward Elena across the table, "The numbers on the screen had a plus in front of them."

Elena shot a look at Travis. "A foreign phone number."

Travis nodded. Foreign phone numbers used an exchange code to identify what country they were in. It always started with the plus sign, followed by three digits.

"Can you remember any of the numbers?"

Jake stared at the ceiling for a second and looked back at Elena, "No, I'm sorry, I can't."

Elena got up from her chair and started pacing back and forth. She stuffed her hands into her pockets, looked at Jake and said, "Okay, one more question. If you couldn't see the woman on the other end of the line, what did she sound like?"

Jake frowned, "I don't know." He paused, looking away from Elena and Travis as if he'd spotted something far off in the distance. "Now that I think about it, she sounded kind of funny."

"Kind of funny how?"

"Like her voice was being modulated somehow. You know how they use those auto tuners for songs?"

Travis nodded, watching Elena's reaction. He knew exactly what Jake was talking about. It was one of his least favorite aspects of new music. Producers would use auto tuners to help musicians stay on pitch. But with the technology, they could also change the octave of the voice radically, taking what sounded like a male, and making it sound like a female. Travis blinked. He'd been in a bar a few months earlier, four guys in the corner singing cover songs from Fleetwood Mac and Britney Spears. At first, he thought it was a woman singing and that he just couldn't see her from his vantage point, but then he realized it was a man, complete with a beard and a bun of thick curly hair on the top of his head. "An auto tuner. Voice modulation."

Elena nodded. "Jake, you said it sounded like a woman, but it sounded fake. Anything else about the voice? Any speech tics you can remember?"

"No, not really." Jake's voice drifted off. He looked away for a second and then back at Travis and Elena. "There was one thing though. The voice had kind of an accent."

Elena scowled, "Are you sure it was a woman?"

"Now that you mention the auto tuner, I can't really be sure. But there was an accent. I'm sure about that."

"What kind of accent?" Travis asked.

"Maybe Middle Eastern? Whoever was talking had good English, but they didn't talk like they were raised in America. Not British. And not Asian either. Yeah, I guess Middle Eastern."

Travis shot Elena a look. She raised her eyebrows. Had the voice that had given Jake the password been Raashid himself?

## 64

Before Travis could say anything else Elena's cell phone pinged. She stared at the men across the conference table. "We gotta go."

"Eli?" Travis said, picking up his backpack.

"Yeah. He's got something."

Travis followed Jake and Elena out of the makeshift offices above the bookstore and the guitar studio and down the steps. As they walked out the back door, Travis saw the same man who'd carried the guitar case in the building coming out again, this time carrying the sheaf of sheet music in his hand. His lesson must be over. He gave Travis a nod, as if they were fast friends. He looked like he was about to say something when Travis looked away. He wasn't interested in any conversation, not even if a lack of one created suspicion. Based on what Elena said, the hastily put together office in Little Bayou for the CIA would be there and gone before the man's next lesson.

Elena strode out to a red sedan parked at the back of the lot. She slid into the driver's seat. Travis rode shotgun with Jake in the back, glancing at the man with the guitar case as he got in.

Elena fumbled in the center console for a second after

starting the car, handing Jake a notepad and a pen. "I need you to write down that password for me. Can you do that?"

Jake's eyes went wide, "I was told not to give it to anyone."

"Write it down, Jake. If something happens to you, we may need it." Travis growled. As Travis turned forward in his seat, he realized his fists were balled. There was something about Jake that made him want to alternately protect the guy and throttle him. At that moment, throttling seemed like a better option. Travis pressed his lips together. All Travis could hope was that Jake took the threat rising in front of them as seriously as Travis did. Their lives might depend on it.

A few seconds later, a sheet of paper appeared over Travis's shoulder. He stared at it. Glancing back toward Jake, Travis asked, "Is this all of it? The whole password? You're not getting cute are you?"

"No, no. Of course not! That's the whole thing." His eyes were wide, his mouth hanging open.

Elena nodded at Travis, "Send me a picture?"

"Yeah, sure." Travis pulled his phone out of his back pocket, snapped a picture of the piece of paper, and texted it to Elena. He shoved the paper in his pocket.

"What do we do now?" Jake said.

"We go see Eli," Elena said.

## 65

Elena pulled the red sedan in front of a small café in downtown New Orleans after weaving her way through the side streets. There seemed to be barricades everywhere. Mardi Gras was ramping up. The parades were increasing in duration, frequency, and attendance, as they neared the two days before Ash Wednesday. They were the busiest in the city. While the city's website boasted that Mardi Gras was a two-week celebration of fun, frolicking, and revelry, anyone who had lived there for longer than a few years knew that it was really only a few days before Ash Wednesday when the most riotous fun was to be had. During that time, the streets were lined with visitors and natives to New Orleans. Crowds littered the streets, the businesses open nearly all day and all night, serving colorful drinks to anyone who wanted them, music blaring as the latest community band paraded down the road. In the background, the echo of sirens screamed off in the distance as the New Orleans Police Department and ambulances were dispatched to take care of any bouts of revelry that had gotten out of hand.

Pulling into the parking lot behind the West End Café,

Elena gasped and slammed on the brakes, nearly hitting a group of three loudly dressed people, wearing satin outfits in turquoise, lime green, and orange, as they crossed in front of her car, one of them pounding the hood with a smile. She pressed her lips together and stared at Travis. "Dumb drunks."

Travis didn't say anything. He just shook his head.

"How are we going to find my sister in the midst of this mess?" Jake said. His voice sounded sad, lost.

As Travis slipped out of the car, he glanced back at Jake, who seemed frozen in the backseat, "Come on, Jake. It's not time to lose hope yet. Let's go."

Elena led the way into the café. The door of the West End Cafe was perched at an angle on the corner of the building as though someone had sliced off the sharp edge. Above it was a porch with a finely detailed black wrought iron railing, a line of mismatched folding chairs ready for a parade watching, though they were empty at the moment. As Travis stepped inside the door, he could smell the combination of coffee brewing and something sweet baking. His stomach lurched. He hadn't had much to eat and he realized how hungry he was. He saw Eli huddled in the back corner of the café sitting at one of the tables, his fluff of hair visible. His watcher, the same young man with the dark hair, sallow skin, and long nose from their last meeting sat with his headphones on in front of his computer, as though the entire scene had gotten transported from when he'd met Eli in Austin. Travis walked over to the table where Eli was sitting and sat on a chair across from him, feeling the sticky red vinyl seat under his fingers.

"This café has the most delicious crumb cake I've ever had," Eli said, using a single finger to pick up a few scattered crumbs on his plate. "You should try a piece, Travis. Put a little meat on your bones."

Travis's stomach soured. "No thanks."

Elena sat next to Eli. She narrowed her eyes. "How are you, Eli?"

"Fine, fine. Busy. A little too busy." He scratched the back of his head.

Travis looked at Eli. He looked like he was wearing the same clothes as the last time, the same rumpled shirt and pants, the fluff of his hair threatening to go rogue at any moment. Travis imagined Eli as a child, his mother licking her hand in an attempt to stick Eli's wild hair back down on his head to make him seem presentable. "What's going on, Eli? You wanted to see us. We're here."

Eli narrowed his eyes at Travis as if insulted by the quick pace of questioning. He glanced at Jake, ignoring Travis. "You must be Jake. I'm Eli."

Jake frowned; as if confused by the pleasantries. "Nice to meet you," he said, as if he was unsure what else to say.

"I have to say, I'm sorry that we are meeting under these circumstances." Eli's eyes settled on Jake's arm. "I hear you had a minor procedure done earlier today. I'm assuming you are feeling well?"

Jake touched the bandage that Dr. Scott had put on his arm after removing the implant with a single finger. "Yes. Fine enough. Glad to get the implant out of my wrist."

"You should be." Eli glanced at Travis, "As instructed, your Dr. Scott is currently entertaining several FBI agents in her office. They are having quite the field day with the implant, so I've heard."

Travis raised his eyebrows and then glanced at Elena. A smile tugged at her cheek. Travis looked back at Eli, "That's what you've heard, huh?"

"Yes."

Travis shook his head. He'd forgotten how wily the Mossad could be. They always seemed to be three steps ahead of everyone else, with eyes and ears everywhere. Travis chewed the inside of his lip. He couldn't tell if Eli sharing with them about the FBI was meant to be braggadocio or a warning. He blinked, pushing the thought away. The near-constant threat to Israel's sovereignty had made them the best at what they did.

Before Travis could say anything else, Eli leveled his gaze at Jake. "I suppose you'd like to know what's going on with your sister?"

Jake's face brightened, as if a ray of sunshine had broken through thick clouds somewhere in his soul, "Yes!" he blurted out.

Travis elbowed him. "Not so loud."

"Sorry."

Eli smiled, "That's perfectly all right, Jake. A little enthusiasm once in a while isn't a bad thing, right Agent Bishop?"

Travis didn't bother answering.

"Your sister was taken a few hours ago from a street near the Old South Hotel where she's been working to help set up a conference for Explority Biotech. I believe you are familiar with this company, no?"

Jake nodded. "Yes. I work for them too."

"So you know Keaton Callahan, the CEO?"

Jake shrugged, "Not exactly. I work for him, but I don't ever see him. He sends me emails with issues to fix."

Eli stirred what was left of the liquid in his cup. Whether it was coffee or tea, Travis couldn't tell. "What kind of work?"

"I was dealing with a software issue. I'm in IT. Keaton was having trouble with the implants reporting their locations back to the system accurately. First, he said he just wanted them to report back every few hours. Then it was every hour, then after that, he wanted real-time data streaming someone's location down to approximately three meters."

"Yes, yes. I'm aware of this."

Travis blinked. When he'd met with Eli, Eli had seemed curious about the information he had, never letting on how much the Mossad knew. Now, it appeared that Eli and his team had far more information than Travis ever suspected. What had started as giving Jake information about his sister had quickly turned to Eli grilling Jake.

Eli leaned across the table, pushing his ceramic mug forward by a few inches, wrapping his hands around it and staring at Jake as if he was about to tell him a very important secret. He lowered his voice, barely above a whisper, "Your sister was taken several hours ago as she left the hotel. It looks as though she was injected with something and then put into a van. She's currently being held on the outskirts of the city in an apartment."

Elena watched Jake's face pale. She frowned. "How do you know all of this?"

Eli smiled, "Luckily, my dear, we were following her. Saw the whole thing happen right in front of our eyes. Our teams are positioned outside of the hotel, watching."

"Why haven't you retaken her?" Travis said, feeling his jaw harden. If they knew where Gia was and that she was in danger it didn't make any sense to let her sit. They were just giving whoever had her the opportunity to take advantage of the situation. Maybe even kill her.

"That's what we need you for."

## 66

"What are you talking about?" Travis leaned forward, staring at Eli.

Eli sighed, "Our agents can't retrieve Miss West without causing an international incident. Tel Aviv believes it would be better if you handled it."

Travis frowned, "Tel Aviv? Are you saying your bosses think it's better if the United States handles it, is that what you're saying?"

"No, Travis. Tel Aviv believes it's best if you handle it."

Elena interjected, "Eli? Travis doesn't work for the CIA anymore..."

Eli held his hand up, stopping Elena. "Elena, with all due respect, I can only give you the information that is passed on to me. I believe that's part of the reason why Tel Aviv has made a very specific request that Agent Bishop go in and retrieve Gia. We will take him to the location. Him alone."

Travis leaned back in his seat, feeling the muscles in his neck tighten. Something was up. "Okay, say I agree to this. I want to know two things."

"What's that?" Eli said, cocking his head to the side, the words coming out of his mouth slowly.

"Why me, and what kind of support do I have?"

"Why you? That should be obvious. Agent Bishop, you have a certain skill set that few others have. There are only two men staying with Gia at the moment. The more time this little interview takes, the more it is likely others will show up. You have the training to deal with these types of issues on your own without creating a big stir that involves strike teams or quick response units. In and out. Silent. Just the way we would do it if we could."

Travis narrowed his eyes, "And the support?"

"We have a van parked in the lot. A plumbing truck. The building, unfortunately, has had a rough day with their pipes, so the plumbers have just arrived to help the inconvenienced apartment residents."

Agencies like the Mossad had shops throughout the cities they operated in, with teams deployed to help disguise vehicles, quickly applying removable labeling to vans they'd rent, the teams slipping in and out of cities before anyone was the wiser.

"In that van, you'll find some of my associates. They will be more than happy to outfit you with any equipment that you might feel necessary in order to retrieve the package."

"And what about the implant? It has a kill switch." Jake stammered, staring at Eli.

"Excellent follow-up question, Mr. West." Eli smiled. He looked back at Travis, "Once you retrieve Miss West, we have a Mossad physician standing by, actually a team of them, ready to remove the implant from Miss West's arm immediately, to prevent the deployment of the kill switch."

Travis glanced at Elena. "One more question. Why isn't Elena invited to this party?"

"Tel Aviv wants to keep her clean." Eli's face was relaxed and calm as if they were discussing nothing more interesting than the local sports scores. It was a strange juxtaposition given what they were really talking about.

Travis sat back in the booth for a second staring at the ceiling. What Eli was asking him to do was to go in and retrieve the hostage from two hostiles on his own with no backup. The men holding Gia West were likely heavily armed and even more dangerous. If their reconnaissance had been correct, Travis was immediately at a disadvantage — two of them to one of him. That was problematic, though it wasn't an insurmountable position. He would have to be quick. Very quick. He cracked his knuckles, thinking. "And the cleanup?"

"The plumbers will take care of it."

It was an interesting situation. The Mossad had set the entire thing up. They had people in position, knew who they wanted to run the operation, and had sidelined Elena, likely to leverage her for some future use. Tel Aviv was always ahead of everyone else, ready to take advantage of whatever asset they could find when they needed it. Today was his day.

"I'll do it."

## 67

Gia became conscious momentarily, the room swimming around her, a sour taste in her mouth as if she'd slept for a week. On the ceiling, she could see the outline of a fan spinning slowly, the feel of a thin lumpy mattress underneath her. She was sprawled awkwardly on her side, her arm prickly from laying on top of it, the blood pooling under her own weight. She grunted, trying to push herself up into a seated position. A shadow passed across the room. As it covered her, a male face came barely into focus. She blinked, trying to make words come out of her mouth through what felt like a thick curtain of confusion. "Where am I? Who are you?" Terror gripped her stomach into small knot.

"It doesn't matter, Gia. Go back to sleep," the voice said as she felt a pinch in her arm.

The world went black again.

## 68

After agreeing to the mission, Eli gave a curt nod to David, his watcher, who quickly pulled the head-phones off of his ears, closed his laptop, and stowed everything in his backpack. Standing up, he headed out of a back entrance Travis hadn't noticed. "Go with young David, Agent Bishop," Eli said, taking a sip of his drink. "We will see you shortly."

Travis didn't say anything as he walked away, not goodbye, not even a see you later. Nothing. To someone else, it may have appeared that he was a dead man walking, but Travis felt nothing but a sense of calm and confidence. Not that the mission would go exactly as Eli had described, but if he was Gia West's only shot at getting rescued, then so be it.

David walked about five yards ahead of Travis and didn't stop and didn't check over his shoulder. Travis didn't make any effort to catch up. He trailed David halfway down the block when David darted through an alleyway to a side street where a black sedan was parked. David got inside and started the engine just as Travis opened the passenger door and slipped inside, joining him. David pulled the vehicle away from the curb without saying anything. Travis tossed his backpack in the backseat and fastened his seatbelt, waiting.

"As Mr. Segal said, when we get to the venue, you'll enter the plumbing truck. You'll receive further instructions from there." David's voice was thick with an Israeli accent.

"Fine."

Seventeen minutes later, after a silent ride to the location, the black sedan pulled up at the South Shore apartment complex, three identical buildings set in a U shape, positioned over a wide swath of concrete parking. The parking lot was approximately a third full, Travis estimated. Most people were probably at work, or if not, they might be downtown getting ready to watch one of the parades. The late afternoon sunlight glimmered through dappled shade from the single island of scraggly trees in the center of the parking lot, the developers nod to natural beauty in the midst of the bulky buildings.

Travis stared ahead of him. Parked in the second row from the main entrance of the center building was a white plumbing van with bright green lettering on the side. "Mr. Plumber," it read with a small tagline printed underneath, "We fix your clogs or your job is free!" There was a phone number listed underneath that Travis was absolutely sure was fictitious. It was likely staffed by a Mossad agent somewhere in the world, who was waiting to receive calls for plumbing work that would never be completed.

David glanced over at him. "Give two short knocks on the back entry doors. They're expecting you."

Travis nodded and slipped out of the car.

As he got out, Travis realized the afternoon had become hotter than he expected. It wasn't Texas hot, at least not in temperature, but with thicker humidity, as if the air itself was charged with raindrops that had yet to be expressed from the sky. He jogged to the back door of the van and knocked twice, his stomach tightening. The door opened.

A young man, not much older than David, let him inside. Travis crawled in and sat on one of the bench seats in the back as the young man closed the door. "Welcome, Agent Bishop. Thank you for joining us. I'm Lad and this is Hannah. We're ready to get started as soon as you are."

Travis glanced around the interior of the van. There were no windows. A privacy curtain had been installed between the front and the operational area in the back. It wasn't fancy, a simple tension rod with a thick black curtain split down the center, but it did the trick. Hannah, a small woman with bobbed red hair and long lavender nails, was neatly positioned in front of a laptop, her fingers tapping on the screen.

"Let's get this done." Travis looked around the van. Other than Hannah's laptop positioned on a small suspended desk held up by two thin chains, there didn't seem to be much else in the van. Travis frowned, "Eli said you'd have equipment for me."

Lad nodded, "We do." He slid his stool to the side and lifted up a hatch in the floor. Inside, a light flickered on, showing a wide option of handguns and two rifles. Travis raised his eyebrows. "Nice selection here."

"We aim to please, as you Americans say. What would you like to take with you?"

Travis stared at the guns for a moment, "What do you know about the layout of the apartment?"

"I can show you," Hannah spun the laptop toward Travis. She pointed with a long fingernail, "Here's the floor plan. Pretty basic. They are in a two-bedroom unit. When you enter, the living room will be in front of you, the kitchen and bathroom off to your right. The bedrooms are straight ahead. Gia is being kept in the second bedroom. It's the door on the left." Hannah flipped over to a surveillance video. How they'd managed to get feeds into the apartment, Travis had no idea. "We have live streaming video through their television and a couple of small

cameras we placed when we did their plumbing inspection."
She pointed to the screen again. "There she is. Looks like they
knocked her out again. If you can rid the apartment of these
guys, we can come up to help."

Travis sucked in a breath. Based on the spacing of the two
men at that minute, it wouldn't be a difficult proposition to take
care of them. The problem would be removing Gia from the
apartment without suspicion. A man carrying an unconscious
woman out of her apartment might raise some eyebrows. He
shook his head. He'd have to risk it. He glanced down at the
gun selection. He pointed to a full-sized Beretta nine-
millimeter that had a suppressor attached. "How many mags do
you have for that?"

Lad raised his eyebrows, "That's a good choice. How many
would you like?"

"It shouldn't take more than one shot a piece, but I'll take
two mags just in case." To anyone else, he probably sounded
callous, but he knew he had a job to do. In his mind, it was that
simple.

Lad reached down and handed Travis the gun. He checked
to make sure it was unloaded and then took the two magazines
that Lad extended to him, loading one of them and racking the
slide. They were already loaded with hollow-point
ammunition.

Lad glanced back at him. "Ready to go?"

"Yep. Which building am I going to?"

Hannah swiveled from her position on her stool, folding
her long fingers in her lap, "Building three. That's the one on
the left. Apartment 309."

As Travis moved toward the back of the van, he saw a
couple of safety vests hanging on hooks. He glanced back at
Lad and Hannah, "Mind if I take one of these with me?"

Lad raised his eyebrows, "Not at all. We'll see you in a little
bit."

Travis slipped out of the back of the van, closing the door behind him, laying the gun on the bumper for a moment, and checking over his shoulder for anyone moving in the parking lot. There was nothing happening. He pulled the fluorescent orange safety vest over his shirt, straightened his baseball cap on his forehead, and tucked the gun underneath the vest as he strode toward building three.

There was no movement in the parking lot, save for a single white SUV leaving. Travis stared at the vehicle as it drove away, the woman inside on her phone, clearly not paying any attention to Travis. The only other noise was Travis's footfalls as he picked up a jog, moving towards the front door of building three. As he got to it, he saw a long metal panel installed on the glass door and realized it had a buzzer. Before he could glance back at the van, the door vibrated open. "Thanks, guys," he muttered under his breath. Lad and Hannah really did have the building under control. How they managed to take care of things so quickly, he had no idea. At that point, he wasn't sure he wanted to know. What he did know as he strode through the lobby and walked toward the bank of elevators, pressing the button to go upstairs, was that he needed to get Gia back, and fast. They had to know what was going on with Raashid, and getting Gia back was the first step.

## 69

T he elevator doors slid open with a whoosh. As Travis stepped inside and pressed the button for the third floor, he did a mental run-through of what he was about to do. He could see the motions in his mind, how he would breach the door, raise his gun and end the two men holding Gia hostage. It was a well-worn track in his thinking from his time with Delta Force. He didn't feel nervous or anxious in any way. In his mind, he imagined a square, his breathing slowing as he focused on the outline of it as he rode up in the elevator. Combat breathing. It was one of his favorite techniques. People did all sorts of things in order to stay calm in high-stress situations. Luckily, Travis had only ever needed the minimum. Some people might have said he wasn't sensitive, not compassionate to the loss of lives. That wasn't the case. He was just excessively good at compartmentalizing and convinced that good and evil operated in the world.

As the doors to the elevator slid open, Travis stepped out, his hand still hidden under the safety vest, gripping the Beretta. He sucked in a breath. This wasn't the type of operation that would take a lot of time. In and out. Quick as lightning.

Striding down the doorway, he stuck to one side of the hallway, though he didn't want to make it obvious that he was on a tactical approach to the apartment in case the men inside had surveillance. Hannah did, so it only would make sense that somehow the men might too. The last thing he needed was them waiting on the other side of the doorway, ready for him.

The hallway in the South Shore apartment building where Gia was being kept was a study in gray. Gray tile flooring and gray walls with cheap metallic light fixtures mounted crookedly on the wall near each doorway. It could have been any apartment or hotel hallway anywhere in the world for its lack of distinction. There was nothing interesting or notable about it. Not that Travis was there to critique the decor. The building branched off into three separate directions. Following the signs, Travis moved quickly, locating the door for 309. He paused for a moment; as if waiting for a silent command that never came. Weighing his options, Travis knocked, announcing loudly, "Mr. Plumber! I'm here to fix your clogged drain!"

He had no idea whether they had a clogged drain or not. It didn't matter. He needed them to open the door, even just a crack.

A second later, he heard the locks on the door rattle as they opened. A man appeared behind it, about Travis's height, with dark hair and the scruff of the beard on his face. "We don't have a clogged drain," he said gruffly.

Travis didn't give him a chance to close the door. He lifted the gun in one smooth movement, leveled it at the man's heart and pulled the trigger. The suppressor prevented the loud pop of a normal report of a gun. The man slumped behind the door in relative silence, the only noise the thump of his head hitting the carpet as he dropped. Travis stepped over him, seeing the second man, his eyes wide, staring from the doorway of the bedroom where Gia was being held. The man tried to retreat into the bedroom, but two bullets intercepted him, dropping his body to the ground. Travis closed the door to the hallway behind him, quickly giving each man an additional head shot. They didn't need to survive.

Striding toward the bedroom, Travis held the gun down at his side looking carefully as he went. Lad and Hannah said there were only two men, but if they were wrong it was his hide that would be in a sling. Not theirs. Quickly clearing the second bedroom, the kitchen, and the bathroom, Travis realized he was alone.

He went into the bedroom where Gia was being held, moving slowly, the gun still dangling at his side. He pushed the door open, hearing it creak on its hinges. The images in front of him were exactly the same as what Hannah had shown him only a few minutes before, save for the addition of two dead bodies. Gia was out cold on the bed. Travis went to her side and checked to make sure she was breathing. She was. He shook her a little bit, grabbing her arm, "Gia? Wake up! We gotta go." Hannah and Lad hadn't said anything about other men keeping an eye on the apartment, but if these were Raashid's people, Travis had to assume there were more of them close by. Whoever had taken her wouldn't be happy that she'd been rescued. He had to get Gia out of there, and now.

After watching her for a few seconds, Gia only managed to roll her head back and forth on the bed. Travis didn't have time to wait. He set the gun down, scooping Gia up and throwing her over his shoulder. He grabbed the gun as he did. He didn't want to leave it behind.

Leaving the apartment with Gia over his shoulder, he looked left and right for the entrance to the stairwell. Taking the elevator would've been easier, but it also would have required explaining if he bumped into anyone. Travis didn't have time for that. To his right, he saw a red exit sign, lit from behind above a metal door. "Bingo," he muttered, striding down the hallway. Shouldering the door open, he could smell the stale air of the stairwell. He moved slowly at first, trying to shift Gia's weight so he didn't stumble. Luckily it was only three flights of steps and he was going down and not up.

Two minutes later, he emerged in the lobby and bolted for the front door. The minute he emerged in the afternoon sunlight, the plumbing van was in front of him, Lad and Hannah dressed in matching safety vests, the two of them helping to load Gia into the back of the van. Lad stared at Travis. "Let's go."

The van doors slammed closed behind him. Hannah jumped in the driver's side and the van pulled away from the curb. Lad sat in the passenger seat. Travis looked at Gia. While he was upstairs, Lad and Hannah had rolled out a soft mat on the floor of the van, complete with a pillow and a blanket. Her head was already resting on the pillow. Travis pulled the blanket over her. She started to stir, her eyes wide. "Where am I?"

"Gia, stay calm. My name is Travis. I'm a friend of your brother Jake's. He sent me to come and get you. You are okay. You are safe."

Gia started to struggle to sit up, her eyes wide as if she didn't believe Travis. Travis heard Hannah in the front of the van, muttering something in Hebrew to Lad. What it was, he wasn't sure, but he guessed it was either relief or frustration. Which one, he wasn't sure.

Travis glanced back at Gia again. She'd gone pale, but her eyes were half-open. "Where am I?"

Travis repeated the story. "You are in a van. I rescued you from the apartment where you were being held. I am a friend of Jake's." People who were drugged often needed to hear things more than once in order for it to sink in. "Jake?" Gia blinked. "Where is he?"

"He's here in New Orleans. You're going to see him soon. We're taking you there now." Travis glanced at Hannah. "How are we doing, Hannah?"

"Fighting with the traffic, but we should be there in a couple of minutes."

By the time Travis looked back, Gia had settled down on the pillow, not looking quite as frightened as she did before. Her eyes were closed again. He grabbed her hand. "Hang tight. We're going to get you someplace safe and have a doctor take the implant out of your wrist."

Gia nodded, keeping her eyes closed.

After what Travis learned was a good deal of swearing in Hebrew as they dodged Mardi Gras traffic and road closures, the van pulled into a darkened garage through a rusted overhead door on the side of a building on the other side of New Orleans. Travis watched from his position on Hannah's stool in the back of the van. Gia was alternately in and out of consciousness. As soon as they pulled in, the back doors opened, and a woman and a man wearing scrubs pushed a stretcher up to the back of the van. The woman, her black hair tied in a knot at the back of her neck nodded to Travis, "Help me get her out?"

Travis nodded, lifting Gia's shoulders up and hooking his hands under her arms. The male attendant lifted her ankles and they walked her forward, setting her gently on the stretcher. The woman immediately covered her with a blanket. A man wearing a white doctor's coat stepped forward, looking at Travis, "Has she been conscious at all?" He said, lifting Gia's eyelids and flashing a light into them.

"A little. Seems to go in and out. It's like she's trying to come out of it, but she's not there yet."

From his pocket, the doctor pulled an automatic syringe. It was the kind that allergy patients carried who might need a dose of epinephrine. He put it on Gia's thigh and pressed the stopper. A second later, Gia sucked in a deep breath, her eyes

wide. The doctor muttered, "Welcome back," putting a stethoscope on her chest.

Travis hopped out of the van and stood near her head,
looking at her. "Gia, do you remember me? I'm Travis. I'm Jake's
friend. You are safe."

Gia shook her head as if she was trying to push the cobwebs
out. She blinked a couple of times and then looked at him,
licking her lips, "Yeah. Sort of. Where am I?"

Travis looked at the group of people assembled in front of
him and then back at Gia, "These are some friends of mine.
They're gonna take you in a minute and get that implant out of
your arm. I need to ask you a couple of questions though first."

The doctor laid his hand on Travis's arm, "Our instructions
are to get that implant out of her right now so they don't flip the
kill switch."

Travis nodded, glaring at the doctor. "I get it. Give me a
second."

"Gia, I need you to focus on me. You were working for
Keaton Callahan, right?"

"Yeah. I came here a few days ago to work on a conference."

"Is Keaton in town? Or is he still in Miami?"

The doctor put his hand on Travis's arm again, "I really do
need to…"

"One minute," Travis hissed. The doctor was trying to save
one life. Travis was trying to save many. It was a calculated risk,
one Travis hoped would pay off. He stared back at Gia, "Gia? Is
Keaton here? Is he in New Orleans?" Travis knew if they could
locate Keaton they would most likely be able to figure out what
the next part of Raashid's plan was.

"Yeah. I think he is. He's somewhere close to the conference
center, I think. I overheard him when he was talking to Edward
on the phone. Said he's going to be close by for the festivities."

"Do you mean Mardi Gras? Was he coming here on
vacation?"

Gia shook her head, her eyes wide, "I don't think so."

## 70

The doctors didn't give Travis any more time to interview Gia and he still had questions. Without asking, they rolled the stretcher to the other side of the garage, the wheels clattering on the rough concrete floor. Travis narrowed his eyes. They pushed aside some clear plastic sheeting that had enclosed what looked to be a makeshift medical bay filled with lights and equipment. Travis stood and watched for a minute until one of the doctors looked back at him and gave a nod. He felt his body relax. The implant was out. At least Keaton, or whoever had control of the implants, couldn't kill Gia. As he turned away, he saw a young man carrying a brown paper package out of the building. Within minutes, the implant would be on its way to Tel Aviv, Travis was sure.

But that didn't explain exactly what Keaton Callahan was up to and how Raashid was involved.

Travis turned on his heel and walked back toward the van intercepting Lad who was deep in discussion with Hannah. Lad had his arms folded over his chest. "David is waiting outside for you."

Travis nodded. "I'm assuming you guys are working on the cleanup?"

"As we speak. Thanks for your help." Lad offered his hand and Travis shook it.

Outside, David was leaning against the black sedan. He nodded at Travis as he slid inside. David didn't say anything.

"Thanks for picking me up," Travis said sarcastically as though he was a kid getting driven home from practice by someone else's mom.

"No problem. Things go okay at the apartment?"

"For Gia. The other two guys? Not so much."

David glanced at him out of the corner of his eye, "That's good to hear."

"Where are we headed to?"

"Back to the café. Elena needs you."

As they drove, Travis's mind reeled. Gia was safe. They had half of the code from Jake. And if Gia had the other half, they'd have the entire password. But the password to what? Things still weren't quite adding up. The questions in Travis's mind knotted in his gut. He felt like he was stuck in a smoke-filled room, not able to see the entire space. As they got the information, it felt like they would clear temporarily, but only for a moment. That's how this entire situation had been, ever since Sheriff Burnett and Dr. Scott had approached him at Sarah's. It seemed like a lifetime ago, and yet it was only a few days. He wanted to get back to his life in Texas — rebuild the barn, get things back to normal — but he knew he needed to get answers first.

By the time they got back to the café, it was late afternoon. Eli, Elena, and Jake were sitting in exactly the same positions as they were before they left. The only difference was the empty plates in front of them. Jake jumped up when he saw Travis, "Everything go okay?"

"Just fine. Your sister's safe. She's with the doctors right now."

Eli cleared his throat, "Yes, I just got a message. They successfully removed the implant. It did have the same kill switch as the one you had. She also provided the password she'd been given." Eli glanced at Elena. "I sent you an encrypted message with it."

"Thanks."

Eli looked at Jake, "We will get you reunited with your sister in a few minutes. Young David and I will take you. Why don't you go outside and wait with David for a moment while I do a little business here with Travis and Elena?"

Travis watched as Jake looked at Elena and then back at him as if he was looking for some sort of verification that it was okay for him to leave. Travis nodded, "You can stay with David. Eli's right. We have a little business to finish."

With that, David appeared at the edge of the table, motioning for Jake to follow him outside.

As soon as they were out of earshot, Eli hunched over the table, his face staring at the surface. Travis knew it was a counter-surveillance move, one designed to prevent anyone from reading his lips. "Elena, if you could send me the other half of that code, I would be most appreciative."

"Already did."

"Many thanks." He cleared his throat and then looked up at the ceiling for a moment and then back to the table as if he was gathering his thoughts, "Now, the question becomes what are the codes for?"

Elena shook her head, "Clearly, they have something to do with Explority Biotech and possibly Raashid. That part just isn't clear yet. It's also curious that a brother and sister have them. Reminds me of Raashid and Sadi."

Eli nodded. "I was thinking the same thing." He glanced at

his phone again and muttered. "We have a location on Keaton if you would like it."

"We already have it. I just got it." Elena looked down at her phone and then back at Eli, "Hotel Montefiore?"

Eli nodded, pushing his chair away from the table. "Exactly. I'm assuming you're heading there next?"

Elena nodded, "Correct."

"You'll keep me updated?"

"Of course.

Without saying anything else, Eli walked toward the back of the café, his hands shoved in his pockets, his shoulders slumped. Travis looked at Elena, "I guess that leaves the two of us."

"I guess it does." Elena raised her eyebrows, "Ready to go pay a visit to Keaton Callahan?"

"I can't wait."

## 71

H otel Montefiore was one of the oldest hotels in New Orleans. It was the kind where they still had bellhops and doormen dressed in uniforms, with plush carpets and long velvet draperies in the lobby. It wasn't a new school hotel where there was self check-in and a sleek bar where they served the hottest new drink from mixologists in New York. No, Hotel Montefiore looked as if it had been preserved in a time capsule, Travis thought, walking in the front door. This hotel was a place to sip whiskey and smoke a cigar in front of a roaring fire eating surf and turf.

As the lobby doors closed behind him, Travis took in the space. In front of him was a luxurious bouquet of flowers displayed beautifully on a marble-topped table complete with scrolled gold legs. The scent of roses hung in the air. The check-in desk was at the back of the space, the sleek computers the only nod to modern technology. To his left, he could see a polished oak bar behind a set of stained-glass doors, a peek of the brass railing welcoming people to step inside along with the hum of a jazz song barely audible above the voices bouncing off the high ceilings.

Elena and Travis made their way to the elevator, the attendant asking where they would like to go.

"The presidential suite, please," Elena said in her sweetest tone.

"Are they expecting you?"

Elena flashed a badge. "No, but that's okay."

"Of course, ma'am. As you wish." The attendant didn't say anything else, quickly swiping a keycard over a reader and pushing a button on the panel, taking a position on the side of the elevator car, staring at the ground.

Travis tried not to smile. Frequently, the CIA issued badges, although they didn't read CIA. They were brass, stamped with the words, "Federal Agent." It wasn't as if agents used them all the time, but in situations like these, people became very compliant in the face of a badge. Any badge, it seemed.

As the elevator doors opened, the white-gloved elevator operator held the door open and pointed down the hallway, using a voice that sounded more like a ride operator at Disney than someone accompanying them to see Keaton. "The Presidential Suite is at the end of the hallway. It's the one with the double doors. Have an enjoyable visit."

As Travis stepped out of the elevator following Elena, he mumbled, "Not sure it's going to be enjoyable."

Elena led the way, walking down the plush maroon carpet, flanked by matching maroon walls and gold sconces. It was a far cry from the dingy apartment building Travis had been in a few hours earlier to rescue Gia, that was for sure. The scent of roses hung in the air. For a second, Travis wondered if that was manufactured or real.

Elena knocked on the door, waiting for Keaton to answer. She looked at Travis, her eyebrows raised, as if to say, "I hope he's here," but the words didn't come out of her mouth.

A moment later, Travis heard the door knob rattle as if

someone was trying to open it. One of the heavy wooden doors creaked open and Travis got his first look at Keaton Callahan.

"Who are you?" Keaton scowled.

Travis didn't bother to wait to be invited in. He stepped into the doorway, pushing his way through, "Nice manners, Keaton. Why don't you try being more polite next time?"

"Wait! You can't just come in! Who are you?"

Elena flashed her badge again, "We don't need an invitation, Mr. Callahan. Why don't you have a seat."

Travis quickly searched the suite, walking through the bedrooms and checking the bathrooms. "It's clear," he said, rejoining Elena. Now that he knew there were no other threats, Travis scanned his surroundings.

Hotel Montefiore's Presidential Suite was expansive, with a floor-to-ceiling bank of windows on one side of the suite, the walls painted in a light gray accented by contemporary art, and sprawling white leather couches over navy carpet. It was nothing like the elaborate lobby of the hotel, but was probably designed for up-and-comers who wanted a more modern aesthetic. Travis noticed Keaton had taken over what was supposed to be the breakfast table for his desk. A laptop, backpack, a pile of pens, and a few papers were scattered over the surface, along with dirty plates and cups pushed off to the side. It appeared Keaton hadn't left his suite in a while. Travis sized him up. He was neither tall nor short, with extraordinarily pale skin and wavy dark hair, covering deep black circles under his eyes. Glasses with thick, stylish frames sat on the top of his nose. Whether he needed those for vision or they were simply an accessory, Travis wasn't sure. Keaton was dressed in a pair of dark wash jeans and a T-shirt. He was barefoot. If Travis had to guess, his jeans cost more than Travis's entire wardrobe.

"Why don't you have a seat, Mr. Callahan?" Elena said, pointing him to a chair at the kitchen table. "I think it's time we have a talk."

"Who are you?" Keaton demanded.

Elena stood, her arms crossed in front of her chest looking at Keaton, "Who we are is not nearly as important as what you have been up to, Mr. Callahan. We have Jake and Gia."

Travis saw Keaton lunge for his computer. Travis took two steps, putting his hands on Keaton's shoulders, shoving him back into his seat, and clucked, "Not so fast, Keaton. If you're thinking you're going to flip their kill switches, that's not going to happen. Their implants have been removed. And, we have the codes."

Keaton narrowed his eyes, "Good for you! But I don't need the codes anymore." His tone was sarcastic, the voice of a schoolyard bully with nothing to back it up.

Elena pulled out a chair on the other side of the table and sat down across from Keaton. Travis kept his position behind him, out of his line of sight. "And why is that?"

"I built a workaround."

"Aren't you clever. For what?"

Travis held his breath. What happened next was critical. Keaton could either clam up and tell them nothing, or he could spill all of his secrets.

There was a pause for a second, Keaton staring at the screen. "If you don't know what it's for then I'm not going to be the one to tell you."

Travis moved off to the side, where he could see Keaton's facial expressions better. Keaton had his jaw set, his eyes riveted downward. He had the face of a guilty man. He'd done something, something he shouldn't have and it was beyond the implants. They had to get it out of him before it was too late.

Elena picked at one of her cuticles and then glanced up at Keaton, "You know, we can sit here all night long, or you can just tell us what we want to know and we'll get out of your hair."

Keaton shot up from his seat, "Sit there for all I care! My life is over anyway. And there's nothing you can do about it. No one can!"

Elena glanced at Travis and raised her eyebrows. It was as if she was saying she could work with that. "What do you mean your life is over?"

Keaton started to pace back and forth, waving his hands in the air. Travis had the urge to grab him by the shoulders and slam him down in the chair, but he held back. He knew from past interrogations people having emotional outbursts provided some of the most fertile ground for exposing facts. Emotion loosened lips.

"You really don't know, do you? Keaton bellowed. "You don't know what kind of a hell I've been living through for the last year!"

Elena didn't move, sitting stock still, still staring at her fingernails. Very slowly she lifted her head, "Why don't you tell me?"

Keaton paced back and forth in front of the windows a few more times. He ran his hand through his dark hair. Travis noticed he looked gaunt, almost skeletal, as if he hadn't eaten in weeks despite the dirty plates on the table. Whatever he was going through was eating him up from the inside out.

"You're right. This does have to do with something bigger. That maniac Raashid Sharjah. He basically took over my company a little more than a year ago. Offered me capital to get some new projects off the ground. I was stupid. I took it and now look at this!" Keaton bent over his laptop and hit one of the keys. Travis glanced at the screen. It showed an old man half curled up in a bed, the side of his face drooping. He was alone. "Who's that?"

"My father. He had a stroke. He was on the mend. I thought everything was going to be fine and then Raashid..." Keaton shook his head. "If I don't do what he says, he will kill my dad. He's invested so much into my company, he pretty much owns it. He's got control over my whole life. I've got nothing left."

"Then maybe we can help," Travis said quietly. "Give us the full picture, Keaton. What's going on? Why are you in New Orleans?"

Keaton narrowed his eyes for a second at Travis and then his expression loosened as if he'd just had an epiphany. "Wait! I know you. You're Travis Bishop. You're the one that had the other implant for a while."

Travis nodded slowly, "That's correct." Travis waited to see if Keaton would say anything else.

"All of that, none of it was supposed to happen," he said, starting to pace again. "The dead guy, I mean. I don't even know what his name was. Raashid said the guy was on the run. His guys killed him. Then Raashid made me hire this guy named Edward. His real name is Abdul el-Hadi. He's one of Raashid's guys. He was working at the coroner's office by you. Somehow Raashid got him a temp job there to try to get the body back. But by the time we did…"

"Dr. Scott already had the implant."

Keaton shook his head, staring at the floor, "I thought it had the other half of the code on it. But it didn't. Gia had it the whole time. I just didn't know."

Travis balled his hands into fists thinking about the fire that had taken his barn and Scarlett. "Who came after my ranch?"

Keaton froze in place. His eyes got wide. "I hired them. Sent Edward and Malcolm, but Raashid made me do it," he stammered. "Raashid was mad that someone knew about the implant. They were supposed to stay a secret. Sorry about that."

The apology did nothing for Travis's anger.

Travis watched as Keaton threw himself down in the chair in front of his computer. "This whole thing. It's all messed up. And now, there's nothing I can do."

"About what, Keaton?" Elena whispered.

The room was so quiet that the hum of the air conditioning seemed loud. Travis swallowed. Keaton had admitted to being involved in the missing dead body that pulled Travis into the case in the first place. Keaton admitted to knowing about the implant and the kill switches already and to the fire at his barn. Travis narrowed his eyes. That was a lot to admit to. If that was the first pass, there had to be more – something bigger he was hiding.

Travis waited for another second, watching Elena. She was staring at Keaton, her eyes boring holes through him. "Keaton? About what? What is there nothing you can do about?"

"The bombs." The words came out as a faint whisper, Keaton looking away from them as if he couldn't bear to make eye contact.

Travis shot Elena a look. The pieces suddenly began to fall into place. Raashid, his need for a caliphate, his fury over his brother being taken – he was using his wealth to push his own agenda forward. Elena's mouth sagged open slightly, her face relaxed. "The bombs. Is that what you said, Keaton?"

"Yes," the word came out barely above a whisper.

"Where are the bombs?"

"Everywhere. I don't know. They're already out there. There's nothing anybody can do. Raashid already armed them."

Travis frowned and cocked his head to the side, "Keaton, you gotta do better than this. Are you saying there are multiple bombs?"

Keaton shot up out of his seat, "Yes! What are you people dumb? Yes. There are multiple bombs in the city. Raashid wanted me here to make sure that they got armed. I thought he needed the codes to do that so I made a workaround, but he's already armed them. I don't know where they are. I don't know how many there are. He's been using my technology and my company as cover. The whole conference is nothing but a show.

He's put tracking implants in all of my people, but I don't have any idea who they are or what they're doing."

Travis watched Elena. She blinked. It was the only sign he saw from her that she recognized what a dire circumstance they were in. "And Raashid wants to detonate the bombs during Mardi Gras?"

"Yes. Tonight, I think. I mean, I guess." Keaton stared at the ground.

Travis felt a shiver run down his spine. There were literally millions of people rushing into the center of New Orleans at that very moment, lining the streets for one of the biggest nights of Mardi Gras. Depending on where the bombs were positioned, thousands of people could die.

Before Travis could say anything, he heard a hum from outside the windows of the suite. He watched as Keaton turned slowly toward the window, his face paled. "Oh no. He's here…"

## 72

"Who's here?" Travis said, pulling the curtain aside. A black drone was hovering above the railing on the other side of the balcony. Travis dropped the drape and looked back at Keaton.

"Raashid."

Travis narrowed his eyes, "What are you talking about? There's a drone outside. Probably just some kids."

"No. It's not. It's him."

Travis watched as Keaton walked like a robot to the patio door, pushing the curtains aside and opening the slider. The buzzing got louder as the drone entered the room, slowly spinning around. Travis backed up, eyeing the machine suspiciously.

"It looks like you have some visitors, Keaton." A tinny voice came from the inside of the drone. "I didn't think I would find you entertaining guests on such an important day."

"I didn't... Please!" Keaton begged.

"I know you didn't, Keaton. Not with the life of your father in your hands, not to mention the future of your company, but that's an entirely different issue."

Travis watched as the drone spun toward him, "Nice to see you in person, Agent Bishop," the voice from the drone said. "And I see you've brought a friend with you. I don't think we've been acquainted."

"And I don't think you need to be. Raashid, is it?"

A deep, gruff laugh came from the other side of the drone, "So you figured out who your adversary is, Agent Bishop. Congratulations. I was warned that you are very good at what you do. A hunter by nature. Very interesting. Not my particular area of talent, I have to admit."

Travis narrowed his eyes, "What is your particular area of talent?"

"Strategy, Agent Bishop. And I'm very good at it. You see, I play every game for the long haul. I'm not interested in short-term wins."

"What is it that you want, Raashid?" Elena said, standing up, crossing her arms in front of her chest.

"World peace, an end to hunger, you know, all the good stuff."

Raashid was playing with them. He stared at the drone. "Keaton said you've planted bombs all over the city. Is that true?"

The drone swiveled, facing Keaton, "Oh, Keaton. You didn't! Did you share our little secret?" The voice dripped with sarcasm.

"They made me. I didn't have a choice." Keaton blathered. "I want to be done with this. I want my life and my company back. I want you to leave my father alone."

"Keaton, if you thought your life was ever going to be the same after you started working with me, you were mistaken. Have you checked on your dad recently? From my records, I don't think you've gone to see him in a long time. You should show some respect."

Keaton ran over to his computer, staring at the screen.

Travis stood behind him. A woman wearing a surgical mask walked into the room, glancing up at the camera in the corner as she did. She injected something into Keaton's dad's IV line and then stood for a second, watching. Keaton yelled, "No!" as his heart monitor flatlined.

"I warned you, Keaton. I warned you not to tell anyone and not to talk to anyone."

"But I gave you the workaround for the codes. I'm sorry I couldn't find them! It wasn't my fault!"

Raashid laughed, his voice echoing out of the drone, "I didn't need them. The passwords are nothing but nonsense. It was designed to keep you busy and focused on the project, which you did, until right now. What is it that you call it? An idle threat? So, now that I don't need you anymore, goodbye."

Travis watched, his mouth open as he saw Keaton glance at his wrist and then back at Travis. His eyes rolled to the back of his head as his body dropped to the ground, white foam dripping from the corner of his mouth.

The drone hovered over his body, laughter coming from inside of it, "See, Agent Bishop? See how much control I have? There are dozens of people that have these implants. I could kill all of them right now if I wanted to. You Americans, you think that you know everything. That you have the best lifestyle. But you don't. You don't honor Allah. And you stole my brother from me and gave him to the infidel Israelis. That is something I will never forget. Tonight something will happen that you will never forget either!"

As the drone pivoted to fly out of the room, Travis picked up the chair that Keaton had been using at his desk and launched it at the drone, catching the propellers in mid-air. It crashed to the ground, smashing into a pile of black plastic confetti.

Travis ran over to Keaton, staring at him. Elena was already kneeling next to him. She held her hand up. "Don't touch him. It can kill you if you get it on your skin."

"I know."

Elena stood up and turned toward Travis, smiling, "Nice work with the chair."

Travis grimaced, "Thanks. But what do we do now?" Travis's mind was pounding with questions. Both Keaton and Raashid had admitted to the fact there were bombs planted throughout the city. They had to get them before more people died.

A knock came at the door, followed by the door to the suite creaking open. Eli strolled in, David following, wearing his backpack, his earphones around his ears.

Eli stopped and stared at the pile of plastic on the ground and Keaton's dead body. "Well, I guess that gives us some answers. Can't say I've ever seen a drone used this way before. Glad to see you put it out of its misery, Agent Bishop."

Travis shook his head. "You knew about the bombs?"

"No. I didn't know that, but I'm not surprised."

Travis started to pace. "But how are we going to find them? Keaton said there are bombs all over the city. As in plural. Tonight. We're talking about thousands of casualties. We can't let that happen!"

Eli nodded, "Easy, Agent Bishop. Let's see if young David can provide us some assistance."

By the time Travis glanced at David, he had pulled one of the other chairs from the table around behind Keaton's laptop and had plugged in his own. "Give me a moment. I need to hijack the system."

"Hijack the system?" Travis frowned.

Eli shrugged, shoving his hands in his pockets, "It's tech-speak for he's going to take over."

The patio door was still open from when Raashid had flown the drone inside. Travis stepped outside looking at the street below. Raashid might be in the city, he might not. The level of technology they were using was something Travis hadn't seen before. Normally a drone operator had to be relatively close, but with Raashid's billions of dollars behind him, or he could be halfway around the world and operating the drone. Travis's gut told him Raashid was close though, close enough he would be able to hear the sirens if the bombs went off, maybe even the screams. Travis stared off in the distance, gritting his teeth. Raashid was somewhere out there, watching.

A moment later, Travis heard the beats of drums as the early evening parade began, the cheers of the crowds roaring up between the buildings downtown. A tingle ran down his spine. They were running out of time.

# 73

"I have good news and bad news," David said, looking up at Eli, who nodded. "I can tell you there appear to be five bombs. Two of them look like they were dropped off in buildings and three of them appear to be car bombs. Sacred Heart Academy and Gallier Hall."

Travis swallowed. Car bombs made sense. It was one of the hallmarks of Middle Eastern terrorism. Load up the vehicle with plastic explosive, set off the bomb and the twisted metal and glass plus the gasoline in the tank would become a fireball complete with shrapnel that would kill and maim people for fifty yards on either side of the blast. "Five?" Travis lifted off his baseball cap and ran his hand through his hair, replacing it. "How are we ever going to find them?"

"I have the building addresses here."

"I'll call it in," Elena said. "We can get bomb units out to those two buildings."

"If we aren't too late." Travis stared at David, "What about the cars? Three of them?"

David nodded. "Keaton has the information in his notes here. It doesn't look like there's any way to track them, but we do have makes, models and license plates. Looks like they're rental cars."

Elena looked at Travis, holding her phone off to her ear, "They have to be along the parade route. That's where they would do the most damage."

Travis felt every muscle in his back tighten. "We gotta get out there. Now."

## 74

Carrying the piece of paper David had given him, Travis ran down the hallway and got into the elevator, Elena following. He turned as the elevator doors closed. "What about Eli and David?"

Elena shook her head, her face stony. "Let Eli do his thing. He'll call if anything pops on his end. We need to move. Now."

By the time they made it outside, the parade that was curling its way in front of Hotel Montefiore had already begun, dusk settling over the city. Everything from community bands to tractors to cars pulling handmade floats made of tissue paper and flowers crept slowly past them. Music pumped out of the vehicles as they passed, scantily clad dancers on top of the floats, smiling and tossing colored beads at the bystanders who all seemed to grin back. Little did they know what was happening in their midst. With all the people clustered in the city, there was no way to evacuate. It would cause chaos, chaos Travis knew Raashid was counting on. Travis stopped after running outside, staring left and right. "This thing goes for miles. How are we ever going to find them?"

Just as the words came out of his mouth, he heard a large

boom, the thunderous roar of an explosion vibrating in his chest. Off in the distance, he could see a cloud of smoke billowing its way into the air. Travis glanced at Elena. She covered her mouth with her hand. Dropping it, she said, "Oh my God. It's starting."

"Raashid must've moved up his timeline now that he knows we're on to him."

The parade kept going, although the noise of the explosion had caused the parade watchers to stare in that direction rather than celebrating the floats in front of them.

Travis glanced at Elena. "Now the question is when the next one will come. We're going to have to split up if we have any hope of finding the cars."

Elena nodded, walking away from him, disappearing into the crowd of people. Part of Travis wanted to stay with her so they could work together like they used to, but he knew she could handle herself. She would watch the streets, trying to spot one of the other vehicles on her way to see what happened at the explosion.

Travis took off at a jog going the opposite direction, stopping every few feet to look over his shoulder, staring at the vehicles on both sides of the road. He pulled the piece of paper David gave him out of his pocket. David had scrawled the makes, models, and license plate numbers of the vehicles on it. Luckily, they were all the same type of car – American-made, four-door sedans. Travis quickly memorized the plate numbers as he moved along, dodging his way through the flow of parade watchers, carrying folding chairs and drinks, wearing T-shirts and shorts decorated with layers of colorful beaded necklaces they'd collected.

Travis made it down another block before the next eruption occurred. This one was louder, closer. The people around him stopped and stared, shadows of concern passing over their faces. Travis kept moving. Then his phone rang. Elena. "I found one of the cars!"

"Stay away from it! He's gonna blow them all." Just as the words came out of his mouth, Travis heard another boom, this time one coming from Elena's direction, the noise echoing over the open phone line. "Elena!" he yelled, feeling his heart drop. He ran toward the direction she'd disappeared. His breath caught in his chest. If anything happened to her, he wasn't sure he could ever forgive himself. He was the one who had gotten her drawn into this case. Although, knowing her, she probably would've gotten pulled into it anyway.

Travis dodged and weaved through people who were scattering away from the explosions. The noise and smoke had thinned the crowd out significantly, some of the floats stopping where they were in the middle of the road, the drivers abandoning them, snarling traffic.

Half a block from the hotel, Travis could see the smoke gathering in the sky near Elena's location. He took off at a sprint, running as fast as he could toward the explosion.

By the time he got there, it was chaos. What was left of the sedan was on fire, the metal twisted, acrid smoke hanging in a thick cloud between the buildings. People were running away from the area, some of them limping, blood running down their faces. There were bodies on the ground. Lots of them, parts of them too. Seeing the stump of a foot near the curb, Travis looked away, his stomach lurching. This shouldn't happen on American soil. Never.

Gritting his teeth, Travis searched frantically, looking for Elena. He glanced over his shoulder to see her sitting on a step in front of a building behind him, her head hanging. He ran to her, "Elena!" he yelled, grabbing her face in his hands and lifting it up toward him. She had blood running down the side of her cheek from a cut in her forehead, black smudges of soot on her face and arms. Her clothes were torn and dirty. "I'm okay. I'm okay," she panted. "You gotta find the other ones. More people are going to die if you don't."

More people are going to die...

As Travis watched people struggle away from what was left of the car, he realized Raashid was probably watching the chaos unfold, laughing somewhere and celebrating, hiding out while other people suffered. He gritted his teeth and scanned the area. Then he saw it.

Across the street, he spotted another one of the cars. "Elena!" he pointed.

"No, Travis! Don't!"

Travis took off, sprinting for the sedan that had been parked down the street from the first one. Travis glanced around him, opening the door. It was the perfect setup. Put two car bombs in close proximity to each other. Detonate one and then wait for first responders to arrive. Once they were clustered on the scene, detonate the second one. Raashid was right about one thing. He was a good strategist and a cruel one.

Travis slid in behind the wheel and touched the ignition. The key fob was still in it. He turned on the engine and threw the vehicle into gear and sped away from the scene as fast as he could. He glanced behind him. There was a trail of wires leading into the trunk. He swallowed. That made sense. The trunk was closest to the gas tank. It would make for a larger explosion.

And he had no idea how much time he had before it went off.

---

## 75

T ravis tromped on the accelerator, winding his way through side streets that weren't blocked because of the parade, dodging the screaming sirens of police cars racing to the explosions. He said a silent prayer that Elena was okay and out of danger. Off in the distance, he heard another bomb go off. He swallowed. There was only one left. And it was the one he was driving. If he had to guess, Raashid knew he was in the car and was waiting for the opportune time to set it off.

Getting clear of some of the traffic, Travis glanced down. There had to be a timer or some sort of remote device that would control the detonation. It would probably be close to where the driver was. Keeping one eye on the road, he flipped open the glove compartment to see a display with red numbers on it. It was ticking down, twenty, nineteen, eighteen, seventeen, sixteen..."

He had only seconds left before the bomb would blow.

Ahead of him, Travis saw the wide blue waters of Lake Pontchartrain. He gripped the steering wheel more tightly and rolled down the windows of the vehicle as he sped up. He'd have only one shot to get the car into the water, drowning the detonation device, only a few seconds to spare if he could make it work. If. He flattened the accelerator to the floor, staring straight ahead. He could barely breathe. He counted the numbers down in his head.

The car hit the guardrail going eighty miles an hour, the thin metal fencing no match for the car barreling through it. The sedan launched itself into the end of the water in a wide arc slamming against the surface as though it hit a concrete wall. Travis felt the impact, the cool of the water on his skin, and then nothing more. Everything went black.

## 76

The next thing Travis remembered was being dragged up the bank of the lake, coughing and sputtering. His head was pounding. He rolled over on his back, feeling someone put a hand on his shoulder, "Travis? You okay? Are you with me?"

He opened the eye that wasn't swollen shut to see Jake hanging over him, smiling, a grin stretched from ear to ear, water dripping off his clothes. "You like to make things dramatic, don't you?" Jake chided.

Travis rolled to his side, every inch of his body aching, "A little, maybe." He glanced at Jake, who had stripped off his shirt and was ringing it out, the water cascading onto the rocky bank of the lake. "How did you get here?"

"Eli." Jake laughed. "They spotted you on surveillance when you took the car. I told them I could get you out. I've spent a lot of time scuba diving. Man, you should see David drive. Practically took out an entire float filled with clowns getting here."

Travis shook his head trying to picture it. "Well, however it happened, thanks."

Jake slumped on the bank next to him. "It's all good man. It's all good."

# EPILOGUE

On his second morning in the hospital, Travis had visitors. Eli came in trailed by Elena. He set a beautifully wrapped brown box with a fluffy white bow on Travis's tray table. Travis tried to ease his way up in the bed, grimacing from the pain. "What's this?"

Eli grinned, chewing away at a piece of gum. "Some of that delicious crumb cake from the West End Café. I thought you might need something other than Jell-O by now."

Travis winced. He'd broken six ribs in the crash and given himself quite a concussion. But neither of those reasons was why he was still in the hospital. The impact of the car hitting the water, which the doctor said was as hard as if he'd hit a wall of concrete, had caused his spleen to bleed. They'd waited for a few hours to see if it would resolve on its own, but then ended up dragging Travis into emergency surgery to get it out. The doctors had promised he'd be able to leave the hospital that afternoon. It was a promise Travis intended on making them keep. He held an ice pack up to his eye. The swelling had finally gone down enough that he could see out of it, though it still hurt.

Elena walked to the side of his bed, giving his hand a squeeze, "How are you feeling?"

"Like I've been hit by a Mack truck. Any updates?"

Elena shook her head. "I don't have a lot more information than we did yesterday. Unfortunately, a lot of people died, but our agencies are all over it. Jake and Gia are together. Both are doing fine. We've located three dozen people with implants that have been removed."

"Did they find Raashid?"

Eli nodded. "Sort of. Your American FBI found a house he was renting on the Gulf. Seems the speedboat the owners left behind is missing."

"So he got away."

Eli nodded, "Indeed, but we still have a card to play. Sadi."

Travis sucked in a breath, "Good. Keep it that way."

Elena smiled, "And even though it was crazy, you did manage to save a lot of lives. If that second bomb had gone off after first responders had arrived it would've been catastrophic."

Eli nodded and eased himself down in a chair at the other side of the room, "That was truly a heroic maneuver, Agent Bishop. Tel Aviv is impressed."

Travis raised his eyebrows, at least as best he could with how banged up his face was. "Well, I guess that's something."

Eli leveled his gaze at Travis. "So, Agent Bishop, what's next for you?"

"I'm going home."

Elena laughed, "I'll bet you are."

Later that afternoon, Travis walked out of the hospital wearing a fresh set of clothes Elena had purchased for him. It was nothing fancy, a new pair of jeans, a t-shirt that read "Mardi Gras" on the front, and a baseball hat. Wincing as he pulled the cap down on his head, Travis sucked in a deep breath. From the news reports he'd read over the last few hours, the city was still in chaos, nearly every agency from across the country deployed to downtown New Orleans to help with the cleanup. Mardi Gras had been effectively canceled, but Raashid hadn't won, at least not in the long term, even though people had died. He was now being hunted by the CIA and the Mossad, not to mention many of their other allies.

It was only a question of time before justice was done.

A sleek black car pulled up in front of the hospital. The window rolled down. A young man glanced over at Travis, "Need a ride?" It was young David.

"Sure."

"Where are you going?"

"Home." Travis smiled as they pulled away.

*The CIA wants Travis dead.*
*Can he get bounty off his life and stay alive?*
*Get Tainted Asset now!*

# A NOTE FROM THE AUTHOR

Thanks so much for taking the time to read *Threat Rising*. I hope you've been able to enjoy a little escape from your everyday life while joining Travis on his latest adventure.

If you have a moment, would you leave a review? They mean the world to authors like me!

If you'd like to join my mailing list and be the first to get updates on new books and exclusive sales, giveaways and releases, click here! I'll send you a prequel to another series FREE!

Enjoy, and thanks for reading,
  KJ

# TRY THESE OTHER BOOKS BY KJ KALIS:

**Check out these series and add them to your "to be read" pile today!**

Investigative journalist, Kat Beckman, faces the secrets of her past and tries to protect her family despite debilitating PTSD. Visit the series page here!

Intelligence analyst, Jess Montgomery, risks everything she has — including her own life — to save her family. Visit the series page here!

Former detective, Morgan Foster, is on the run from the people who tried to kill her, until trouble comes knocking at her door. Visit the series page here!